HAMR BROT...
ROMANTIC ACTION ADVEN...

WRECKED

Sam "Partyman" Leclair

DIANNA LOVE

Cover Design and Interior Format

© **KILLION**

DEDICATION

*To my amazing romantic suspense readers
who waited for this series. You rock.*

CHAPTER 1

S AM HAD HIS NVG MONOCULAR flipped out of the way so he could see everything in natural colors as he died.

He kept waiting for this old-as-hell helicopter carrying his HAMR Brotherhood FALCA team to sputter and crash into the waves below. An early evening storm pounded the fuselage as if the chopper needed help nosediving.

An August to remember.

Thick foam rolling along the Venezuelan coast would be a stunning photograph for tourists.

The only sight he cared about capturing was W in cuffs and leg irons. Few international terrorists had eluded security forces and military in every country the way W had for five years.

Sam would never forget the bloody images of citizens, especially children, killed in the attacks. In his mind, he still saw the eyes wide open and body parts missing. One teenage girl who had looked so much like Sam's sister kept visiting his nightmares with her half-blown-away skull and eyes wide open in fear.

Had his sister looked as terrified when she'd died?

Bile ran up Sam's throat. He forced his mind back to the here and now. Stick to the mission.

He couldn't screw up on this one, not after the last mission where he'd made a misstep. Logan, leader of all HAMR Brotherhood teams, understood what his men faced, but he expected everyone to stick to their duty and keep the team strong.

Sam still felt justified over rushing through enemy fire to save a woman being dragged away. Sam freed her and handed her off to another woman then rejoined the team.

Nitro had chewed him into pieces. Yes, Sam had no one to cover his six for those seconds, and yes, she could have been hiding a weapon, but he'd seen true terror in her face and had a plan to return safely.

The fact that his plan had worked failed to spare him from Nitro's wrath.

Sam would do the mission tonight by the book no matter what crossed his field of vision.

No one wanted to lose a spot in HAMR Brotherhood, and Sam lived for operations with his FALCA team.

His seat dropped suddenly in an air pocket. Muscles in Sam's gut clenched even though it was only inches.

Having spent an hour helping the forty-something pilot get this bucket-of-crap-parts running, Sam had up-close knowledge of the flying death trap.

He didn't mind flying at night and low to the ground. That was perfect for a stealth approach when he had faith in his ride.

Nothing fazed Pablo, their intrepid pilot, not even lightning streaking across the sky and rain hammering so loud Sam should be deaf by now. Sadly, he wasn't. Was Pablo even the pilot's real name? Thick, curly hair sprang out in every direction. He wore flip-flops and one of those Hawaiian-print shirts with a string of seashells around his neck as bright against his deep tan as the white around his dark eyes.

Didn't matter what he looked like so long as his reputation as a former hotshot Army pilot held up.

The team medic, Blade, sat in the co-pilot's seat, but he couldn't fly this thing if Pablo fell out the opening on his left. As the largest of their four, Blade had to ride shotgun. If not, somebody would have been hanging off the side of Pablo's OH-6A chopper, a Vietnam-era relic like the one his revered Army colonel father had flown.

The LOACH, which pilots and crews had nicknamed this chopper, had the exact attributes needed for tonight's mission. It had flown in low, fast, and quiet to flush out the enemy during the Vietnam conflict. When the speedy little helo took on enemy fire, a larger, noisier, and deadlier Cobra AH-1 hanging back on their ass would sweep in and break up the party.

But that had been sixty freaking years ago.

"You enjoyin' the ride, Partyman?" Nitro asked, his voice coming through Sam's headset. The leader of their FALCA team found most things amusing until show time. Right now, his eyes gleamed with amusement as if they were on the way to a bar.

That would be the day. For Sam to go barhopping would surprise all of them.

Sitting between the two of them, Angel's lips curled, but the Spaniard stayed out of this.

Positioned behind the pilot and with an open door on his left, Nitro was not one to show any concern. Always cool on the outside. Of course, Nitro would find flying in this rattling bucket of bolts funny if Sam gave the least indication it got under his skin.

Not happening.

Sam wanted no one on this team to question his commitment at any time, but especially tonight. He would nail his part without bitching. He grinned at his leader.

Nitro smirked, not buying the grin one bit.

Angel, one of their snipers and the master of impossible stunts, held his HK 416 assault rifle in a relaxed grip. Sam, Nitro, and Blade held identical weapons. They all carried Baretta M9 handguns with suppressors as well.

Sam had thanked Esteban for damn good weapons, ammo, NVGs, and tactical gear. Sam had vouched for Esteban when Logan needed an in-country arms supplier close to the target on short notice.

Hard not to vouch for someone who helped Sam survive being a prisoner in a Libyan drug-running and terrorist camp three years back. Trust ran both ways after Sam took a shot to save Esteban's life during their escape.

The chopper engine groaned and skipped.

Sam gripped his rifle, muscles kinked in his shoulders. He silently asked to not go diving into the black ocean. He had no idea if they were so close to the beach that they'd hit too shallow and break into a thousand pieces or sink a hundred feet the minute the chopper smashed into water.

Blade's neck muscles flexed. Yeah, he didn't like this either.

As if sensing tension, Pablo held up a hand and spoke into their headphones. "Not long now."

Sam ground his teeth to keep from yelling at Pablo to put both hands back and keep this thing airborne. They could have used Slider on this mission. He could fly a tin can with two wooden wings and orange juice for fuel.

Pablo leaned forward quickly and tapped at a gauge.

Blade's head whipped to the left, sharp eyes watching him.

The motor coughed and sputtered.

Ah, shit. Sam moved his boot closer to the opening, preparing to make a quick jump and get out of the way for Angel.

Pablo's flying dinosaur dipped for the longest second of Sam's life before the engine caught again, blades whining at full power once more.

Pablo grinned and pumped his fist. "She's old but solid."

Sam cursed. He couldn't be the only one holding his breath until they landed. He'd made HALO jumps from thirty thousand feet that were less dangerous than this.

Angel cursed lividly in Spanish.

From the team daredevil?

Oh yeah. Bad sign there.

If they landed at the designated spot, they had to hike five klicks. On the other hand, if the motor cut out one more time, Sam was ready to set this chopper down immediately on the nearest strip of beach and hike the additional distance.

Lightning crackled and fingered into jagged zaps of power.

They had been flying straight into the rain, but Pablo banked sharply toward the coast. Hallelujah. Sam gripped the side of the fuselage. Water bullets drilled into his body, battering the right side as the chopper continued angling west. He didn't care. Wind buffeted him, lifting and pushing the egg-shaped cabin around.

The helicopter neared a narrow strip of beach and raced across it, closing in on the drop point.

Nitro clicked into mission mode, reminding Pablo what time to return and to not land if he did not see a flashing signal from the team. They either made it in and out on time, or something had gone FUBAR.

Sam flipped his NVG monocular down and lifted his rifle to his chest, ready to get rolling.

Pablo slowed the beast then hovered only seconds and touched down as softly as if he had been carrying dynamite.

Bailing out first, Sam's boots hit solid ground. Relief.

Now they had control of their mission.

He strode from beneath the rotor wash with Angel right behind him.

They met up with Nitro and Blade on the other side as the chopper lifted off, flying away toward the coast.

Rain fell in a heavy drizzle, soaking Sam until he felt at one with the dark Venezuelan forest they entered. He didn't give a damn about bad weather.

It came in handy sometimes.

His first concern was always keeping his team safe as they extracted the package—a kidnapped US senator.

This op had been pulled together with plenty of talent but rushed. Opportunity rarely cared about time when it knocked. No one to date had been this close to nailing the international predator known only as W, who his FALCA team believed held the high-value hostage in a reclusive location.

This was not a kidnapping that required a monetary payment.

If W did indeed have the senator, there was no amount of gold that would save the politician. Senator Turner had publicly vowed to bring W to justice. Special Force teams were already following other leads in multiple countries. One of Logan's intel specialists turned up intel pointing at W possibly being in South America.

Hell yeah, Sam had wanted to go for many reasons the minute he knew the plan, not just to cement his position with FALCA moving forward.

Moose, another FALCA member, one who handled intel gathering for multiple teams, had hit paydirt while searching for anything on the senator's kidnapping.

Logan had activated FALCA immediately.

They all wanted W. None more than Sam. The word *crimes* failed to describe the hideous murders and destruction committed by that sick monster, W.

They went wheels up knowing every detail could not be flushed out.

No op went exactly as planned.

Sam kept waiting for the mission calm to settle over him. He lived for that moment when his world made sense, but he could not shake the foreboding sensation of spiders with sharp claws crawling up his spine.

CHAPTER 2

———◆———

HALLENE SQUINTED TO SEE AHEAD where an endless
darkness waited and paused to listen for any sign she'd
been discovered. If they caught her in this dirt tunnel, she had
no chance of outrunning bullets.

Her jeans and long-sleeved black T-shirt had been soaked by
the time she parked the BMW 1200 GS motorcycle built to be
used on or off-road. She'd been fortunate to even find a dual
sport bike to ride, which could handle dense woods as easily as
the highways in Venezuela.

Money solved most problems in a foreign country, but only if
a product was readily available.

She breathed slowly and had to push away claustrophobia
needling her, then strode forward on the hard-packed dirt path.
An LED light hidden in a ring she wore bounced over the hard-
packed ground with an occasional thick root bulging up across
the path. Roots in the wrong place could compromise an old
tunnel like this built centuries ago without engineering plans.

Dirt in here smelled of old wood and damp mulch, two things
that deteriorated. If this tunnel caved in, she'd die here, and
no one would ever know. *Nice, Hallene. Why not think about
running into a slumbering anaconda and being strangled to
death?*

She had hacked at vegetation for over an hour to reveal parts
of the crumbling shack that had collapsed over the closest access
point to the ocean for this underground passage.

This tunnel would likely not be the only one along the
northeastern coast of Venezuela from back when pirates stashed
their stolen goods.

She didn't want gold and jewels.

She was here to save a seventeen-year-old girl then beat the crap out of the kidnapper who had dragged her here.

According to her intel techie, a big-time pirate historian and enthusiast, this seventy-hectare, or two-hundred-seventy-acre location had once been a sugarcane plantation. But time changes everything. The plantation had been left in ruins for almost a hundred years. Then two years ago, a US businessman who had lost his entire family acquired the decaying mansion along with twenty acres the government allowed him. He spent nine months remodeling the structure back to its glory days and kept the place up without any domestic help. A loner who raised his own food as well as goats and chickens.

A sophisticated hermit.

A dead hermit by now.

She shook her head at someone who looked at a reclusive South American location and thought *sanctuary*. The government might have no interest in him so long as he paid taxes when they came due, but cartels were another story.

The person her intel indicated was currently squatting in the mansion for two days. He would not fear cartels nor be here long enough for a tax collector to show up.

Kidnappers frowned on paying taxes.

She only needed this world-class scumbag to be here one night. Just for a few more hours, in fact.

She'd been mentally counting steps in groups of fifty and bent a fourth finger into her palm. The tunnel exit leading into the basement of the remodeled mansion should be before she tucked the fifth finger.

Her head bumped something hard. She cursed and rubbed her head. She'd hit a rare crossbeam installed for support. Damn pirates. She was five-nine. Had the men back then been that much shorter than her or just too lazy to carve out a taller corridor? Ducking her head, she kept moving.

Wouldn't a taller tunnel have made carrying trunks of gold and jewels easier?

She would not go through this hell tonight for all the lost treasures in the world.

Only for Phoebe, a seventeen-year-old girl with a bad attitude who had been a pain in Hallene's backend since Phoebe's birth.

Still, no girl deserved the fate her half-sister faced.

Hallene rarely had regrets in life, but she now had a few when it came to Phoebe.

Without missing a step, she peeled open the Velcro cover shielding her black watch face turned to the inside of her wrist. Closing in on half past nine at night.

Two and a half hours should be enough time if she had a team with her, but doing this solo felt as if she cut it close. Her plan required inserting and extracting Phoebe before midnight. The infamous Collector never spent more than seventy-two hours at any location once he had a captive. He'd arrived here at midnight two nights back.

Now that he'd been located once, he could be found again, but that didn't mean Phoebe would still be in his possession or alive by his next stop.

Her intel resource had gained a tip when the Collector stopped in South America and traveled to the remodeled home. Her techie told her there was a high probability the Collector was headed to this mansion.

If that was true, Hallene would never tease her friendly hacker about his obsession with pirate lore again.

She pushed her legs harder.

Everything about this half-assed plan went against her sense of preparation. Worry climbed across her shoulders at the fear she'd make a mistake and either die before she could free Phoebe or get them both killed.

Discovering the location of El Coleccionista, aka the Collector, had been too good to pass up or to wait on backup, which she no longer had. Hacking the computer of Phoebe's father sealed the deal when Adam Kovac received a message about an unspecified task he had to perform once details were delivered if he ever wanted to see Phoebe again.

Resources were everything.

Her tech also supplied information to UK military such as SFSG, Special Forces Support Group, where Coop had been a respected member. His buddies had been nice to her after Coop's death, but she'd told them nothing about this or they would have hauled her away and taken time to recon the area before any insertion decision.

An excellent idea if time had any part in this equation beyond running out too quickly.

Any interference would blow her chance at rescuing her half-sister.

She'd trusted Coop to a point. He'd been an elite operative after all, but Coop would not approve of her being here. She understood. Without rules, there would be chaos in his line of work.

Phoebe didn't have time for someone to bless this. Coop's team sure as hell wouldn't bless her take-no-prisoners plan.

Hallene's fingers curled into a tight fist with the urge to make the kidnapper pay. She hadn't decided the exact definition of making the Collector pay yet, but it had to be more than sticking him in a jail cell where he'd find a way to slither out.

Monsters could not be rehabilitated.

She'd reached forty-five steps.

Her blood pressure jumped. Where was the end of this tunnel?

She clicked the light in her ring to the lowest setting, a bare glow that should not give away her position by leaking through an opening to the mansion. She just hoped some entry point still existed. With her eyes adjusting to the ambient light, she took one step then another, always reaching forward.

Her fingers bumped something solid hanging away from the wall. Lifting her ring, she had a tiny thrill at finding an old wooden ladder. This was where things got dicey.

Her heart thudded.

Would she have a welcoming party?

Sweat drizzled down her face and neck even in the cool temperature down here.

How many times had Coop said, "In the world of special operations, hesitation gets you killed."

So would a bad decision, but sometimes that was the only option.

Climbing carefully and praying the wood was not rotted, she made it up six steps, constantly feeling above her head. Her fingers hit a solid surface. She moved her hand over the texture and found parallel lines in the rough surface.

Wood planks.

She pushed. Nothing moved.

Hooking her leg over a rung, she used both hands to push up.

She grunted from straining until the covering began to give. Dirt rained down on her face. She closed her eyes and spit out debris, pausing to listen. No light bled through from above. Demanding more from her arm muscles, she gritted her teeth and shoved harder. The trapdoor began lifting.

Her vision blurred from perspiration stinging her eyes. She kept going until she had the wooden covering a foot high and paused to swing her light around quickly to search the opening.

No one stood there pointing a weapon at her.

It took some maneuvering, but she managed to ease the heavy covering over to one side before hoisting herself through the hole.

She sat there breathing in and out as quietly as she could until she'd regained her energy and pulled her legs up, turning to kneel. That gave her leverage to lower the cover. It fit perfectly back into the floor, but with a snick of sound.

Heart thumping, she waited.

No voices. No footsteps came her way.

Sweeping her light over the cover, she could see where thick dust had been undisturbed for many years prior to her opening the hatch. She had just enough room to turn around in the space without hitting a wall.

Where was the way out? She ran her hands everywhere until she touched a thick piece of wood that had been slid through two wooden loops. Yes!

She removed the heavy board that felt hand-hewn and tugged on a loop, inching the door inward. It squeaked. She held her breath. Chills ran up her arms.

No one attacked her. No bullets flew by.

Only dark met her on the other side.

Her ring light could stay on longer.

She squeezed through as soon as she had enough room and pulled the door back in place. It fit into the wall in a way that camouflaged the access.

She sniffed, expecting the musty smell. What else was she picking up?

The room stank. Body odor and something worse.

Then it hit her. Dried blood.

She pinched her nose and breathed through her mouth as she swept her light to inspect the closet-sized room. Her foot bumped into something that didn't move. The body of a man in khaki pants and a white cotton shirt was lying in a dried pool of blood from his throat being slashed.

He'd been dead more than one day.

Very likely the hermit owner.

That meant any options were on the table to get Phoebe to safety, even burning this house to the ground to send the Collector's security running to find the threat.

But only if she located Phoebe and knew she could free her.

Moving around the body, Hallene found a walk-in door, which opened to a larger room ... the basement she'd been hoping to find. Disappointment slammed her in the chest at the silence.

An empty room.

Phoebe was not here. No one was.

As much as Hallene wanted to hammer the Collector into the ground, she'd hoped to find Phoebe kept in the basement. If so, she'd pass on any payback to spirit the girl away to a safe place then send law enforcement to look for the property owner.

She walked around to determine all exit points. Only one besides the tunnel route. A set of stairs led way up to a landing easily thirty feet up.

That had to be higher than ground level.

She pulled out a lipstick camera and found a place to put it near the exit to the tunnel then headed for the metal stairs.

She climbed fifteen steps, then turned and climbed another twenty steps along the wall to a landing when the stairs turned left.

A modern-looking light fixture had been mounted at the side of a door she hoped opened into the living area. Rushing across the landing on her soft-soled shoes, she paused to carefully open the door and peek out.

Yet another closet. Big one.

Passing through that ten-foot-long by six-foot-wide space, she opened the second door into a grandiose ballroom.

The distinct smell of lemon polish replaced the stench clogging her nose.

While the tunnel appeared to still be a secret, the basement was not, but access to the basement had been somewhat hidden.

Where would they have put Phoebe? In a bedroom?

Where were guards set up to patrol?

She lifted a powerful stun gun from where it had been hooked on her belt. She'd brought it into South America broken apart with pieces hidden in her luggage contents, a camouflaged set Coop had created for her.

This gun was not even on the market yet.

Coop had always been getting his hands on the latest and greatest but warned her to stay in top shape. Never depend on the stun gun for more than gaining a moment's edge in a fight.

She stuck to that rule.

She pulled off her shoes and continued in her socks. Any sound could get her killed.

Her pulse quickened. She hurried into the ballroom where she found only two other doors on her right. The farthest one opened to reveal a long set of steps going down.

She'd save downstairs for last. Bedrooms were normally upstairs. That seemed a logical place to hold a captive.

Closing that door carefully, she moved to the other door, which opened into a small kitchen. Vintage cooking utensils were hung on a wall rack and stuffed into a ceramic vase sitting on a long prep counter with white cabinets below. More white cabinets were above a porcelain sink. The small refrigerator and free-standing gas stove with two small ovens all appeared clean and just as old as the cooking utensils.

Nothing appeared to be in use, which made sense for a single occupant. Probably a larger kitchen downstairs.

Could this have been the servant's access to upstairs living quarters for the domestic staff at one time?

Crossing the galley kitchen, she opened another door to find a long walkway overlooking a wide foyer. She inhaled fresher air here, thankful not to find the copper penny smell of fresh blood.

No sound came from below in the foyer. At the end of the walkway, a curved set of stairs with a polished wood railing descended to the main floor.

Deep breath. Then another.

Go time. She stepped out onto a wood floor and glanced over the railing, patiently waiting to locate a guard before moving into the opening.

A man dressed in dark fatigues and carrying a high-powered rifle finally walked by outside beyond the tall glass windows on each side of wide mahogany double doors. Exterior lights spaced along the walkway tossed beams across the marble floor inside where a circular table held a vase of dead flowers.

Her heart squeezed at the poor guy who had come here and worked so hard.

As soon as the guard went out of sight, she lifted her stun gun and moved quickly across the carpet, staying close to the wall on her right. Once she passed the staircase going down, she stopped at the first door. No lights shined out from beneath.

She opened it carefully and kept her voice low. "Phoebe?"

No one answered. Closing it softly, she opened the next door.

Someone gasped in a high-pitched voice.

Hallene whispered, "Phoebe?"

Loud sniffling, then Phoebe begged in a trembling voice, "Go away. Leave me alone."

Hallene's heart broke at the terror in the girl's voice because Phoebe couldn't see who entered. Still, her heart pounded, excited to have found the girl.

She took a step in, quietly saying, "Stay calm. It's me—"

"*Nooo!*"

Something hard slammed Hallene in the side of her head. She went down to the sound of Phoebe screaming.

CHAPTER 3

NOW FULLY IN COMBAT MODE, Sam left his misgivings behind as he moved through the dense vegetation, blending with the black night. He continued to sweep his surroundings just as his teammates were doing.

Almost five klicks covered.

The rain had just dwindled to a drizzle again, which disappointed him. Until now, a heavy downpour had shielded any noise of them pushing hard through thick vegetation.

They should reach their anticipated observation point in six minutes.

He hadn't hiked so fast in the rain since the Bamako operation where they'd had to track down a traitor to the US. Loser thought no one would find him in Mali after he'd stolen secrets from one of the largest aerospace companies in the US.

That had been bloodier than expected with the small army the traitor had hired to protect him.

The HAMR Brotherhood made sure he'd wasted his money.

Nitro's hushed voice came through all the comm units. "We're close. Should have visual in another fifty yards. Spread out."

Sam moved to his predetermined position just far enough away to see Nitro on his left and Angel on his right painted in greenish-gray tones from his NVG monocular.

All at once, the rain and wind died down.

Like cemetery quiet.

Blood surged in Sam's ears. His senses sharpened. He listened for even a leaf to flutter.

Nitro lifted a hand to signal where he would stop.

Sam and the other two dropped low, creeping up to join him.

Man, what a house. This compound hopefully held a kidnapped

US senator and the elusive W, the man behind extraordinary deadly events.

Deaths in the creative attacks normally ranged well over fifty and injuries into the hundreds.

Every August for the past five years, W orchestrated a heinous crime against humanity. At each event, someone barely alive, but chosen specifically to send a message, was left hanging in a macabre setting with the letter W slashed into their abdomen.

Allowed to be visible long enough for photographs and videos to be taken. Then kaboom.

This monster wanted the world to fear his power.

That's why Moose and Logan believed W might be the one who orchestrated this kidnapping. Senator Turner sat on the Foreign Affairs committee in congress. He'd made stopping W the center point of his last campaign, which got him reelected. As a frontrunner to become the next US president, Turner was pulling out all the stops to destroy W.

The senator had a pair of steel balls, but he'd challenged a vicious criminal and might end up paying the ultimate price.

Sam and this FALCA team would love to drag W back to face justice but rescuing the senator was paramount to everything else.

Nothing came before that mission.

On the other hand, if W turned his firepower on Sam's team, the murderer's notorious legend would end here.

They were far enough away from the mansion for them to talk quietly through their comm units. Sam took in the huge structure sitting on an island of landscaped property surrounded by miles of forest and jungle. "Looks like a good place for a cartel to hang out, Cuz."

Nitro replied, "True, but Moose would have found out by now if any were involved."

"Agreed." Sam nodded. Moose had coordinated everything they needed for this mission. He would not let them walk into a cartel nest.

Angel added in his Latin accent, "Does not fit the way W operates either, based on what little we know of him. This mansion is privately owned by a man who lives here with no staff."

"*Lived* here. He's likely dead," Blade interjected. "W would send in an advance team to secure the property before he arrived."

A grim truth. Sam had heard bits and pieces about the owner. Poor schmuck had built a multi-million-dollar business in the US housing industry and walked away from the civilized world to clean up an abandoned property out in the middle of nowhere.

Why? Because, in one day, he'd lost his wife and two children, who were caught in the crossfire of two gangs.

Poor bastard had no other family and snapped.

That's why Sam would never get involved with anyone. Any op could go badly, and he wouldn't return. Why put a woman through that? He'd already let two women down and that alone had broken him. Why risk failing someone else?

He'd hit his limit.

"Let's sync and get this show rolling." Nitro gave them the time on his watch.

Sam, Blade, and Angel signaled they were good.

"Only one guard has passed the front of the house since we arrived," Angel pointed out.

Sam tracked the heavily armed guard walking east to west in front of the wide steps to double mahogany doors. Lights were on in two upstairs windows at the east end. Most of the ground floor had the soft lighting of a house gone to bed.

Why did that look right and wrong at the same time? Sam muttered, "Seems like there should be at least two covering an exterior area that wide." It wasn't as if anyone on this planet had intel on how W ran his operations. "Could be to make them look vulnerable with more guards hidden inside."

A trap if anyone was expecting company.

That was almost impossible, based on how fast the FALCA team had gone wheels up on short notice. They entered the country on a private jet as five businessmen here for holiday.

Nitro studied the scene for a long moment. "Or W is overconfident someone wouldn't find this place so quickly after the kidnapping. He's not known for staying anywhere long for that reason."

Sam concurred. Moose had been digging nonstop for any intel on the kidnapping when he came up with this lead after decrypting dark web chatter, a place where he kept a secret presence. Logan immediately reached out to his people in US intelligence. They had teams in four different countries following tips and other intel on the kidnapped senator. The multiple leads could be a smokescreen to confuse everyone, but that would not stop any of them from going after the senator.

When Logan confirmed to military intelligence that he had a team ready to go wheels up and a rundown of their plan, he was asked to execute the extraction, but it would be off the books.

Most of what HAMR Brotherhood did was off the books.

That was the beauty of not being part of a large military force tasked with protecting the entire US.

Blade scratched his neck. "W is an ultimate prize, but if our package is still breathing when we extract him, anything else is a bonus. Right?"

Grunts of agreement followed.

It wasn't as if they weren't going in, but the single guard brought back a niggle of Sam's misgivings. He had no idea why since everything had run smoother than expected.

The helicopter hadn't crashed. That had been reason enough to feel positive. They'd even made it here eight minutes ahead of 20:00 as planned.

Still, the senator had been taken from a hotel in Virginia almost forty hours ago. An eternity with most kidnappings, but this was no standard snatch and grab.

Not if W was at the wheel.

Nitro gave the signal to head out. Everyone had a job.

Each of them would clear one side of the structure. Then Angel would deactivate any alarm system, if one had been installed, and send two clicks five seconds apart through their comm units before they entered on the ground level.

Nitro and Blade would insert past Angel who stayed in the downstairs at the front doors while Nitro searched the upstairs east wing and Blade went through every first-floor room.

By the time Sam heard the "all clear" clicks, he would have taken down anyone outside the west end of the building and entered the garage to disable the vehicles. Then he'd clear the west wing, which intel indicated had no bedrooms.

The moment he rounded the corner to the west end of the building, he hesitated.

No guard walked sentry here at all.

He'd be thankful not to deal with a guard, but there had to be more of them somewhere.

This smelled wrong.

He couldn't change what was. Not spending time neutralizing a guard allowed Sam an extra minute if he didn't encounter any inside. Angel's two spaced-out clicks came through Sam's comm just as he reached the walk-in door for the garage and turned the handle.

Not locked.

That would make sense if there had been a guard outside.

He couldn't call to check on the rest of his team. They had to be radio silent inserting. Hell.

Turning the knob all the way, he stepped inside.

CHAPTER 4

———————

SWEAT POURED OVER HALLENE'S FACE and naked body. Her wrists screamed in pain from being tied with rope to hold her weight on a chain hanging from the ceiling. Terror had gripped her mind when she'd first regained consciousness. She'd cringed at discovering she'd been stripped and strung up like a side of beef.

Her feet had been submerged ankle-deep in a wooden barrel of water. She'd never experienced this gut-wrenching sense of despair and fear.

Then Coop's training kicked in. He'd once shouted at her, *"Don't you fucking dare quit on living! EVER! Never give up!"*

When she could finally draw a breath, she'd forced herself to use his mental exercises to remain positive and ready to escape.

But he would not be proud of his student now.

The scuff of boots over the basement's dirt floor reminded her she was not alone.

Don't whimper, she coached herself.

She clamped her lips tighter, determine not to make a sound and give Cyclops any satisfaction. She'd given that name to the bastard with one unravaged eye in his ugly mug who took joy in his task.

She hoped the other eye had been gouged out with a dull spoon. He didn't physically compare to the giants of ancient lore. This creep topped out at just short of six feet and with a wiry body that smelled worse than any homeless person she'd ever met.

He liked flexing his muscle when he had a defenseless woman hanging by her arms.

Sweat inched down through her eyes, taking its time annoying her.

Cyclops had been musing once more over his assortment of torture tools laid out on a filthy table. He turned to her with excitement rising in his soulless eye. A thick black mustache hid most of his toothless grin. She hoped his disgusting body stench would not fill her last inhale.

Before he arrived, she'd been hung for an hour. Her feet had turned numb in the icy water. She lifted weights and trained constantly to be in shape. Her arms could handle the pain if that was all she had to endure.

As if. This was not as bad as it would get.

"Again, puta?" Cyclops asked in a seductive voice as if he intended to massage her and not fry her body.

Can't think about that. Think about anything else but the pain. "Never give into victim mindset," Coop had told her if she ever got caught.

Glaring down at Cyclops, she saw him as a tiny man. A nobody. That wasteland of humanity was only a tick on the back of the mongrel she hunted.

Much better. She had to keep coming up with ways to feel powerful.

Cyclops enjoyed taunting her, convinced he could wield a psychological game when he lacked the brain cells to bob for apples.

She hoped her glare televised that insult.

He scoffed at her. "You think you are better than me. Many have this foolish notion at first." His heavy boots pounded the cement floor as he circled her like a land shark closing in on its prey. He went out of view on her right and returned on her left, never slowing his drivel in a heavy Latin accent. "But none ever outlast me. To withdraw intel while prolonging your life, this is an art. Not what you see in movies."

She sighed, expecting his resume next.

Neither of them had time for this. She'd overheard two men talking a short while ago. One was Russian, a language she was adept at interpreting. He addressed the second man as Collector, who talked about their next move.

This idiot below her smirking clearly could not translate Russian and thought he'd been left in charge after the Collector told him to take his time and call when he had everything.

What the Collector and the Russian had discussed was the mansion being wired to explode.

If she didn't get out of this jam soon, she'd end up dying with Cyclops. Now, to just magically remove the ropes cutting into her skin and she could escape.

She'd get on that any minute now.

Cyclops rubbed his hands together. "Just remember, I give you chance to end this quickly and you waste it."

She tried not to shiver and encourage him, but this was a dank basement despite being late summer in South America plus her icy foot bath.

Shock from the pain wasn't helping either.

Cold was cold no matter what you were doing.

He paused, seeming to weigh a decision, then reached for the two battery clamps he clicked against each other. Sparks flew. Plenty of power.

Lifting the leads slowly, he started for her.

She worked on sending her mind somewhere else, somewhere far from this place, to withstand what she had coming.

That hadn't prepared her for the first time he'd shoved the ends into the water. If not for being dehydrated, she'd have embarrassed herself.

Her first electric shock had been just a tease. She'd bit down hard and flinched, keening in pain.

He'd howled with pleasure as if he'd personally created that form of torture. The Collector and the Russian had entered, interrupting him. Cyclops had stood at attention, his gaze fixed on a spot high up and behind her. Sounding as if he stood at the top of the stairs behind her, the Collector told this idiot he'd have thirty minutes once the green light flashed on the wall Hallene faced.

That had not been the truth.

She recalled the Russian saying the minute a black ops team entered, opening any door would trip an alert to the Russian's phone. A green light would flash on the wall Hallene stared at, which would indicate a timer on the bomb had been activated with enough time for the team to be deep inside when it blew.

With Cyclops now heading for her, she had a choice. If she clued him in that his time alive was dwindling, he'd attack her with all he had. She'd die before him, then he'd likely escape alive.

Not acceptable.

He paused and clicked the wires together again.

She arched an eyebrow and stared him down.

He lost his smile.

That was the opening she needed. "I know my death is going to suck, but you should get done and not be late contacting your boss."

"I control time," he snarled.

"Nope, your boss does. I'm not sharing a thing so you might as well kill me now. At least you don't have time to rape me. Every dark cloud has its silver lining, right?"

His brow wrinkled with an obvious question. He was too stupid to realize she'd insulted him.

He stood there debating if he should torture her now and possibly kill her or if he should rape her first while she was lucid.

Tough question for so little mental capacity.

She'd done as Coop taught her and kept her mind locked on defeating Cyclops. She was not going down without a fight.

She had an idea.

Just thinking of a plan helped, even a bad one.

Time to sell it no matter how much bile ran up her throat. She let her legs dangle open, drawing his gaze to her triangle of blond curls.

Disgust rolled through her in waves, but she had only one play. "If you don't grow a pair of cojones and do something soon, your amigos will know you didn't touch me. They're watching all this on video. They'll wonder if you even like girls or if your dick was too short to reach."

She hadn't found a camera down here, but Cyclops' head spun from side to side searching.

Ha! Made you look. Juvenile thought, but it kept her positive.

Hands shaking with fury, he bared his teeth and threw down the wires, decision made.

She swallowed hard, praying she had a chance. Even a small one was better than just giving in.

CHAPTER 5

NO ONE IN THE GARAGE attacked or shot at Sam. He would like to be happy about that, but it was just one more sign of something off with this setting.

His head kept warning him he should go watch his team's back, but Angel was more than capable. They all had specific tasks to complete. This was not the time to do anything except execute his orders.

Sam got busy with the vehicle, slowing long enough to flatten two tires on each side of the black Suburban by sticking his knife tip into the valves.

They might need a vehicle later or he'd slash unfixable holes.

Why only one vehicle?

Probably because W had a chopper coming in to lift him and the senator out, making it harder to track them.

Sam pushed to get his part done quickly. He'd bet Nitro would find someone in the upstairs library or master bedroom, but Sam might bump into a guard taking a break in the kitchen to rummage for food. That didn't sound possible in his head, but stranger things had happened on ops.

That's why he had a Beretta M9 with a suppressor in his side holster.

He held his HK up, using the rifle barrel to lead his way as he headed for what should be entry to the mansion from the garage. Moose had found photos posted in a blog from hikers who had located the dilapidated mansion and spent a night here. There was no way to confirm any changes made by the new owner, but his team had a decent idea of the architectural layout.

Quietly opening the door, he entered a hall with a laundry room and half bath.

Instrumental music, something jazzy, floated from hidden speakers along his path. He searched for cameras to disable but found none so far.

Didn't mean there weren't some hidden.

He passed through a fully updated kitchen with new appliances. From paint to new wood cabinets, this place smelled new. He cleared the huge dining room with tall glass windows trimmed with fancy curtains he'd never had in his home. If the loner had entertained, he likely lit up the patio outside for his guests. At the moment, everything beyond twenty feet out from the patio remained shrouded in shadows.

His area required him to circle back to the kitchen and look for access to any other rooms before going upstairs. He crossed the kitchen to a door that opened to twelve steps rising to another door. His boots sank into thick carpet as he climbed them.

Not like the threadbare carpet he'd slept on as a kid.

When Sam reached the top step, he pushed the half-open door all the way and found a freaking ballroom.

This guy must have needed a map to get around.

Clearing the huge ballroom lit by two sconces with puny lights and an unlit wrought-iron chandelier, he came up emptyhanded again. On the far side of the room, an antique mahogany bar that belonged in an upscale hotel stood ten feet tall and stretched over twenty feet wide. Damn room could easily hold a hundred people.

The guy who remodeled this mansion could have turned the place into a bed and breakfast for tourists wanting to visit remote locations. That's what Sam's aunt had done. Angie built a moderate-sized inn in a remote location in northern Maine but never advertised it. That had made no sense.

He started clearing the room and checked the first door on his left.

Another kitchen. This one belonged in a house from the early nineteen hundreds with small appliances. Old crap, but nice in its own way. This kitchen did not appear to be in use. No sign of food like bananas, vegetables, or even canned goods.

Closing that door, he surveyed every nook and dark space quickly. Prepared to head back down to the main floor to help

Angel, he swung past the last wall on his right and noticed an alcove.

There were too many places to hide in this house.

He stepped into the dark space, expecting a storage space for servicing this ballroom with shelves of cleaning supplies and equipment.

Nope. It was a closet with yet door number bazillion on the other side of the narrow room.

He stepped in and his boots bumped something on the floor. Looking down, he found a pair of dark sneakers with a smooth bottom. Not for running. Hard to say if they belonged to a man or a tall woman. The senator had been in a suit when he was taken.

What were those shoes doing here?

Taking in every inch of the room, he found a thin strip of light squeezing through the gaps at the bottom of the second door. If he had not taken his time looking, he would have missed it.

Would that be a hidden room?

He froze at the muffled sound of voices. His pulse went into overdrive.

Could this be where they kept the senator? Sam would have to confirm first before knowing his next step.

Palming his knife, he slid it into a gap on the side of the door and pried it away from the frame without making a sound.

No squeaking. There was a bit of luck.

Weapon in hand, Sam slowly opened the door wider and heard a sexy female voice challenging, "If you don't grow a pair of cojones and do something soon, your amigos will know you didn't touch me. They're watching all this on video. They'll wonder if you even like girls or if your dick was too short to reach."

What. The. Hell?

Sam flipped up his NVG because of light glaring from above that scene. He saw the attractive backside of a naked female strung up by her wrists.

An insane naked female taunting her captor.

The single lightbulb hung above her cast a harsh glow over her smooth skin. She looked to be five-nine or five-ten and muscles in her back and legs had come from serious weight work.

She had likely worn the shoes he found.

This place could be an ancient dungeon. It didn't belong to the opulent structure viewed outside the room.

Sam needed a clear shot to take down her captor.

No chance.

The male, blocked by her body, flicked into view for a second when he stepped back and tossed aside wire leads from a battery. Her feet were in a full tub of water.

He'd been about to torture her. Or maybe this was just continuing with a new round of torture.

Challenging him to rape her would only make her situation worse. Was she trying to die quickly?

Fuck that.

Ugly bastard had one good eye and a thick black mustache. He started for her, snarling, "You will pay for your mouth, puta. I will hurt you in ways you ..."

"Blah, blah, blah," she scoffed at him.

Sam had entered the dark top of the stairs and started moving down slowly. If she'd shut the hell up and give him a chance to get closer, he could take out the male with a shot that wouldn't put her at risk. Moving as fast as he could but silently down the stairs, he hung close to the wall, hoping not to announce his presence.

Not yet.

This place had to be thirty feet down from the ballroom.

Four more steps and ...

One-eye reached for the naked woman.

Two seconds dragged by as Sam's heart power-punched his chest. He lunged down the steps to reach her faster.

Her hands twisted and her fingers gripped each side of the rope tying her to the chain. Blood ran from her wrists. Every muscle in her back and legs flexed when she snatched her feet from the water, drawing those long limbs up together fast.

She first kneed her captor under the chin.

When his head snapped back, she kicked the heel of her foot out to smash his face.

The guy howled and fell backward with blood spraying from a broken nose.

That all happened in seconds.

No reason to be quiet now. Sam raced over to her.

She struggled with her grip on the ropes, trying to use one hand to hold her body weight and shake her other hand free of the binding. Impossible.

He yelled, "Hold up. I'll help you."

A laser gaze of fury shot to him. "*Who are you?*"

Not the reaction he'd expected. "I'm not with *that* guy moaning on the floor." Said guy was trying to get up. Sam took a step and kicked his booted foot at the creep's head.

Down went One-eye again.

She sagged with relief, then muttered, "Took you long enough."

What did that mean?

Sam didn't have time to find out. He glanced around and found a metal wheel with a chain wrapped around it next to the wall. Hurrying over, he grabbed the lever and released the tension on the single string of chain. The links ran through pulleys hung from the rafters and then down to the rope. He leaned his back into lowering the chain slowly to keep from dropping her hard and breaking an ankle.

Water in the three-foot-tall wooden tub still splashed when she hit. Her knees folded against the edge. She groaned as her arms dropped and she fumbled with the ropes.

Sam ran over with his knife out to cut the rope from the chain. He pulled the pieces from her raw wrists and hissed at the damage. "Hang on. I'll get you out." He used both hands to grab her around the waist and hoist her out, pinning his gaze to her gorgeous gray eyes the whole time. Loose hair had fallen from a twisted-up style, probably from having it grabbed.

He stepped over to a dry spot and lowered her feet to the floor.

"Can you stand on your own?" he asked gently.

"Yes." That had come out as a croak.

Guessing at what she'd suffered turned his stomach.

She put her hand on a tall wooden table next to her that held an assortment of torture tools.

Disgust tore at Sam.

He released her then unlatched his tactical vest, keeping his rifle and handgun where he could reach them immediately. He dropped his vest on the nasty display of tools still covered in dried blood, then pulled his black T-shirt over his head and handed it to her.

He would understand anyone in her situation falling apart, but this woman shifted between flinching with pain and fury crossing her face.

She startled at being handed a shirt. Red-rimmed from what she'd been through, her gray eyes still met his straight on, but her face softened.

She was tall and a looker. A tough female from what he could see.

Why had she been kidnapped?

She swallowed hard and pulled the shirt over her head. "Thanks."

He wanted to make everything better for her and hear that sweet voice without the underlying pain. It was all he could do to not stomp the one-eyed cretin to pieces.

A groan and scuffle sound yanked Sam around. He automatically lifted his Baretta as he turned.

One-eye dragged a weapon from behind him, yanking it up.

Sam double-tapped the torturer's forehead out of natural reaction before One-eye could pull the trigger. Sadly, no intel from that one. Sam hoped like hell the rest of his team managed to keep someone alive.

Preferably W.

Turning back quickly, he took in the woman's face to see if what had happened to her had begun to sink in. Was she about to break in half?

She was calm. In fact, seeing her dead attacker washed away her fury.

Sam hadn't allowed his gaze to look at her naked body. She may be tough, but she had to feel vulnerable. He managed a quick sweep from head to toe, assessing her for injuries. She had bruises along her arms and neck. Her long-ass legs hadn't been treated any better. The rest of her body filled out his shirt in a way that would stay carved into his mind.

While he'd taken stock of her damage, he'd snatched up his vest and put it on over his undershirt. With all his weapons back in place, he nodded at her. "Can you walk?"

"Yes. I'm good." She seemed to regain her composure then pinned him with a suspicious look. "You haven't said who you are."

How could she see him as the enemy? "Me? I'm the one who just got you out of a jam." Then he yanked his head out of his ass to tell her what she needed to hear. "I'm with an American special operations unit. Please give me your name and my people will get you home." His team had been told nothing about another captive, but it wouldn't be as if W released a kidnap guest list.

She started backing up.

Sam could not believe his eyes. Did she feel threatened by him? "Wait a minute. Where are you going?"

"Not going with you."

"Really? You think *I'm* a bad guy?"

She shrugged. "No, but I can't even see your face with that mask and headgear."

Was she serious? Still, Sam had to get her stable so he could go to his team. He lifted the NVG monocular headgear and pulled his black mask down. "Feel better?"

She sidestepped and backed up again. "I still have no idea who you are. What's *your* name?"

Just kill him now.

What a shame for a woman that hot to be certifiable. Time to dial up his no-bullshit mission voice. "My name is classified, but I can get you returned to your home. I just need to know what's going on, your name, and how you ended up here, Miss. That's fair, right?"

She blew out a sigh as if this had become tedious.

What? Was he holding her up for a lunch appointment?

She had a husky voice that might star in his next fantasy, but it turned all business and dismissive. "Thanks for lowering me to the ground. I'll pay you back right now by warning you to get your team moving and leave immediately or die. See? Debt paid. I'm out of here."

An operative? She had skills and sounded too under control to not be. She backed up another two steps toward a grungy wall piled with boxes and clothes.

Now she had his suspicions pinging all over the place.

"What makes you think I have a team?" He stepped toward her and kept his voice calm as he put his headgear back on. He kept his assault rifle at the ready and hoped he would not have to use it. "Slow down because I don't understand what's going on with you or why you're here."

She raked a hand over what looked to have once been perfectly styled blond hair in a bun and snapped, "Try to keep up. That dead guy's boss left two guards and Cyclops as bait to draw you and your team in. The minute your team inserted, you triggered the green light up there which came on for fifteen seconds just before you came running up to me."

Sam followed her pointing finger to a small green light high on a wall that wasn't currently illuminated. He swung back quickly to keep an eye on her.

Sounding in control, she continued. "That was a warning for any guards they wanted out of the house before a bomb detonates in ... crap. What time do you have?"

Bomb? Should he believe her?

He peeled the cover off his watch then put it back. "Twenty-two-hundred-twenty-three or ..."

"Twenty-three minutes after ten at night. Got it. Based on what I could see of Cyclops' watch, I'm guessing you might have ninety seconds, plus or minus, to get out before everything blows."

Pressure expanded in his head. Should he believe her? "Why would One-eye's boss blow this house?"

She fisted her hands and spoke in a furious snarl. "You got a leak in your group. They knew you were coming. He's blowing up the house to get rid of evidence and take out your team, probably so he won't face any of you again. That's it for a news brief."

She turned to leave.

He had to alert his team. No reason to keep radio silence now.

As he cast a fast glance at Cyclops, who was definitely dead, he warned the team, "*Exit now!* I repeat, *exit now!* No extraction. Package not here. Structure wired to blow in less than ninety seconds." He turned back to the woman, expecting to see her climbing the stairs.

She was nowhere in sight.

What the ever-loving hell?

Sam raced across the room and climbed the steps two at a time. He paused at the top and snatched the door open. Nothing had been disturbed. She hadn't come this way.

The shoes were still there.

Shit. Covering the mic for his comm, he shouted, "Hey you! This is the only way out."

Maybe. Or maybe she knew another way.

He wasted precious seconds.

Nitro's quiet voice, the one that came out when he was deep in a mission, spoke in his ear. "What the fuck, Cuz? Over."

"They knew we were coming. When we entered, we tripped a signal to remotely trigger a bomb. Over." Sam gave the room one more look, shook his head, and got busy getting his ass out.

"From what intel? Over." Sharp noises coming through with Nitro's voice meant he was knocking things out of the way. He would not leave until his entire team was out.

Sam scrambled through the ballroom and headed for the stairs to the main kitchen. That was the quickest way he knew to reach the ground floor. "More in debrief, but I believe the intel is sound. Over."

How many seconds had passed already? Sam couldn't waste time checking his watch.

Nitro said, "I'll wait at our insert point. Over."

Heaving breaths as he pumped his legs, Sam said, "I won't make it that far. Get out. See you at the meet point. Over and out."

A deep curse vibrated Sam's headset.

Where had the hot crazy woman gone?

He couldn't help someone who didn't want to be saved but leaving without her twisted his insides.

He'd never leave a female in trouble.

Sam lunged down the last four steps to reach the kitchen and grabbed the doorframe to swing himself around toward the dining room. Every second counted. A quick slide and his boots had traction again. Running into the dining room, he looked left at the huge windows and ran that way, unloading the HK in a constant blast as he did.

The window burst open with glass flying everywhere.

His legs felt heavy as lead. That was his body's psychological reaction to expecting a bomb to blow him to pieces at any second.

He leaped through the shattered window, catching jagged pieces across his arms. His body was big and muscled but slamming the ground with no way to break his fall hurt. He rolled, got up, and forced his legs to move again.

Reaching up to pull his NVG back in place, he grinned. Hot damn. He'd made it out in—

The bomb exploded.

Pressure from the blast sent his body flying forward, flipping around in the dark. The back of his head slammed something hard, coldcocking him.

His body hit water with a splash.

He sank as he blacked out.

CHAPTER 6

———◆———

HALLENE'S LEGS AND ARMS ACHED as she scurried through the dirt tunnel that ran over two hundred feet from the mansion to what was left of the access shack. Her intel had been good on this insert and escape route, but the minute that bomb went off, she'd end up buried alive in this death trap.

When she'd heard the Russian tell the Collector a black ops team was en route to the mansion, she hadn't expected someone to come to her aid.

The team could have been a rival group with orders to capture and punish, or kill, the Collector for any number of crimes.

Hallene had been worried Phoebe would get caught in the crossfire. Now the Collector was moving her to a new location.

If only Kovac gave a shit about his daughter and their mother. Hallene would find out who blackmailed him and hopefully use that to find Phoebe again.

She stumbled, stuck her hand against the dirt wall to stay upright, and kept moving. Her leg and arm muscles were strained. She kept thinking of anything but feeling weak.

Maybe she'd have been better off leaving with that hunk.

No, he would have continued his sixty questions and she'd have been hard-pressed to escape from him and his team in this country. But he'd been the backup she'd needed tonight.

Six-feet-two of badass attitude. Then he'd yanked his shirt off and handed it to her.

Her eyes had tracked all of that lean and cut body as he'd put his tactical vest back on.

Calendar shot right there.

He'd gotten gold stars for handing her the shirt and never letting his eyes drop below her neck for a sneak peek.

It had been a long time since she'd had a man care for her needs, mainly because she allowed no one close.

No one to lean on. No one to lose again.

She'd spent a lot of lonely nights over the last few years, but she kept telling herself she was stronger alone.

Coop hadn't been hers, but he'd filled some of that hole in her chest as a friend for a long time.

She followed the bouncing glow of the small flashlight. They hadn't taken her ring.

Just her clothes and her dignity.

She still left with intel. She'd done okay and would have gotten Phoebe out if they hadn't planted a guard inside the dark room.

She had her moments.

Coop would still be yelling that her plan had been nothing short of suicide. He might have had a point, but she'd really expected to be successful, or she wouldn't have gone in alone.

Would Coop have anticipated the hidden guard?

Maybe, maybe not, but he'd argue that he'd have had someone watching his six as he entered.

Point taken but ... she had no one anymore.

Too bad she couldn't have had her badass savior on this mission. He would have covered her six and then some.

Coop would be shaking his head at her logic. She didn't even know that guy. He'd tell her to only take someone she trusted. That narrowed the field to ... no one.

Even if she could ask someone from his team, which she couldn't, she wouldn't risk losing any of Coop's people. They had treated her as family when Coop died and would step in at a moment's notice for a normal request.

Saving Phoebe was her responsibility. Hallene had sworn to her mother that she'd protect the girl. When she made a vow, she intended to keep it.

She just hadn't planned on Phoebe being captured by someone who didn't even ask for money.

Her bouncing light reached the partial ladder as it came into view. Of the original eight steps rising three feet off the ground, only the bottom six remained. Jumping down into this hole earlier had been simpler. She hadn't really planned to be outrunning a bomb when she came back this way with Phoebe.

Someone had stacked rocks for makeshift steps so long ago, it took her a second to figure that out due to mold and vines crawling over the stones.

She jumped to the top stone, which was just large enough for both feet.

It rocked on an uneven base.

"*Whoa!*" She waved her arms to keep her balance then landed a hand on the edge of the rotten floor above her. Wood broke free. She danced on the stone again then caught part of the floor with both hands.

The rocks wobbled but not as much as before.

Pulling the ring off her finger, she tossed the light through the opening and hoped it did not break or fall into a hole.

The bright beam glowed over the opening.

A muffled boom sounded behind her. The ground shook and rumbled. She fought to keep a grip on the floor.

Noise boiled through the tunnel, heading her way.

Adrenaline zinged through her body. Hair lifted on her arms.

The rocks shifted back and forth faster.

She bent her knees, dipped down, and shoved up, gritting her teeth against the pain inflicted on her body. Growling for more boost, she forced her body up on exhausted arms and threw a foot over the edge to hold her in place with one leg dangling. Sweat burned her eyes and slid over her skin.

The floor vibrated and made cracking noises.

She took a breath and went for one last push to drag her body over the edge and fell forward. Her face smacked a filthy wood floor.

Partial walls left of the shack leaning over her shook. This should be too far from the mansion for that to happen, right? Maybe not. A house of cards would have been more substantial than what was left of this place.

She mustered another bit of strength and rolled away from the hole, then flipped onto her back. She dragged air through her strained lungs and wheezed, feeling much older than twenty-nine.

The tunnel rumble grew in volume until her escape hole

belched out a cloud of dirt that blew all over her.

She covered her face and kept her mouth shut.

Sweaty grime slicked her body.

She'd gone through worse today but still spit dirt to the side of her face and started breathing through her nose.

Amazingly, the decrepit structure around her remained intact after all that.

More loud noises boomed.

Could that be another bomb? Rain began falling through the canopy of leaves, sneaking past the holes above her.

She listened to the repeat of the second boom. Ah. That last noise had been thunder.

The drizzle picked up speed, splattering her face and body. She welcomed the refreshing feel of fresh water. It washed away the mud and vulnerable feeling from being in that basement.

She'd survived this attempt. A win was a win.

But she still had to get back to Phoebe.

What about the green-eyed badass? Had he survived?

She'd heard him calling to her and, like an idiot, she'd paused. Bigger idiot, she'd almost gone back to warn him again to leave. But she could hear Coop screaming in her mind to never slow down when on the run.

If he stood here now, Coop would hug her even as he admonished, "Too close, Hellie."

Those days of having him to comfort her were gone.

He might be here if he had been more cautious, but that had never been his nature. That was why he'd kept her at arm's length as a friend only.

Wandering around in that mental minefield would only get her hurt. Again.

Hallene had to stay focused on finding Phoebe. If she didn't get Phoebe back, she'd end up burying another part of her soul. Her mother had kept Hallene up on Phoebe, constantly trying to connect the two of them. No telling what she'd told Phoebe about Hallene since they only had polite conversations when visiting their mother.

With adrenaline draining away, Hallene's body ached from personal treatment in the Cyclops salon. Her head throbbed where she'd been hit when she found Phoebe. She lifted her fingers to the cut on the side of her head. The blood had dried around a goose-egg shape. Not too bad. Hair would cover it.

Time to get moving even if her body wasn't onboard yet.

She'd leap to her feet the minute she felt that renewed burst of energy.

Slowly struggle her way upright would be more like it.

Maybe just one more minute to catch her second or third wind. Seconds ticked by as she reveled in being alive. Her hand dropped to her chest, reminding her she wore the soft black T-shirt.

After being ogled by that scum Cyclops, her hot rescuer had treated her like a fully dressed woman. She still couldn't believe he had kept his gaze up on her face. Not because she considered herself a knockout, but she knew men. Their eyes sometimes separated from their brains in front of a naked woman.

Not her badass. He seemed to understand how a woman in that situation would feel even worse to be ogled.

Respect was sexy in a man.

She'd been mentally ordering herself to not feel like prey, to not give Cyclops a second of pleasure, and to avoid any thought of not leaving that basement alive.

Like Coop had said, mind over matter is often the only thing between dying and walking away from a bad op.

In that moment, when the stranger had handed her his T-shirt, she'd been surprised at not being treated as just a naked victim.

Badass with a moral compass.

After she'd knocked Cyclops backward, that operator's initial expression had been one of seeing her as a peer. But he'd been confused, which meant he'd likely heard her taunting Cyclops to rape her. That might not be what he'd expect a peer to do in her situation, but he hadn't questioned her reasoning.

Points to him for not wasting time asking her.

Rain slowed to a steady drip off the leaves and branches. Tired or not, she had to climb out of this dark place both literally and emotionally. She shoved up to a sitting position, careful to not catch splinters in her exposed butt.

Grabbing the hem of the shirt she'd tied into a quick knot, she wiped mud off her face and away from her eyes, then inhaled deeply. The rugged masculine scent infused into the shirt by heat brought a half-smile to her lips.

She loved the manly smell.

Some women might be turned off by a man's lingering perspiration scent ground into a piece of clothing, but she'd spent a lot of time around men training for dangerous ops.

Real men didn't smell like fancy models.

Real men got dirty, sweaty, and banged up.

This T-shirt attested to all that and more about her mysterious badass.

What had he said into his comm unit right before she snuck into the tunnel entrance? "No extraction. Package not here."

What person had his team inserted to rescue? She doubted it had been Phoebe since Kovac was being blackmailed to do something nefarious.

That guy's team had not only located the Collector but had also come there looking to rescue someone.

If mystery guy's team found this location, they might be able to find the Collector's next location.

If so, they'd know where Phoebe had been taken.

Phoebe was alive. Hallene had to keep telling herself that.

Energized by that hope, Hallene twisted around until she located her LED and shoved the ring on her finger. She untied the knot at the hem of his shirt, which held the lipstick camera she'd placed in the basement. She checked it quickly and released a long sigh. This one survived.

If she got decent images, this camera had the power to put her back on Phoebe's trail as soon as Midnight Ferret performed his electronic magic. He could access hidden data that some intelligence agencies could not.

Unfortunately, the small camera could not pick up images at the top of the stairs where the Collector and Russian had stood.

She hoped Midnight could come through one more time on this mission.

If her techie could not find the Collector's next location, maybe he could pull a clear enough image off this lipstick camera to locate her sexy badass.

Then she'd find out if that operator was willing to help her.

If not, she'd find a way to convince him.

One of Coop's sayings had been, "All things might not be fair in love, but they are in war."

CHAPTER 7

———

"COME ON, PARTYMAN. OPEN YOUR eyes."

Who was slapping him?

"Cuz? Can you hear me?"

That sounded like Blade. Sam waited for his scrambled brain to rearrange itself back to normal. He blinked.

A bright light blasted fire into his eyes.

He swatted at the evil glow. "Get that out of my face."

Blade's wide body blocked out the world. He sighed heavily. "He'll live, Nitro."

Nitro. Blade. Angel. The FALCA team. Brain coming back online. Sam tried to sit up. "Is everybody okay?"

Blade topped Sam by another two inches and a load of muscle. The team medic held him down with big hands used with precision to heal or kill, depending on the situation. "*We're good. All but you, Cuz.*"

That's when Sam realized he was soaking wet, laying on grassy ground and surrounded by trees.

Was this their meet point in the woods? How had he gotten here?

Blade's watch face glowed as he checked Sam's pulse, but not enough light to see anything clearly beyond Blade's face.

Sam felt his head. No night-vision gear. When had he lost that?

Back of his head hurt like hell. He coughed. Raw throat as if he'd been throwing up. His undershirt was soaked. "Why am I wet?"

The resident daredevil's grinning face came into view above him. "You land in the pool when the house blew up. Wish I had seen that stunt, *Primo*." Angel often reverted to Cuz in his native language. "You must have *ángel de la guarda*."

Guardian angel? Sam's memory sharpened.

Gray eyes came to mind.

That woman had been no angel. He couldn't decide if she'd been a godsend that had saved his team with her warning or if she was the very reason their op had been exposed. Was she part of W's world? If so, what the hell had she been doing in that basement being tortured?

She seemed to know a lot about W and the mansion.

She hadn't exited by any obvious escape route.

Maybe she'd crossed her boss, and he'd left the one-eyed goon to teach her a lesson before W wiped out her and the torturer.

But how had anyone known Sam's team was coming in?

"Let me sit up, Blade," Sam grumbled. He had to prove he was still able to continue with this mission. He accepted the hand his buddy offered and sat up, waiting for his head to stop imitating an out-of-control amusement park ride. Clamping his teeth together prevented heaving. For now. His vision cleared more. He could make out Nitro and Angel getting ready to leave.

Blade dropped down and used an antiseptic wipe to clean cuts and a few burns on Sam's arms and shoulders. If he hit the pool that fast, the burns were from flying pieces of debris.

Sam's vest had likely saved most of his back.

"What happened to your shirt, Cuz?" Nitro asked on his way over to him.

That's right. He'd handed his T-shirt to the woman.

"First, did you find any survivors?" Sam had to know if she'd escaped.

"No." Nitro squatted down next to him. "The two guards left unconscious outside didn't make it through the blast. After we found you in the pool, we searched the debris and found body parts under rubble in the middle of the house."

"Probably the basement."

"No one mentioned a basement." Nitro frowned, no doubt thinking through the intel they'd received. That wasn't the half of how many things they had to sort out from this clusterfuck.

Sam swallowed hard. "Pretty sure it's the body of the guy I walked in on torturing a prisoner."

"The senator?" Nitro tensed. "We didn't find a second body."

"No second body. It was a woman." Sucking up his courage to move his head again, Sam pushed to his feet, glad his stomach hadn't revolted.

Nitro stood with him as Sam elaborated. "She's the one who told me the building was set to blow."

At that announcement, all movement ceased.

Blade and Angel joined Sam and Nitro.

"Who was she and what happened to her?" Angel asked, sounding as surprised as Nitro looked.

Sam wished he knew the answer to both of those questions. "She'd been hung by her wrists from the ceiling with her feet submerged in a tub of water. Bastard had wire leads from a power source ready to go. Looked like he might have used them on her once already."

Disgusted sounds oozed from the trio.

But they didn't know everything yet. "The basement entrance was on the second floor. Yeah, crazy location I found by accident and that basement didn't fit the house. Looked like it'd been there for hundreds of years. Her body blocked any clear shot of him from the top step. Before I could slip all the way down, she goaded the goon into raping her."

"What?" Blade's jaw dropped. More shocked expressions joined his.

Sam held up a finger. "By the time I got to help her, the fool had jumped at her offer. She made a badass move, jerking her legs up to knee him under the chin then used her heels to slam him in the face. Smashed his nose."

Admiration wiped away their shock. Nitro muttered, "Damn." Then his gaze lifted to Sam. "Where is she?"

Sam washed a hand over his face, still frustrated at losing her. "Once she told me the place was wired to blow, I took a second to alert all of you first then headed for the stairs. That's when I realized she'd vanished and not by the stairs. No way she could have gone up two levels by then. I got to the top and looked around one last time, but she was in the wind. I called to her and got no reply. I'm thinking she had better intel on that building than us, which included an escape tunnel from the basement."

Nitro's mood went south. "That's why you almost didn't make it. You *waited* for her."

Like Sam could deny that. "Only for a moment."

"After you said we had less than ninety seconds to get out. If you had not exited through that window in front of the pool and if I had not been close enough watching for you to show up and dove in after you, you'd be dead right now. You know to treat a female operative like a male in these situations."

Sam's blood boiled. This was not the same as that last mission. "Don't start that crap with me, Nitro. You sayin' you wouldn't have taken a last look?"

"Not with my life on the line and my team at risk of dying."

That just pissed off Sam even more. He leaned in. "I put my team first by contacting all of you before anything else."

Friction shot through the air.

Angel and Blade found something else to do, leaving those two to go at it.

Nitro opened his mouth then caught himself. Raising his voice was out of character, especially on an op. Nitro held a steel grip on his emotions, joking and picking at everyone before he'd devolve into shouting.

Inhaling deeply, the team leader spoke in his low voice. "I was *not* questioning your commitment to all of us, and I never would, Cuz. I would also help a woman in danger, even if it meant risking my life, but everything you said pointed at her being a trained operative, not a defenseless female. Your hesitation stole extra time for you to run from the house. I am not losing *any* of you on my watch for any unknown operative."

Sam hooked his thumbs in his pants pockets and stared at the ground. He'd had the same thoughts of wasting precious seconds but still felt justified in his effort to find her before leaving. He owed Nitro thanks for keeping him from drowning and had to admit that in hindsight his hesitation to leave without her had been a mistake.

Before he could get the words out, Nitro added, "One day, a woman in trouble at the wrong moment is going to be the reason you don't walk away from these ops."

That crushed Sam's moment of understanding. Nitro would

report everything to Logan, which he should.

But Sam could do without being condemned for losing ten seconds. "That's bullshit, Nitro, and you know it." So much for mending their argument. Sam looked around and his head spun. He covered his mouth, inhaled, and forced the contents of his gut back down where they belonged.

"Blade," Nitro called out softly.

When the medic came back, Nitro asked, "What's Sam's diagnosis?"

"Sam is fine, *Cuz*," Sam snapped at Nitro.

Ignoring that, Blade said, "He's got a few nasty cuts from debris, which I've cleaned. Second-degree burns on the back of his arms. I've treated that, too. He's gonna heal."

"See?" Sam snapped.

Blade added, "But he's also got a concussion."

"No, I don't." Damn if Sam's stomach didn't lurch and almost prove him a liar.

"Yes, you do, Partyman. We'll watch you for twenty-four hours, then ..." Blade paused, his gaze shifting to Nitro.

Nitro finished. "You're going home for a two-week R&R."

"What? Hell, no," Sam argued and realized where he'd have to go. "That's no R&R."

"It is compared to what we're doing. I need you a hundred percent."

Sam stopped himself from yelling, "Finish that thought. You need me a hundred percent if I'm still on the team."

He had to do damage control before they returned stateside. This couldn't be happening. Logan would not penalize him over getting hurt in the explosion, but he would have issues with how Sam had barely escaped considering he had been the first one warned.

Sam couldn't go over Nitro's head, not unless he wanted to bring their boss, Logan, into this along with Margaux. Nobody wanted to cross Margaux. She had a lightning-fast temper.

Also, Sam would never do that to Nitro and expect to have any working relationship.

He gave in an inch, hoping by daylight to convince Nitro to change his mind. "Before we go, we have to find the leak.

The woman said W knew a team was coming, which is why he left guards and the torture goon as bait for us to continue into the mansion. He wanted us deep inside before he triggered the bomb. No one knew our plans except Moose and Logan once we left. The leak has to be here."

Angel called over, "Most obvious is the arms supplier."

Sam's mind had already gone there. He'd trusted Esteban for many years now. Hard to imagine that one giving up his team after how Esteban suffered daily in the prison camp and never gave up a word even for a cup of water.

Still, Sam's team had to start at the most obvious point.

Proving he was ready to continue with the team, Sam said, "Angel's right."

Nitro eyed Sam, probably looking for any sign of second thoughts on the arms dealer.

Sam reminded everyone, "We notified Pablo only an hour in advance and he had no idea of our final destination until we were airborne. He's not a good option as a leak. Logan agreed to use Esteban and had Moose run a quick check. At this second, Esteban is the most obvious breakdown point. Once we talk to him, we may learn something new."

"Agreed." Nitro stood.

"I want to go with you to see him." Sam wouldn't plead. He just made it clear he'd like that one concession. If that worked, he'd have time to prove he was healthy enough to stay with the team.

Angel piped up. "Esteban may only talk to Sam, and it will save time for Sam to fly back with us."

Sam sent Angel a tiny head nod that didn't send his head cartwheeling.

Sounding irritated by the whole conversation, Nitro shut it down. "Let's get everything wrapped here and head out. We can be at Esteban's home before 0300."

Sam said, "By the way, thanks, Cuz."

Nitro nodded and turned to the other two who were almost packed up.

Just to look busy, Sam checked his vest. The guys had his

weapons. He'd get those back before going in to talk with Esteban.

Best time to interrogate anyone was when they were deep asleep. If Sam's friend stumbled over any word, he wouldn't be sleeping in comfort ever again.

Going with the team was the first inch.

Sam walked around, getting ready for the hike back to the pickup point. Please let him make it without barfing. Pain blasted in his head, but his brain still worked. He sorted through so many pieces that made no sense.

What if Esteban had sold them out?

If so, he would be waiting for word they'd all died. With lack of confirmation, he'd know they were coming for him. He'd be armed and ready.

And what about that woman?

Did she know the arms dealer?

CHAPTER 8

———

SAM CONCENTRATED ON STAYING UPRIGHT when he wanted to lay down and sleep off this freaking headache.

Riding in a bucking Hummer wasn't helping. Angel navigated his own path through an overgrown forest, which would have been better for migrating goats than this wide vehicle. But Angel handled the sudden curves and dips like a champ.

Better than Sam's stomach.

The first time they'd traveled to Esteban's location, they'd taken a two-lane highway to a four-mile dirt road. That had been a smooth glide compared to this.

This time they wouldn't risk advertising their approach.

Blade road shotgun again with Nitro and Sam in the back where Nitro could throw judgmental glances at Sam.

Here came another one.

Sam turned slowly, taking his time moving his head. He mouthed, *What?*

Nitro shook his head.

They'd been doing that since climbing into Pablo's rattle-trap helo to make another death-defying flight. Sam would give his left nut to lay down somewhere quiet and sleep. Blade would veto that. Didn't matter. Sam had no intention of spending two weeks at home during which his fate would be decided.

He didn't really have a home, just a place he visited once a year. Three days was all he could take and only if forced to go there.

Angel announced, "We are fifty yards away." He slowed and must have driven over buried hippos before parking the Hummer with one side sitting higher than the other. Sam breathed through clenched teeth. He couldn't wait to get out, but he would not be first.

Damn Nitro noticed everything when he was in dog-with-a-bone mode.

Thankfully, that ended the minute Nitro started issuing orders as they climbed out. Then he switched to hand signs, maintaining radio silence while inserting and containing Esteban.

In minutes, Esteban's wooden building came into view. From the outside, it was larger than other homes in the village a half-mile away. The exterior hadn't been painted in years and the roof had been patched, but inside Esteban had reinforced one large room with cement-block walls, half-inch-thick aluminum panels for the ceiling, and a two-inch-thick steel door with a fingerprint-activated lock.

A light glowed in the front room.

As far as Sam knew, the arms dealer lived alone. Esteban said he'd never brought a woman to his home, which was his place of business, and avoided entanglements.

When things got hot, he needed to be mobile with no baggage. He told Sam he'd been down here for around two years.

He'd sounded content, happy even, when they met for Sam's team to buy arms.

Once Sam and the team were within thirty feet of the modest building, Angel pulled away and chose a spot to cover them from outside.

Nitro took the lead, slowly approaching the one-level structure with a footprint of forty by thirty feet.

Robbing Esteban would require knowing his location.

The village believed he was a writer who had been born in Venezuela and spent his days journaling his travels with plans to publish. Esteban had just told Sam he enjoyed volunteering at the local school five klicks away.

A man of many talents, but Esteban had sounded genuinely happy when he'd spoken of the local school.

Sam had contacted Esteban through an elaborate electronic system or Esteban would not have opened the door to Sam the first time.

Would he open it this time?

Nitro slipped through the dark without making a sound before hugging the wall on the right side of the illuminated window. Calling it a window was a stretch. There were two narrow slits a foot wide and four feet tall with a steel bar running down the middle. The glass had to be bulletproof.

Nitro gave Sam the nod to knock on the back door where Esteban had a camera hidden to observe anyone approaching.

Sam walked over to the simple wood door and knocked. "Hey man, I could use a cold one." That had been a code he and Esteban created while imprisoned, which identified a friendly.

A minute later, no one had answered the door.

Damn. That couldn't be good.

Stepping back from the door, Sam waited for Nitro's next move. Hairs lifted along Sam's neck. This operation refused to get better.

Nitro gave a quick signal for Sam to go in, then he and Blade moved into position to protect Sam's back.

Esteban had turned this place into a fortress but had no security alarm on the door. He told Sam it was unnecessary. If an unfriendly found him and made it into his reinforced armory, then all the alarms in the world would not save him. Besides, who would come to his aid?

Sam fished out a set of picks from a pocket on his vest. He moved them a couple times until the tumblers clicked, unlocking the door.

Adrenaline rolled through him on a tide of unease.

This did not fit for Esteban.

Would his friend shoot him or give Sam a chance to talk? Sam repeated, "Sure could use a cold one."

He opened the door slowly and listened.

Graveyard quiet.

Lifting his HK 416, he led the way through the small foyer, pausing to glance in the living room. A half-eaten sandwich sat on a plate next to an open beer can.

Sam swallowed hard.

Where was Esteban?

He kept moving on soft steps. The living area was one

bedroom with a bathroom, a small kitchen, and his television room with a recliner.

Three-quarters of the place was an armory, so it didn't take long to reach the steel door to his weapon storage. Nitro and Blade would be following four steps behind.

Seeing the two-inch-thick steel door ajar chilled Sam's skin.

Light spilled through the opening.

Nitro put a hand on Sam's shoulder, letting him know he was close.

Sam glanced around at Nitro whose mouth had flattened into grim determination. Blade wore his standard stoic look.

Every tense movement felt as if the air had turned into thick pudding. Sam stepped to one side of the door and used the barrel of his rifle to nudge it wider.

No one shot at him.

He risked a peek inside.

Weapons filled every free wall of the room. Others had been stored in a steel cabinet normally used for tools. This didn't appear to be a theft.

Esteban sat in a chair with his head down on his crossed arms. "Esteban?"

Sam drew a deep breath. A coppery stink hit him.

"Ah, fuck." He walked into the room and over to the table where he lifted Esteban up and leaned his back against the chair back. His head flopped to the left, exposing his throat that had been cut from side to side.

Nitro appeared next to him. "Who would kill him and leave all his weapons?"

"Makes no sense," Sam agreed.

"Sorry about Esteban, Sam, but we need to get all the intel we can and head out."

"Copy that, Cuz." Sam swallowed hard. He had so few friends. Losing even one left a huge hole.

As Blade and Nitro moved around hunting for any intel of use, Sam sucked up a gut of pain and started searching around Esteban. When he leaned to look on the other side of his friend's body, a folded piece of paper stuck out from where it was trapped under Esteban's right arm. He pulled out a switchblade and eased enough paper out until he could open it with his fingernails. Maybe Logan's tech people could pull DNA, fingerprints, or both from it. Doubtful, but he would not leave any evidence that might help.

His breath caught when he read: *One down then the final delivery.*

What the hell did that mean? Then Sam saw a photo clutched in Esteban's hand. He pulled it free.

An attractive woman in her thirties with long black hair. Next to her, a small boy with her nose and eyes held her hand. They stood in front of a building with a sign on top saying *Escuela de Sueños.*

School of Dreams.

Esteban had gotten attached to the woman and child.

He'd developed a weakness someone had found.

Sam's pulse thumped hard. Adrenaline surged through him. A trap again? "We gotta get out of here *now!*"

Nitro asked in a tight voice, "What'd you find?"

"Esteban was tortured and—"

Angel's urgent voice came through their comms. "We got company coming in hot. Time to go."

Sam shoved the note in his vest and swung around to find Nitro and Blade with weapons ready.

Nitro angled his head for them all to leave. He started out the door.

Powerful weapons blasted the structure from different directions sending Nitro backpedaling.

"Get in the armory and keep the door open!" Angel ordered.

Sam had to pull up short to not hit Blade, who uttered, "What the hell?"

The front of the building exploded inside with the Hummer crashing through backward. Bullets pinged off the truck.

Sam stepped over and said, "Go!" Then he laid down high cover as Nitro rushed out and opened the front passenger door. Then he stepped up and unleashed cover for Sam and Blade.

The minute the two of them dove into the back, Angel punched the accelerator, driving the Hummer forward as they yanked doors shut.

They drove straight into a barrage of bullets.

Their attackers must have expected them to escape by dirt road out, not try to run them down.

Someone tossed a grenade just as Angel took a hard cut to the right. The blast rocked their vehicle up on two wheels and would have rolled them if Angel had not avoided a direct hit.

That surprise straight-on attack allowed them to haul ass through the woods, side-swiping trees and bouncing through ruts. Nitro and Sam swung weapons out opposite sides of the truck and fired a barrage of shots while Blade shouted into his sat phone.

Headlights jumped all over the place behind them, closing the distance.

Sam grabbed a grenade, pulled the pin, and kept shooting. He shouted, "Slow down like we got hit, Angel."

Without questioning why, Angel slowed the truck as if they'd been hit and were losing power.

Mentally counting seconds, Sam watched as two trucks gained ground on them. He tossed the grenade and shouted, "*Hit it!*"

The Hummer lurched forward and had made thirty feet when the grenade detonated.

The front end of the first truck lifted high and hung there. The second truck slammed the first one, pile-driving the mangled metal into trees.

Angel kept driving with insane control and putting distance between them.

Sam dropped back onto his seat.

Nitro pulled his weapon inside as his butt hit the passenger seat. "What's our situation, Blade?"

The medic ended the call and lowered the phone. "We've got Pablo picking us up in eight minutes."

"Copy that."

Adrenaline pounded for another ten minutes, giving Sam a break from his head injury. But as soon as that washed away, his bad stomach churned, and his head pounded.

He slumped in the seat and sucked in deep breaths, desperate to stay upright and alert. He blinked to clear his swirling vision.

This was not the time to let on that his head wanted to blow off his shoulders.

Pablo would take them to the airport where a private jet waited to fly them home. They'd wipe down the gear and weapons, leaving all of it with Pablo as a service tip.

By the time they reached the airport in an hour and landed a short walk to their jet, no one would notice the four tourists looking like they'd partied too hard.

Sam survived yet another roller coaster ride in that helo and climbed out of the fuselage on his own at the hangar. The world spun a moment then slowed. He could do this.

The other three waved Pablo off so Sam tossed a hand up without looking back. One step, then another. Stay upright.

He swallowed bile back down and kept walking toward the jet.

Another fifty or sixty steps and he could pass out in a smooth-riding aircraft.

Blade fell into step with him. "That cut on your head needs time to heal and you do have a concussion."

Shaking his head would be a huge mistake. Sam dug deep to sound confident and strong. "I'm feeling better already."

Nitro had been last to depart and would be close enough to hear every word.

Blade wiped his face, failing to erase the exhaustion there. "That may be, Cuz, but Nitro wants you to take two weeks, and I agree."

Sam's head ached and dizziness would assault him if he even turned to look at Blade. Not happening. Keep walking to that damn jet. "Nah. I'll get some rest on the flight home. I need to stay with the team and see this thing through."

Angel stepped up on his other side.

What was this? Fucking intervention?

Angel said, "We have a leak, Partyman. Moose is running down every possibility. You can take some time to heal. Nitro will let you know when we have information and a new plan."

The idea of walking away was eating up Sam's insides. If he left now, he had serious doubts about being brought back. Who had gotten to Esteban and why?

Another gut-wrenching thought banged into Sam's headache. He'd vouched for Esteban. Had he been the reason his team almost got blown to pieces?

Sam had to know who was behind this.

What about that woman? How did she fit in?

Thirty feet to go.

Blade took off jogging to the jet with Angel right behind him. Had they done that just to test Sam? He would not take the bait. He could walk, not run.

He'd felt worse before. He just couldn't recall when.

Nitro shouted, "*Sam!*"

Out of natural reflexes, Sam swung around to defend against a threat and found their leader staring him down.

Sam's head spun. His vision crossed.

He bent over with his hands on his knees. He threw up the water and nutrition bars he'd eaten on the flight here. Ah, shit. Just put a bullet in him.

He had to stand up. Had to stand up *now*.

Nope. His knees buckled and he slapped his hands on the ground to not face-plant. "You son of a bitch." He threw up again.

"Sorry, Partyman." Nitro called out, "Blade, need you to help me get Sam on the plane."

Heavy steps of Blade running back came next.

Sam formed curse words and lifted his head to spew them, then he slumped to the side and flopped on the ground.

Blade shouted, "*Don't close your eyes!*"

Too late.

CHAPTER 9

W ENDED THE PHONE CALL AND took a sip of his scotch while the engines on his Boeing BBJ Max 7 jet purred, ready to take off when he gave the order.

The Collector, a late-thirties underworld prodigy with golden hair and blue eyes of Nordic blood, sat in a plush seat across the table from him. The world-renowned kidnapper nursed a crystal glass of twelve-year-old WhistlePig bourbon. "We are good, ya?"

"Of course. Why do you sound concerned?"

"I am alive much longer by being concerned. I would think a Russian can appreciate one who is careful. I would never have made this trip were you not my best customer."

Smiling with the confidence of a man who could pull anyone's string and make them dance, W shrugged. "You were never in danger, comrade."

"The woman heard our voices."

"She is in many pieces, all of them little more than ashes at this point."

Swirling his drink, the Collector frowned. "What do you wait for?"

"Confirmation *every* loose thread has been shredded."

That caused the Collector to cease all movement. "Phone call was not confirmation?"

W had zero tolerance for being questioned. But he had future plans for the Collector and would clear up this one's confusion. "I have many operations in progress at this moment. Do not question me again."

Finally, the man who had arranged the capture of every person W contracted for in the past five years showed respect by lowering his gaze. "My apologies, vän."

Friend? W had no friends, but he tilted his head in reply as if acknowledging their relationship as such. In the next moment, W received the second call he'd been waiting on. His earpiece prevented anyone from hearing the other half of his conversation.

He could have communicated in Russian, but that would have raised the Collector's suspicions. W did not have the patience to keep calming him. He ordered his man to give him a report.

"Targets evaded the mansion detonation," Gregori replied.

Cold fury boiled through W, though he showed no reaction. "Who failed?"

"I do not have this answer yet, Sir, but I will soon. I assigned operatives to neutralize arms dealer and remain until I gave order to leave in case HAMR black ops team returned to Esteban's armory. When this happened, our operatives engaged the HAMR team."

That would mean the HAMR team had survived the explosion. W argued, "Someone tripped the activation wire."

The Collector remained calm, but his fingers tightened around the glass, causing condensation to run down the side.

"This is true, Sir, but until I have reviewed everything and inspected the destruction at the mansion myself, I will not have the answers you require."

"What of their return to the armorer?"

"I am not happy to report the HAMR team escaped. Counter operatives I contracted were highly skilled and came with top referrals, yet they were disappointing. I will ensure this is last time anyone suffers disappointment from their failure."

W would not hold Gregori responsible for this glitch. His man had proven extremely loyal and capable. He had an open checkbook to hire the best.

Evidently, this time, Logan's operatives had been the best.

Not next time.

Until Gregori could report what had gone wrong at the mansion, W focused on delivering the first part of a payment for a future toy. "Do you have evidence of first target termination?" He did not have to clarify which one as this had all been arranged for Gregori to send him a specific death photo.

"I am sending it now, Sir." A silence followed then Gregori said, "Please check your electronic vault."

W thumbed a link to his private electronic vault. There was a photo of the armorer known as Esteban who had broken the heart of a powerful bomb maker. To be more specific, Esteban's as yet unidentified friend, someone on Logan's teams, owed the debt for killing the man's son when the two of them had been prisoners in Libya.

Many powerful people were interested in the new bomb this genius was devising. W would have this bomb without a monetary bidding war.

Gregori never shied away from the truth, making him the most valuable of W's operators. "Although second target escaped firefight, we have video from outside Esteban's building. I am hoping we have clear images from battle. I have sent everything to our intelligence department. We will find him, Sir."

Not the report W had expected, but he could move ahead with his plans and leave capturing the second target in Gregori's capable hands. W thought on what opportunity this might provide. "I want him alive."

No questions asked, Gregori said, "Yes, Sir."

W ended the call and sent the image of Esteban dead with the note – *One down then the final delivery.* Their texts went through a cryptic electronic process to prevent tracking his location or the bomb makers.

After a minute, he received the message:

The second one is most important. Bring me his head and we will make the trade.

Few things could give W a charge of excitement, but he loved the chance to gain a bomb unlike any other that could be carried in three parts no larger than three basketballs. A bomb that would take out ten square miles and leave a two-hundred-foot hole in the ground.

He put his phone down and lifted his index finger, the signal for the flight staff to inform his pilots to take off.

Leaning back with a content sigh, W said, "All has turned out better than even I expected."

Surprise brightened the Collector's face. His fingers stopped strangling the glass. "This is so? Excellent." He lifted his glass. "A toast to your success. I look forward to many more opportunities to work together again."

Beaming a smile worthy of a magazine spread, W met the toast with his glass and took a drink. The Collector had been hunted by military and law enforcement on every continent, but he sat there free and happy because of his healthy distrust in others that had kept him alive.

W would allow him to think all had gone according to plan. The greedy Collector would accept whatever W told him from here on.

Fools. Everyone around him was so easily fooled.

No operation went exactly as planned, which was why W had backup plans for his backup plans and employed the best black mission operators.

Men who would kill anyone—man, woman, or child, so long as the money kept flowing.

W looked forward to meeting Esteban's friend, another captive who had taken the shot that felled the leader of a Libyan drug-running group as Esteban and his friend escaped. That single kill would hand W the perfect attack for next year in August.

It would be like getting the best Christmas gift a year early.

For now, he would enjoy the terror heading for the eastern coast of the United States.

CHAPTER 10

HALLENE HAD THE BURNER PHONE on speaker while she scarfed down the *Viška Pogača* she'd grabbed on the way, surprised to have found the Croatian specialty in Caracas. She paid for two hours in a room at this vulgar hotel. The scumbag behind his bulletproof glass leered at her as if she were just one more *puta* doing her nightly job.

Paying hourly worked for her.

Short of having a gun to her head, she wouldn't touch the mattress in this place even with the stack of clean sheets the manager had passed through the hole to her.

She still wore the navy-blue shorts, gray T-shirt, and running shoes she'd put on at the shack in the woods.

Coop had taught her if she worked alone to always leave a backup escape bag of cash, another mobile phone, and clothes. She'd included a few more necessities like a pair of shoes, thankfully. At the last minute, she'd taken the duffel of clothes with her to the shack in case she found Phoebe naked. The shoes would have been too big, but Hallene would have made them fit the girl.

She hadn't really expected to need clothes for herself.

"Ya thare, Hellie?" her underworld tech specialist in the UK, Midnight Ferret, asked.

"Yep." She swallowed another bite. "Got anything yet?"

"Mebbe. In the last communication, Bahstard swore he'd 'ave his container ship in place by the weekend. Midday Friday local time, to be specific."

She'd assigned the code name Bastard for Phoebe's father, Adam Kovac. What was he doing with one of his ships?

It was just after midnight on Monday here, the same time

zone as the US east coast. Was the ship heading to this side of the Atlantic Ocean?

She had until Friday to find Phoebe but had no idea why or where the Collector had gone. She was basing Friday on Kovac having to execute some plan of action she had no details on.

She couldn't risk cutting it too close in case something changed.

"We need to narrow this down more, Midnight," she pushed. "Do we know which ship he's getting into position?" More than that, where was that ship being sent?

Tapping continued while she thought about the Collector. He had not been known to do more than be the connection between someone who wanted a person kidnapped and delivering on the contract. Nothing had registered about the Collector involved with some sort of attack, but that didn't absolve him of being a dangerous criminal.

"Got it down to two ships that would fit the time frame. One is a day ahead o' the other."

"That first one could be our ship."

He argued, "I won't be sayin' that 'till we figure out where they both be endin' up Thursday."

She rubbed her eyes and shook off the weariness. She paid him well, but she understood how little appreciation someone in his position received since every bit of intel was confidential.

"That's damn good work, Midnight. Far better than I could have done even if I had your computer chops."

"Thank ya, Hellie," came back quietly.

"Okay, so we have something happening in four or five days and maybe a ship in place before that moment." Not information that would help her find Phoebe, but she'd learned from years of hunting lost or captured children that patience often won in the end. If only she had some. Shaking off another yawn, she said, "On to my next question."

"Ya mean the guy wot ya sent me the vid shot of mebbe?"

"Yes. Was it enough to use facial recognition?"

"Found somethin' interestin'," he started slowly. "'Ere's wot I've run up against. The system pinged a perfect match by the name of Samuel Leclair—"

"*Excellent!*" She had a name for her badass muscle-bound white knight without a horse.

"Hode on, Hellie. I cain't find anythin' useful on 'im once he walked out on high school. Looks like he was sucked up by the military and pretty much vanished at that point."

"Crap. You're kidding."

"Not *dooone*," he said in his wait-for-it voice. "I opened a wider search and found yar bloke with a group of people in Nigeria to do water treatment."

"That cover would fit for an operator."

"Those pictures were taken three days ago and posted to a blog claimin' they'd been gone a month."

She lowered her plastic fork. No way. "Did it list his name?"

"Eh ... no."

"That has to be him."

"Someone is goin' to a lot of trouble to keep others from findin' this one."

She straightened. "What else? What about where he grew up and went to school, things like that?" Normally, that would all be bogus information for an operative or spy.

"He carried a 3.9 grade average, but a month from graduatin' he entered the military. No online account. Nothin' helpful electronically."

The first encouraging tingle rippled over her skin. "Oh, that's good."

"Wot? Ya thinkin' wot I'm thinkin', Hellie?"

"Uh huh. If he had nothing to hide, he'd have left a normal trail." She tossed around a couple of thoughts and asked, "What about his family?"

"Standby." A minute later, Midnight mumbled something then cleared his throat. "I sent everythin' for ya to download. At seventeen, the bobbies arrested 'im, and that's probably why he ended up in the military."

Who was this guy? She pushed the food away, her appetite gone. She was on the hunt. "What do you have from his arrest?"

"They locked 'is records ..."

"Not from you."

"Ya didn't let me finish, Hen."

She dropped her head back, wanting to yell with frustration. She couldn't stay here too long. Once she left, she'd have to move toward her next goal.

Her *only* goal. Finding Phoebe.

"Hellie?"

She pulled her chin back down. "I'm here."

"Let's 'ave a look deeper. This won't take hours, just a few ticks."

Now she felt bad because he had picked up on her impatience. He'd helped her since they'd met in college, and she'd agreed to be his study pal. He'd introduced her to the dark side of the web, and she liked his matching dark sense of humor.

"Sorry if I sound upset, Midnight. It's not with you. I'm just ... tired. Take whatever time you need."

"Standby." The line disconnected.

His lack of saying goodbye wasn't rude, just efficient.

That would give her time to shower if she didn't have to fight bugs for floor space to stand on.

Before heading to the bathroom, she shoved a scarred wooden chair in place to block the door. Then she stacked the only lamp on top with the unplugged cord wrapped around the knob. The chair belonged in one of those movies where it broke into a hundred pieces with one good smash.

If someone got the door open, the unexpected noise might slow them down and would alert her.

She left the shower curtain open to keep an eye on the room and showered fast, but the soap and that one minute of hot water had been priceless.

She dried off quickly and braided her hair for stuffing under the tattered blue cap in her bag. Worn jeans, a clean dull-brown T-shirt, and black hoodie covered her bruised body. She lifted mystery guy's shirt and tried to throw it away, but her hand stalled before releasing it.

She sniffed the material and comfort spread over her again.

She'd never been foolish about a man's possessions. Never held onto anything of Coop's.

Just wad up the shirt and stuff it in the tiny trash can, Hallene.

Indecision annoyed her to no end. She threw the shirt on the bed and sat down to put on socks and shoes. Running through the tunnel barefoot had given her a few cuts, but she had a small first aid kit with antiseptic cream.

A ding from Midnight had her grabbing the phone.

Midnight sounded cheerful. "Found more. Could be useful."

Her fingers tightened on the phone. "What?"

"Dug into 'is family. Leclair had a mum, father, and sister."

"Had?"

"Yep. All dead."

Why did that hit her in the chest? She didn't even know this guy, but she had only her mother and might lose her soon. "That's it for his family?" she asked softly.

"Mebbe, mebbe not. No record of 'is mum's family. She was an orphan. 'Is father's family hailed from West Virginia. Not much to scrape up on 'im. Leclair might 'ave been adopted. The other three shared the surname Benson. I 'ave not found Leclair's birth certificate."

"He couldn't go to school without one."

"Auck, we both know 'tis not true," Midnight admonished.

"Okay, sure, but someone had to go all the way back to his birth to wipe his history."

Midnight tapped, stopped, tapped, then quieted. "Me thinks Leclair started out as a Benson. Most o' 'is school records are gone. The rest be electronic files marked as Leclair. E-files probably would not 'ave been used in a small school back then. That would mean someone with juice went back and recreated 'is history after Leclair disappeared in the Army. The school administration would likely not o' noticed once he was gone."

Leclair had lost everything, even his history.

She winced in hurt for someone she didn't even know but felt as if she sort of did know him. At least she knew him better than some stranger walking down the street.

He was an operative. That's all she needed to know.

When she shook off her weird reaction, her gut started talking to her big time to key on how he could be found. "This sounds like it fits the profile of the man I'm hunting. I don't know who set up that Nigerian cover, but I think we're on this guy's trail.

Unfortunately, this is a dead end without any way to research his life after his name change."

"Let's not be rushin' to conclusions yet, Hellion," Midnight said, sounding tired for him to call her that. "I 'ave more. Found a black and white o' Leclair next to an eighteen-foot sailboat on blocks in a yard. Boat was in sorry shape but looked to be o' more value than the house behind it."

She bit her tongue to keep from interrupting because Midnight had a knack for finding stray crumbs leading to a whole loaf of bread. He was also methodical about it and needed the space to work through his thoughts.

She had to sit tight and give him some room to run.

"Usin' that image, a search turned up a photo in 'is school newspaper of 'im standin' on the boat. The caption said *Sinking Treasure*, clearly a dig at 'im. He didn't look none too pleased. The paper didn't identify 'im, but sure looks to be your bloke."

"I'm with you, Midnight, but not sure how this helps."

"Some knob painted the boat name. Hard to read. Looked to be a girl's name. La Jolie Clare or La Julie Clark." Couple taps followed. "I searched boat registration and records for anythin' close. I found similar ones, but then I stubbed me toe on one called *Le Jolly Clerc*. I enlarged the image and played with the resolution. I was dumbstruck. That name matched better than me first guesses."

Her heart jumped. She could feel when Midnight was over the target. "Who is the boat registered to?"

"Woman named Angela Dougherty with a Cape Neddick, Maine address."

The unenthusiastic way he'd said that had her rubbing her forehead where a headache kept building. "Is the boat at *her* home?"

"No. The address belongs to a highly respectable law firm. The kind wot protects wealthy clients from pryin' eyes."

Wealthy? Nothing about this intel pointed to Leclair being wealthy. "If she owns the boat, that doesn't help us find Leclair."

"Patience, Hellie."

The word patience was not in her active vocabulary right now. "Sorry. Go ahead, but can you give me the bullet points?"

He didn't answer at first.

Midnight liked to show all the avenues he traveled to reach a conclusion. "Fine. 'Ere be the bottom line. I searched ever'where for a boat with that name. Hunted rented slips. I mean ever'where. None. Then I searched for an image with that boat name. I come upon a grand openin' announcement from this year where someone rebuilt a marina in northern Maine. 'Tis in a cove settled by a pirate descendant, by the way."

Not pirates.

She'd lose Midnight if he got sidetracked by his obsession. "Please tell me you found the boat."

Midnight grumbled, "'Tis a good thing ya were my study partner in school, or I wouldn't be so understandin'."

As bad as she felt, she smiled. They'd been an odd couple with him five-foot-eight and her a head taller next to him. He'd been her friend more than a study partner. "Waiting on you to tell me what you've found is almost as exciting as us pulling a B in Latin."

He cursed in an oddball language.

"That's still not Latin," she teased.

Ignoring her, he continued. "'Tis believed the pirate hid some of his treasure in that area, but no one has found it."

"I don't have time for a treasure hunt."

"Yar bloody crabby when yar tired. Okay, Hellion, 'ere's wot ya want. The cove be named after the pirate known as Sauville *Le Clerc*. The small community is now called Clercville."

Her brain clicked pieces together. She sucked in a breath and sat up. "Le. Jolly. Clerc! As in the jolly pirate Le Clerc. Midnight, you are truly a bloody brilliant hacker." She smiled and felt it deep in her bones. "What do you have on *that* town?"

"Not much, and ya know what it cost me to admit such, but 'tis a mud puddle town from wot I can find. Boasts a general store, small inn, marina, huntin' and fishin' store, and mebbe a bakery but that be in a home. Ya will 'ave the devil of a time tryin' to approach townies. A stranger will be stickin' out like a donkey racin' at the Royal Ascot. Plus, yar man probably isn't thare if he be an operator."

And just like that, her new-found hope deflated. Time for Plan

B. Hunting for Leclair might cost her too much time.

"My two hours in this room are running out. I have to get rolling." She stood before the idea of laying down overwhelmed her. "You are my one hope for finding Phoebe. I can't tell you how much this all means."

Being redheaded, Midnight was likely blushing. "Be sure to check the vault. This guy be so nondescript lookin' the images may or may not be o' much use."

"I'll go through those. Thanks again. Text me the second you get anything else, okay?"

"Will do. Be careful, Hellie," Midnight warned. "Ya almost didn't escape last time. Ya be needin' someone to back ya up on this."

"Maybe I'll find Leclair. He has a stake of some kind in the Collector." She'd said that just to put Midnight at ease.

"Auck. I do not feel better to 'ear such, plus we both know I'm the best," he admitted, no ego, just honesty. "But someone else can find this Leclair if I 'ave. *Annnd*, if the kidnapper be tryin' to kill this bloke's team in Venezuela, then a contract still be on their heads. Ya could run into the enemy unexpectedly."

He made a sound point, but she would be watching for the unexpected this time. "Gotcha. Thanks again."

She hung up and something struck her as strange. In the earlier texts to Kovac from the person calling the shots, Kovac had been told to remain quiet and ask no questions during the call. Kovac had complied. Why? She put a call into Kovac's office. She had his mobile number but would not use it because he had not given it to her voluntarily. She'd keep that little tidbit to herself.

"Kovac!" snapped through the line. He'd grown up in the heartland of the US, but he had the nasty attitude of a powerbroker.

Would it strain him to say hello? She was just as direct. "Have you heard from Phoebe?"

"No. I told you before, she doesn't return my call for a week or more sometimes. I'm too busy to chase her down."

Hallene tested him. "Did it even occur to you she might be missing ... as in kidnapped?"

"Where'd you get that stupid idea?"

Got him. He answered too quickly. Hallene explained, "She missed a meeting with Mom. I'm worried and think you would be concerned that your *only* child can't be found."

"A kidnapping would mean someone expects a ransom payment. No one has contacted me asking for money. You expect me to call in the authorities and have it all over the news that she's been kidnapped? Then she shows up two days later and the media will not let it go. I'll look like an idiot and my clients will not be happy. Phoebe wants to go to art school in the US. If you or Phoebe cause a negative media frenzy, I am *not* paying for that school."

What a pile of dung. "Clearly worrying about her isn't keeping you awake at night, Kovac."

His voice dropped to a mean level she had heard more than once. "I've made good on my responsibility to take care of her."

Hallene broke in. "Says the man who has no idea where his child is at the moment."

"I can always hire professionals to find her."

"Ah, a checkbook equates fatherly love," Hallene shot back.

"You're wasting my time." His tone changed to threatening. "I suggest *you* find her. If not, law enforcement will question why you told me to not hire a team to find her."

As in, he would make it look like Hallene knew about Phoebe missing and never said a word to him. Threats worked so well with her. Not. "Enjoy counting your money today." She hung up.

What chance did she have to locate Leclair?

Was he even the same guy as her mystery warrior?

Daylight had broken the horizon. This fleabag motel had no business center, but she'd seen a better hotel on her way here. She packed up her duffel, pulled the hoodie over her cap, dismantled her jury-rigged alarm system, and left.

At the far nicer hotel a mile down, she entered looking like a traveling college-age female and walked slowly toward the business center, digging into her pocket, and watching for someone to leave.

Nope, but a man dressed for business passed her and keyed the door.

She pulled her hand free and hurried forward, calling out, "Please hold it. I have looked everywhere for my key. I must send an email." She gave him her biggest smile.

Balding and pudgy, he grinned and held the door. "Come on in. I've had the same problem before."

She thanked him and waited until he chose a computer before she took a seat away from him. Using a prepaid credit card, she activated the computer and hammered keys, entering a complicated password. On the backend of the webpage, she flipped through documents, slowing at the boat picture in the high school paper. No school picture, huh? Sharp cheeks on his handsome face as if food had been hard to come by. Dark hair hung to his shoulders. He wore a five o'clock scruffy beard and his jeans and T-shirt sagged on that body but wouldn't on his bulked-up one today.

How could he be connected to that woman who had the boat?

Hallene enlarged the photo and stared into intense eyes she'd never forget.

Midnight was right. She couldn't do this alone.

Someone in Clercville, Maine had to know something about the woman and that boat. The woman might or might not know Leclair, but Hallene believed Midnight was on the trail.

If she found Leclair, she'd make a deal with him.

A deal he could not refuse.

CHAPTER 11

SAM BANGED THE HAMMER AGAINST a pussy nail that refused to go in straight. He cursed after the third strike then ripped out the bent nail that should have been a staple.

How could Nitro do this to him?

At least Nitro had agreed to only one week.

But that didn't mean Sam would return to the FALCA team next Tuesday. If Sam got a call from Logan this week instead of Nitro, his chance of staying with the team would be too low to calculate.

That was enough for him to have a sleepless week. He could not lose this position with HAMR. He would be given back his original identity. That was the last thing he wanted.

He worked to prove he was not some hothead that attacked his father. Logan knew the truth. Knew seventeen-year-old Sam had been trying to save his mother. He'd failed her. Failed his sister. Hell, he might have failed yet another female. He still didn't know if that long-legged blonde had escaped the mansion, but he would not regret waiting seconds in case she had called to him.

He hoped that one decision had not cost him everything.

One week in Clercville would be cruel and unusual punishment for a criminal.

His team still had to find the senator. Had they located W? Was there a plan to go wheels up soon? Not being with his team chewed on his patience like termites on the rotten trim he'd ripped off this facia.

What'd Nitro think Sam would do with six days more than he needed? Party in the middle of Nowhere, Maine? As if he'd earned the nickname Partyman honestly. What a joke.

He dug out another nail from his carpenter pouch and hammered.

Bent that one too. Dammit.

Flipping the hammer to the claw side, he yanked the nail out and put it in a different pocket of his apron—the one getting fat from rejected nails.

Why hadn't anyone replaced the decaying wood on this house before now? Angie could hire people. It was as if she kept crap work on the chance he'd show up and need something to do.

He'd told her the summer he turned sixteen that he was no carpenter and not cut out for small-town life.

"This is not a small town," she'd replied as they'd walked to the Clercville general store to get paint for that summer's free-labor task. "We'd need a library and city hall tah be an actual town."

That hadn't improved his sour outlook as a teen.

Nothing much had changed in twelve years. He still hated being here.

Angie loved it and believed tourists would flock here to stay in her ten-bedroom inn. That they'd sit in her Adirondack chairs along the wide front porch and admire the panoramic view with a cocktail in hand.

That would never be him.

He'd rather shave with an oyster shell than be that person.

How was he going to survive this week? He never asked for time off. Something Angie complained about every time he did come back.

The last visit hadn't been so bad when he dropped in to check on her. He'd met sweet Janean at the hardware store. She'd been divorced for eight months and had a nice smile. She'd invited him to dinner and that woman could cook. She'd wanted only a friends-with-benefits relationship.

Who was he to say no? Yeah, that would make this week better. He'd give her a call.

That cheered him up.

"What's takin' so long tah fix that bowahd, Sammy boy?" Angie asked in her New England accent.

He'd grown up believing the letter r had been outlawed in New

England. He'd made a point of not speaking with that accent to avoid sounding like his father who adopted it even though he'd been from West Virginia. The ability to alter his speech pattern had worked in Sam's favor when he began special operations training, which required operators to be chameleons.

Angie kept yammering at him. "I made shoh yah had plenty of nails, wood, and paint. Yah fahget how tah replace a simple piece a' trim, Sammy boy?"

He dropped his head to the trim. He hated that name. Angie didn't care.

Sweat ran down his back. Tourists thought the temperatures in northeastern US were always cool. Not in the summer when the breeze refused to find its way here off the bay.

He sighed and lifted his head. "I shouldn't even be out here. I'm supposed to be healing from a concussion." What was the chance she'd buy that?

She made a scoffing noise. "Yah were ovah that nonsense by the time yah woke this mahnin'. That nice young man who braught yah home said yah should be movin' around bettah today. If not foh him and his two buddies, heh, yah'd prahbly be sleepin' in a guttah."

Nice young man.

His traitorous team led by Nitro.

Sam argued, "I'm still bruised and sore." As if that had ever slowed him down? No. He'd have left the minute he woke up in his old room upstairs if not for the risk of drawing Logan and Margaux's attention.

They were all but married without the paperwork. As Logan's partner running the teams, Margaux was a deadly operator and had a temper no one wanted to test.

Sam was trapped. Slipping out of here in the middle of the night would land him on leave for months, or worse. That threat alone would keep him in place. He wanted to go back to the team.

"Bruises? Give me a break." Angie stood to the side on her veranda. "Yah wuh bruised moah aftah ev'ry football game back in high school. If yah hadn't been pahtyin' so hahd yah wouldn't have fallen offa that stage. Thought yah'd grown up some."

He might kill Nitro for the worst injury cover story ever known. He slashed a look over his shoulder at Angie. In polite surroundings, he described his aunt as having a snappy personality.

That sounded so much nicer than calling her an ornery old woman even though she was only fifty-eight.

She hadn't changed one lick in all the years he'd known her.

Meanness must be good for her skin. She had a few laugh lines around green eyes sharp as a hawk on the hunt. Chin-length black hair framed her attractive face with smooth coffee-brown skin. She managed to stay trim even with her high-caloric, but great cooking. Cake recipes started with a pound of butter.

To be honest, she didn't look fifty.

His team had probably thought she was sweet. They had no idea. There stood five-foot-four-inches of steel determination. She took shit off no one, especially him.

He'd have to think of a *special* way to pay Nitro back for delivering him here. He felt sixteen again stuck in this cove.

Angie cocked her eyebrow, a sign she waited for a proper response while she inspected her deep-pink rose bushes growing along this end of the porch.

To push her off the topic of his poor carpenter skills, he changed the subject. "How's Janean doing?"

Angie paused, slowly turning to lift her chin.

Ah, hell. The chin. Worse than the eyebrow. What had he said wrong?

"Janean is *busy* datin' a good-lookin' young man from Pohtland. Someone who stays put."

"Oh." He let out a longer sigh. No relief in sight.

As if Angie had heard his thoughts, she snapped, "Why should she be waitin' foh months at a time, or moah like *yee-ahs*, until yah deem us woohthy foh a visit. She's a fine woman with much tah offah a man."

"Never mind. I just—" He'd turned back to the facia work.

"She doesn't need some playboy toyin' with her."

That was unfair. "Hey. I'm not a play—"

"Maybe one day yah'll see moah in a woman than someone

tah scratch an itch."

He was not going to stand here and take this abuse. "For the love of—"

Angie was on a roll, arms crossed and frown in place. "When Janean asked about *yah* a week ago, I said yah would prahbly be back and I was quite shoh yah had plenty a' women."

He bit down on the curse fighting to get past his lips and dug out another nail. *Thanks for nothing, Angie.*

He tapped the nail in place to get it started.

"Even if she was heah," his aunt continued, "that nice young man, Nitro, said yah should not be bouncin' about on beds while healin'. He said they call yah Paaah-ty Man."

That was it. He would *have* to bloody Nitro. Not kill him. Logan would not understand that, but even Logan had wanted to strangle Nitro at times.

Sam lifted the hammer, pausing only to clear up her confusion. "Let's get something straight. I'll decide *what* I do while I'm here. I may just go on an all-night bender."

"Thought yah needed tah be healin'."

He swung the hammer so hard he drove the nail in with one hit.

"Thah yah go, Sammy boy. I always believed yah had it in yah tah do framin'." She sounded so pleased with herself.

He had to get out of this cove soon or she'd add more to the Auntie List of irritating tasks.

Her phone rang with an odd jangle. Good. He hoped it was one of her gossip buddies.

Her tone turned to sugar. "On mah way, sweetie."

He glanced at her. That had not sounded as if she spoke to a woman. Her eyes lit up and she smiled while listening. Sam took stock of how she'd dressed in a ruffly white blouse that deepened her unusual features she believed had come from a mix of Mexican and Afro-American. Pretty green eyes with curly lashes. She wore a flowy skirt of yellow and pink flower designs with three-inch yellow heels.

Her little beige purse could hold her phone, cash, lipstick ...

Well, damn. He'd missed the deep-pink lipstick on her lips. She only wore lipstick for special occasions.

Not to meet with her lady friends.

"Ayuh, sounds good tah me. See yah in a bit." She hung up the phone.

"Where are you headed, Angie?"

She'd tucked her phone away and there came the eyebrow again. "I have plans."

"With who?"

"Whom," she corrected.

He ignored the critique. "*Who* are you seeing and where are you going?"

"When did yah become mah guahdian?"

"Why are you avoiding my questions?" he countered. Who kept a watch on her to be sure she was safe when he wasn't here? If he'd found out she'd started dating, he'd have come up with a plan to keep track of where she went. Who would know if she didn't return from a ... dinner.

He would not call it a date.

"I'm not *avoidin'* yoah questions. I'm choosin' to ignah them."

He hooked the hammer on his tool belt and turned to where he could lean back on the ladder with his arms crossed. "You're not meeting someone off a dating app, are you?"

She tilted her face to the side. "Let's get somethin' straight. I'll decide *what* I do while I'm heah. I may go on an all-night bendah." She grinned at throwing his words back in his face.

"That's not you." He hoped it wasn't. She'd been alone a long time and deserved a companion, but he had to vet anyone wanting to get too close to her. He really had to show up more often or find someone local to keep tabs on her for him.

That would have been Janean, but not now.

"If yah wuh home moah often, yah'd know what I'm about, Sammy boy." Before he could reply, she added, "Have yah even looked foh yoah boat?"

"What?" Why was she asking about his boat? Sore subject. He'd given it up when he left for the military.

She stared at him with the same look she gave a raccoon tearing up her garbage. "The sailboat yah dragged home at sixteen and nevah finished. Do yah even cayah about it anymoah?"

Why would she bring that up and gut him with a bad memory?

Even so, that didn't stop him from asking, "Have you seen my boat somewhere? Back in Dorchester?" Could it still be in that rundown neighborhood covered in vines?

"I'm runnin' late. Ask about it down at thah hahbah."

"The harbor? We have a new marina?"

She grinned.

Had he really said *we*? Angie would take that one word as him putting down roots.

"See yah." She walked away, rounding the corner of the house out of sight.

He hurried down the ladder. "Angie. Stop."

She waved a hand without looking back as she crossed the fieldstone walkway with brisk steps and got into her red Acura RDX sport utility. She called out, "No time. Dohn wannah be late."

Grabbing the car door before she closed it, he tried again to find out what was going on. "When will you be home?"

She gripped the steering wheel with one hand and turned to him with an unreadable expression. Her voice softened. "If I thought yah asked because yah wanted to spend some quality time vistin', I'd tell yah. Since we both know that ain't thah case, I'm leavin'." She tugged on the door, and he let go.

He could have held it open but would never risk injuring her. She would yank until he gave in, or she'd snap the bones in her wrist. Ornery. So stinking ornery.

The driver's window rolled down before she finished backing around. "Yah dohn get tah show up once a millenneeah and staht askin' questions."

"I was here eleven months ago." Yes, he sounded defensive.

Her eyes twinkled with some secret satisfaction. She rolled the window up and drove out to hang a left onto the main road running through town. Not a town.

Clercville, originally Clerc Cove, boasted four buildings and a bakery in a home. The entire metropolitan area spread over less than a mile.

Oh, and a marina once again.

He cupped his neck, irritated at himself. He should have taken a different approach. He would not fumble with this relationship the way he had others. He may not want to stay here, but he wanted Angie safe and happy. At thirty years old, he was no better communicating with a woman than he'd been at half that age.

He'd saved a woman from being tortured who wouldn't even share her name. For the millionth time, he hoped the hot blonde had made it out safely. He didn't want to believe they were on opposite sides of the law or that she had anything to do with Esteban's death.

He'd like to know how she'd ended up in that basement and any light she could shed on W.

Would the FALCA team go back out to hunt for W without him?

To be honest, if Sam had to keep his head down and wait for a week to return, he wanted them to go. Finding a terrorist before W's favorite party day this upcoming Saturday was paramount to all else.

Hairs tingled across his neck.

The hinky feeling of being watched shook him out of his moment of internal whining.

Even in a noncombat situation, he naturally watched his surroundings. As he slowly turned, he covertly took in every direction. Nothing.

No one lived within a quarter mile of this place because Angie owned sixty acres. She had guests on occasion but spent most of her time here alone.

So why build this big of an inn and not advertise?

That just upped his worry about where she was headed. Had she gone online to find someone for company?

If Sam had arrived under his own power, he'd have a vehicle here to follow her in.

After circling the two-story inn as if he searched for more trim damage but was instead surveilling the area, he noticed nothing unusual. Maybe the odd feeling came from wishful thinking someone had shown up and planned to surprise him with news he could go back to work.

Yeah, he wouldn't bet an empty beer can on that possibility.

Might as well get the carpentry work done.

Then he could check out the marina. What would a marina here know about his boat?

He climbed the ladder and still couldn't shake the feeling of being watched. Nitro had left him a phone.

Sam knew not to call in. For one week, this phone worked one way. Nitro would contact Sam when he was ready.

But Sam would like to know if Nitro had set up a camera on Angie's place. That would explain the hinky feeling of eyes on his back. Knowing Nitro, he had eyes on Sam to save Sam from making one more mistake.

Good luck. Sam had been determined to impress Nitro and Logan on this last mission. How'd that work out for him? Not so well.

By the time he finished the woodwork and showered, then hiked through a shortcut in the woods to the marina, late afternoon light barely broke through the leaves.

He could still navigate these woods with his eyes shut.

When he emerged from the thicket of trees, he could not believe the pristine setting of a new marina building with two brand new docks sticking out into the deep-water cove. Ten individual slips had been built on each side of both docks to serve a total of forty boats.

That seemed like a lot for this cove.

Three boats were berthed along the closest dock, two of which were sailboats at the very end where a dock teed out in both directions in the deepest basin.

His gaze zeroed in on a blue mast like the mast he'd painted on his boat. His heart flipped around in his chest.

What had Angie done?

Even from here, he could read *Le Jolly Clerc* lettered in a fancy script on the stern. Gone were the ugly block letters he'd painted on it before the boat was close to seaworthy.

He headed for the dock.

A female voice called out, "Hold up."

Turning, he took in the nice-looking woman in her thirties with a Maine Mariners ball cap over dark hair, white shorts that glowed in the low light, and a blue shirt tied at her narrow waist. No smile.

He gave her a let's-be-friends grin that had paid off many times in the past. "Hi. Heard someone had rebuilt the marina. Would that be you?"

"Ayuh." Still not even a polite smile. "I dohn allow anyone to wandah around the docks, 'specially when no ownahs are heah."

He strolled over and extended his hand. "I'm Sammy. My Aunt Angela owns the inn." Yes, he was name-dropping and didn't care what that said about him. His hand remained empty.

"Angela hasn't mentioned yah. At all."

Thanks for no help again, Angie. "I travel a lot. She told me to come find my surprise." That had not been what she'd said, but his sailboat was docked here. Surely, this woman couldn't think Angie intended to sail the boat herself.

What was he thinking? Angie could probably pilot an ocean liner if she decided she wanted to do it.

"And what *sahprise* would that be?" the marina owner asked.

Man, she was one tough nut, or he'd lost all his ability to sweet talk a woman. "The sailboat named *Le Jolly Clerc*." He'd said that with pride. He kept his hand out, determined to make her step over that rigid line and shake hands.

She blew out a stream of air, grabbed his hand for a quick shake, then broke free fast. "Did *yah* name it?"

"Yes, I did." He'd admit the name was different but that had been the point back then.

"Hm. Didn't think Angela did that. Ye-ah, she said yah'd be along." She turned back into the office, dismissing him.

Angie got his boat and had it moved here.

He owed her big time. He'd pay her back too, so long as it wasn't in carpentry trade, which seemed wrong since he immediately wanted to work on his boat.

Sam shrugged off the woman's insult, happy to head to the dock. Women here were tough on his ego. First Janean pulled in her welcome mat and now this woman's cool dismissal.

Some days, women were more trouble than facing off with an armed terrorist.

Angie had known him during his awkward teen years and still liked to poke at him to get serious about a female every chance she got.

She'd told him to earn a woman's trust first, then romance her. Good advice if he ever decided to find a partner for life.

Hell, he'd given the female in Venezuela the shirt off his back, and she'd wanted nothing to do with him. Flaky too. She'd bailed on him as soon as he took his eyes off her while contacting Nitro.

How many men would have passed up the chance to take in every sweet inch of that naked body?

He was no saint. Far from it, but he respected women.

Especially a woman in a vulnerable situation.

He stepped onto the plank that dropped at a moderate angle to the dock. Tranquility surrounded him. Water had always been a balm to his soul.

His sister loved swimming as a kid and would have liked this place. She should be here. Not in a cold grave. One thought and he had a hard time breathing. Failing to save her and his mother had torn him to pieces like an out-of-control car skidding into a brick wall.

He was not fixable.

That's why his need to protect a woman overrode anything else in a dangerous situation. He had to be able to face that man in the mirror every morning.

To tell himself he could do better than he had for his mom and sister.

Enough of dark thoughts. This week would never end if he dredged up every bad memory. He got moving again to reach the end of the dock before twilight turned into dark.

Salt air filled the breath he pulled through his nose. His dock shoes slapped the boards as he walked along the hundred-foot dock with galvanized iron cleats for tie-downs. Pilings with black caps had just begun to weather. Water faucets and shore power were well-placed.

Narrow docks jutted out between the boat slips.

His boat sat alongside the last section of dock where it teed off to the right with rubber bumpers hanging between the dock and the hull.

His boat.

He hadn't owned anything he cared about since buying it. He took a moment to appreciate the look of his baby floating in the water. The eighteen-foot boat still needed some topside work, but the craft was clean. He stepped down, grinning like an idiot. Out of habit, he ducked into the cabin and opened the small refrigerator where he used to stash cheap beer.

The refrigerator worked and had a six-pack cooling.

His eyes burned. Angie had been the only person to ever treat him well and make him feel welcome before he met Logan and the HAMR Brotherhood. She'd encouraged him to get this boat and to name it something that was all his.

Opening the beer, he stepped out and walked around to the bow where he stretched out and leaned against the slant of the cabin. Nothing obscured his view falling into twilight with the sun setting behind him.

It would be pitch-dark soon.

He'd too quickly dismissed the joy of watching a day end quietly.

As he took a second swig of his beer, the cold tip of a gun barrel touched his temple.

CHAPTER 12

———

SAM WENT PERFECTLY STILL AND stayed calm. If this person had wanted to kill him, he'd be dead by now. "I'm not armed." He kept his hands where they could be seen.

Who robbed someone in Podunk Nowhere?

And how had that person gotten on this boat without him realizing it?

"I know you're not armed. Do not move or attempt to disarm me if you do not want to be shot."

That husky voice. He knew that deep female timber. This time he caught the hint of a buried accent. British? What the hell was going on?

His heartbeat ticked up and his senses sharpened.

She warned, "Sit very still when I move the gun away. Hate to mess up this shiny boat."

"Understood." Sam assessed the threat level to potential bystanders in the marina. The marina owner had said the boat owners were not here, but he didn't want to put her at risk either.

The office was almost two hundred feet away and uphill fifteen feet if bullets were fired. She should be safe.

The cool metal withdrew from his head.

He cut his eyes to the side but kept every other muscle still. "Hell of a way to thank someone."

The woman from Venezuela stepped into view with her back to the handrail running around the bow. "I already thanked you by warning you the mansion would blow."

"Then what are you doing here?" How had she even found him? He drew in a slow breath, forcing himself to stay calm. With that inhale he discovered she'd showered with a lemon-scented soap. Nice.

Funny the things he noticed when someone was threatening his life.

Nitro would be rolling his eyes.

Sam had enough light from the tall pole at the end of the dock to recognize the length of the gun meant it had a suppressor, which was still pointed at him. No light reflected off the flat black finish.

"I want to know what you were doing in that mansion," she stated.

"I'm not going to pretend we aren't both operatives. Why don't you tell me what *you* were doing there?" He remained still, looking for common ground. He needed her to give an inch first. "In fact, if you want to have a conversation, how about putting the gun down? I'm not as chatty when a loaded weapon is pointed at me."

After a long silence, she lowered the gun to point down but did not put it away. Where would she stuff a gun that size in those tight black pants or that snug matching tank top?

She said, "I was there to extract someone."

That rattled his brain. His heart cranked up to a heavy drumbeat. He cautiously asked, "Who?"

"Do you really think I'll tell you when you have shared nothing?"

Could she know about the senator? Lifting a shoulder casually, he said, "My mission was classified. I can't say a word."

"Classified did not stop someone from giving you up."

"He didn't—" Sam snapped his mouth shut. He could not say a word about the arms dealer.

Her voice held amusement. "You are so quick to defend someone, but you had a weak link somewhere in your intel chain."

The minute he was on a mission, every nerve and thought process geared up, like now, but for some reason, he was enjoying this insane conversation. That's what happened when he'd been denied female company for so long.

Lifting his beer to test her knee-jerk reaction, he took a long drink then lowered it back.

Nope. This one had ice in her veins. Confident she could take him down if he made a wrong move.

He considered all the reasons she'd show up here and still had no idea. "You wouldn't be here unless you needed something. Want to start there?"

"Not yet. Tell me what you can about being in the mansion without breaking your team's rules."

That was an interesting way to interrogate. He'd tell her nothing, but he had to find out what her play was. "Like you, we were there to extract someone. Maybe the same person."

"No, that is not possible." She answered without hesitation and sounded truthful.

He kept his voice conversational and infused it with sincerity. "How can you be so sure?"

"Because I am the only one searching for the person I'm hunting."

Had someone else besides the senator been kidnapped? That was a plausible explanation for her presence, but it didn't mean she spoke the truth. "Do you know for sure your person was there?" Until she stepped over a line he'd mentally drawn, he'd treat her as if he would any other unexpected intel resource. Listen, but question every word from her lips.

"I located my person," she claimed. "The room had been set up as a trap."

"That's how they captured you," he said more to himself than her. "But you *did* see your target?"

"Yes."

Sam ran a hand over his hair, trying to think through his next question. Had she seen the senator? "I know you're going to bark at me about asking more but was the package you were after a high-profile individual?"

"No." Another quick answer. This sounded personal if she was the only one after that second person.

Her face showed that she'd taken in what he said and processed it. "It makes sense that your team had been there hunting a high-profile prisoner."

"Mm-hmm." He kept hearing something in her diction that wasn't entirely American but couldn't put his finger on it.

She made an irritated sound that hissed out between her lips.

"If you spend our time playing games, neither of us will find who we hunt."

He couldn't argue that point. This was no civilian he could run circles around in a conversation. Might as well get to the point and see if this meeting would end with any actionable intel.

"Fine." He put the beer can down and crossed his arms. "Yes, we're hunting a high-profile prisoner." That could be anyone in the world theater and still not point to the senator since his kidnapping had not been made public.

Could not be made public.

Her lips almost curled into a smile, but whatever thought had caused that passed quickly. "Now that we've cleared up that confusion, I can tell you without a doubt that we are after the same kidnapper and our goals intersect instead of conflict."

He wouldn't agree to that right away, but she was talking. "I'm listening. Why are you here?"

"I have a lead on the kidnapper."

His muscles tensed, but he was in no position to interrogate her. Staying quiet would produce more than demanding to know what she had.

She said, "I take your silence as understanding I will not hand over that information for no gain. That's a good start."

Good start for what? He fought the urge to grab his head in frustration, but he had nowhere to go and would play the crummy hand he'd been dealt for now. "We're back to the same question. What are you doing here?"

"Giving you a chance to extract your package before yours dies."

He had to tell Nitro everything and felt certain now that Nitro had not sent someone to watch him. The eyes Sam had felt on his back had been hers. He'd love to know how she got from Venezuela to Clercville when no one outside of his team should know he was here.

No one should know he'd ever been here.

She huffed out a breath, sounding impatient. "I've told you enough. Here's my offer. You will join me in this hunt, but you can't contact your team." She laid those terms out as if he'd jump at her ridiculous offer.

"You think I'm just going to go along with you to find my missing person and not say a word to my team? You should know how a special operation team functions. In fact, where's *your* team? Why are you here asking me to join you?"

"I'm running solo for my own reasons and need backup this time to avoid a problem again."

"Getting captured, tortured, almost raped, and killed is *just* a problem?" he said, irritated at her description.

She lifted a shoulder, appearing cool and confident. "He would never have raped me. I might have died in the blast or if he shot me, but he would not have gotten any farther than his first attempt."

Gutsy woman, but crazy too. He had the worse luck with women these days. He faced a sexy female who had his body humming just by listening to her voice but who also might have cost him his position with HAMR Brotherhood if he couldn't convince Logan for a second chance.

That alone was the reason she wasted her time coming here.

He was not taking one step out of Clercville and destroying his last chance with Logan.

She tapped the weapon against her thigh. "Don't you want to find the kidnapper?"

"Of course, I do. But I can't do anything without informing my team."

"Why aren't you with them now? I assume you suffered an injury and were sent home to heal. Am I right?"

"This isn't my home. My personal business is not part of this conversation. I'm not going with you. If you're willing to share information with my team, you'll have the best chance at rescuing your person."

"That won't work." She cocked her head with a new thought. "If this isn't home, then you won't care if anyone comes here hunting me, correct?"

His heart hit his feet.

He sat up and she tensed.

He didn't care. In a deep warning tone, he asked, "What exactly are you saying?" No more Mr. Nice Guy. Just like Nitro said, this woman was an operative.

That could mean she was the enemy.

Her fingers on the weapon remained relaxed, but she handled it with confidence and could pull it up quickly. "I have a system in place that tracks everywhere I go. If I do not post an update at specific times, which are different every day, someone will come hunting me. That person will send a team and not stop until they learn what happened to me. They will turn over every rock and interrogate everyone along the way. The last time I posted a location was this one."

What the hell? He unfolded his arms. His hands clenched into fists against the hull. He needed something to beat into a pulp. Not her. He wouldn't harm a woman but shaking some sense into her brain might happen. "You'd put civilians at risk? What kind of operative are you?"

That got her back up. She leaned forward and said, "I'm someone who will *not* stop until I find who I'm looking for!" Her eyes flared with the fury of an avenging angel. "Do not test me or cross me. I *asked* you to do this first, but I would not come here without a way to get what I want. Know this. If you don't have the backbone to join me then I'll continue alone. If I am successful, then no one will show up here. If I am not, you were warned, and nothing will stop the people who come hunting me."

His heart was using his chest for a punching bag.

What to do? What to do?

No good ideas. If he turned her down and contacted Nitro, what could he tell him that would be of any use?

Nothing.

Even if he stayed in Clercville, he couldn't protect everyone twenty-four-seven.

That would leave Angie and this cove open to a possible black ops team coming through hunting this woman because based upon her last attempt to rescue her person in Venezuela, she'd likely end up dead next time.

Gut check time. He had one sure way to keep this cove safe and get intel. He'd be the only one to lose.

Maybe if he found W and the senator, Logan would understand his reason for leaving without authorization. That was a big maybe. Logan's teams ran like precision clockwork because no one took off on their own.

He swallowed, frantically trying to come up with a second option. None. "I'll go." Those two words burned his throat. To go with her meant handing Logan the last straw.

"Wise decision." She tilted her head at him as if giving him a thumbs-up. "Don't play me. I will know if you contact your team or tell anyone here that you're leaving. You can't tell even the woman who runs the bed and breakfast."

Now he was in a nasty mood. "It's an *inn*. I'll have to tell her something. Just so you don't think I'm playing you, as you put it, I'm sure my team has a camera somewhere watching the inn. They're keeping an eye on me just in case someone like *you* shows up. I have no idea where the camera is, but I'm giving you full disclosure."

She moved her shoulders enough for him to think she'd shrugged. "We play roles in our work. You and I will play the role of leaving together as a couple for some time alone."

He no longer cared that she was hot.

She boiled his blood in the wrong way.

"There isn't enough time to set up those roles." He kicked his chin up at her in challenge.

"I already have the plan mapped out. Go back to the *inn*," she emphasized. "Stay near the front door."

What the hell did she have up her sleeve this time?

CHAPTER 13

W STUDIED THE MAP ON THE computer monitor covering the wall of his Virginia headquarters for this week. He uploaded the most recent coordinates for Kovac's ship headed to the US, hit Enter, and watched the update.

So far, so good.

When he clicked to end the display and turn the monitor black, his reflection stared back at him. He did not look like the rat that had climbed out of a Russian sewer to hold the world in his hands. He brushed his fingers over his hair, which was starting to grow out. Time for a trim and facial. He could wait until next week.

His phone buzzed. He activated the speaker phone. "What do you have?"

"Positive news thanks to our techs," Gregori replied. "First, I wish to give debrief on South American operation."

W leaned back on the long, black glass table in a conference room that easily accommodated twenty people. "Go ahead."

"We found three bodies in mansion rubble."

"Oh?" That was as close as W ever came to an outburst.

"Three guards the Collector left. No sign of female."

W stood. "She escaped being hung from chains?"

"It appears so, Sir. Chains were there. She was gone. Also, black ops team entered our trap at Esteban's but escaped with no loss I can find."

"I am waiting for this positive news," W said, unwilling to hear any more of what sounded like a failure all the way around.

"Yes, Sir. I mentioned surveillance filming Esteban's place. All but one face was covered. I sent that image to our people. They find nothing right away, but one of them searched for others on net by hunting similar face in underworld."

W had pulled Gregori from the same Russian gutters when W escaped. He took pride in hiring the best intel people even though Gregori paid the techs, protecting W's identity. "I take it you received hit."

"Yes, Sir, one man from black ops team. One you want alive."

That was more like it. "Who is he?"

"Only intel I have at this point is name Samuel Leclair, but that is based on our initial search for him. Does not mean it is valid ID."

"Where is he?"

"We have no location yet. Was no trail to follow when we found where electronics expert had matched Leclair's photo to picture taken inside building with little light. I challenged our intelligence researchers. First one who locates this Leclair before midnight Thursday eastern time will receive ten thousand bonus."

Gregori had been groomed to understand how to use money to produce results quickly. That gave the team two days. W rewarded his man with, "Well done."

"Thank you, Sir. I also have identity of woman."

W stood, truly impressed. "Who is she?"

"Hallene Clarke, Kovac's stepdaughter. I have not determined how she discovered mansion. Impressive intel for this woman. Possibly Kovac had hand in this. She was clearly there to rescue Phoebe Kovac."

Few things stunned W, but that shocked him. Was Kovac trying to double-cross him? Did that fool think if he found Phoebe and brought her home either of them would be safe?

"How do you wish for me to move forward with this information, Sir?"

"Stay on track. I want her alive as well as Leclair."

Leclair and that woman would regret not dying in South America. Then Kovac would find out just what a mistake it was to cross the wrong man.

CHAPTER 14

———

S AM HUSTLED UP THE DRIVEWAY to his aunt's inn where the gaslight atop a metal post near the porch showed him the way.

Too bad it couldn't show him the way to climb out of this mess. Did he want to capture W and rescue the senator? Of course. He'd also like to know who was behind Esteban's killing.

If this blonde would allow him to contact Nitro, this new development could weigh in his favor to come back on the team.

On the other hand, if he left here with her and it blew up in his face, life as he knew it would be over. He would not expect Logan to be that understanding.

Sam ran a hand over his hair, wishing for a simple out. He couldn't risk her leaving here without him and a black ops team rolling into Clercville.

Where the hell had she gone after they parted ways at the boat?

He'd made that two-mile hike to Angie's place in a quick jog once he'd counted to fifty, as instructed, which allowed the blonde time to vanish.

One mistake with this plan and she'd be in the wind.

Part of him wanted her gone forever and to have never met her. He'd moved way past any sense of worry or desire to protect *that* female anymore.

Damn her for using Angie and this cove as collateral.

He still couldn't figure out how she'd found him in Clercville of all places.

That sent his thoughts back to the leak that almost got his team killed. Did she know who the leak was? Could she be using the same resource to find him?

He couldn't convince himself she was connected to what happened at Esteban's. If so, why warn Sam to get his team out before the building exploded?

He walked up the steps to the front door when a new thought hit him.

Could his people have a snitch *inside* HAMR?

Nitro and Logan knew all the men better than Sam.

He shook his head at the traitorous thought on his part. Trust ran deep in the HAMR Brotherhood. He may not know many operatives outside his FALCA Team, but Nitro and Logan would sniff out a traitor.

He entered and closed the front door, leaving lights off in the living room decorated tastefully with comfortable chairs and a wide sofa, a fireplace, and a card table. No television. He didn't watch it anyhow. He strode into the kitchen for a towel to dry his head and face. The beer had soured in his stomach. He grabbed a cold bottle of water and downed it while returning to the living room.

Stay near the front door.

He'd rather be outside keeping watch over the front door. Nitro finally got what he wanted—for Sam to see her as a trained operative. Threatening Angie was all it had taken. If anyone harmed his aunt, they'd suffer the consequences.

No punches pulled.

Headlights turned onto the driveway.

He rushed to the window. Angie coming home. Relief at knowing she was home soothed the beast in him for now. He turned on the lights in the living room and opened the door as she climbed the steps.

She stopped short of the door. "Awh yah really waitin' up fah me? It's only eleven or so."

He forced his face to relax. "It's a school night. You should be home early." It was Tuesday and she used to tell him that as a kid on any weeknight when he visited during summers.

Laughter twinkled in her eyes. "So incahrigible."

He'd had to look up incorrigible the first time she'd used it. This time he smiled, hoping he could keep her safe.

"I'm off tah bed. We shall catch up in the mahnin'."

Would he be here then? He had yet to find out what, uh ... damn. He still did not have a name for that woman. He still didn't know what she expected him to do tonight.

But he couldn't let on.

He closed the door and said, "Wait." Angie had been heading to her downstairs bedroom, which was closest to the living room and kitchen. He stayed in the farthest corner of the upstairs.

She waited for him. "What?"

Now cooled down, he stepped over and pulled her into a hug, whispering, "I know I suck at visiting, but I am glad to see you and we will find time for that chat."

Her arms wrapped him in a tight hug, the one that had held him together after his world had broken into a thousand pieces. His mother had met a good woman in the orphanage. Strange how the two women had ended up on paths so far apart.

Angie patted him on the back, and that touch also reminded him of being sixteen again. When she released her, she smiled and lifted onto her toes to peck a kiss on his cheek. "Yah wuh the best of them all and still awh."

With that, she turned and walked away.

He paced the living room so much he might have worn a spot in the large rug.

Hour after hour passed with no reason to be close to the front door, but here he stood in the dark still waiting. In another ninety minutes, the sun would rise.

Low beams glowed as a vehicle came up the driveway.

Had to be *her*. Miss No Name.

He walked to the door and opened it. The gaslight offered enough illumination to see that she drove a dark sedan. She parked at an angle then stepped out and closed the door softly.

This was her plan? To just drive up to the inn? Hadn't he told her his team likely had cameras covering this house?

She wore a yellow sundress that glowed against the dark along with shoulder-length blond hair styled to draw every eye in a bar. The strappy heels clicked over Angie's stone walkway as surefooted as a dancer in a ballroom.

He'd thought she was stuffy on the boat. This was a different woman.

He must have looked dumbstruck holding the door open since none of this made sense.

She sashayed right up the steps and dove at him. He grabbed her out of reaction, and she melted against his chest then proceeded to kiss him brainless.

Her hand came around the back of his head. Her lips took possession of his mouth with hungry kisses. Sweet Maria, she felt even better than he'd imagined. That sexy body woke up every inch of his.

Every. Inch.

She laughed as she broke the kiss. "I told you'd I'd come back and surprise you. Are you surprised?"

Ah. Now he got it. His body was humming for a booty call, but his brain was shouting at every part of him to stand down.

He had to do his part. Smiling, he said, "Sure am, baby."

Her eyes narrowed at being called baby, but no camera outside would pick that up. She tousled his hair. "I've been driving for six hours. I'm in dire need of a shower and someone to wash my back."

He knew she was acting but his stupid dick didn't. It loved that husky voice talking about taking a bath with her.

Sam smiled. "I'm in desperate need of one myself."

Her eyes flickered with surprise at the smile. For a stretched moment they stared at each other. Something strange filled the air. If he didn't know better, he'd say it was animal attraction.

He pulled her inside and closed the door then stepped back. "Now what?"

And back was Miss Hard Nose. "Just as I said, I want a shower. Let's go to your room. The one upstairs at the end of the hall."

This had FUBAR written all over it.

CHAPTER 15

———◆———

"HEY, YOU NEED TO SEE this," Moose called out.
Nitro had been making a cup of coffee in the kitchen of a HAMR Brotherhood stash house in Durham, North Carolina, one of many they used for different things. At this moment, the place had been turned into intel central as everyone hunkered down to find a lead on the senator's kidnapper.

That there had still been no demands yet was not an encouraging sign. W had plans for the senator, which probably coincided with his annual death and destruction date coming up at the end of this week.

Nitro strode into the great room where computer monitors of mixed sizes had been mounted around the walls.

Angel leaned back in a recliner with his elbow propped on his chair and head held up by his hand. He murmured quietly into the headset connected to the computer on his lap. He tracked down leads Blade, Nitro, or Moose handed him. Research was not Angel's strong point. Risking his life on a mission suited him more.

Blade had gone to pick up supplies. Since walking in and setting up his equipment, Moose hadn't moved from his seat more than the time it took to hit the bathroom.

Placing a hand on the back of Moose's chair, Nitro asked, "Whatcha got, Cuz?"

"I've got an alert set up for any movement at Sam's place at night. He came back from a walk at ten, then his aunt showed up around half past eleven. The lights went out in the living room next."

"Okay, what's weird about any of that?"

"Not a thing." Moose tapped and the video cued up. "Until

this just happened."

Nitro leaned in, squinting to view the video filmed after dark. The time stamp showed just before four in the morning. A black or dark blue sedan had pulled into the inn driveway and a tall blonde got out.

No lights were on inside the house. Outside, a gas lamp offered enough to see the porch area.

Moose tapped more keys and the resolution improved, brightening the image to better see her once she walked near the gaslight. He muttered, "She's hot."

No argument from Nitro. She looked to be five-ten and blond. That bright dress hugged every curve from her neck to her waist then stopped just past her ass. She carried a shoulder bag that Nitro didn't think was only a purse. Just the right size for a change of clothes and other overnight needs.

Sam had opened the door and looked shocked.

She hit the bottom step and ran forward to jump in his arms.

Nitro felt Angel hanging near his shoulder. Angel muttered, "*Tabaquismo!*"

"Yeah, that'd be smokin' even for your women," Moose agreed. "Where the hell did Partyman find *her*?"

That comment shook Nitro loose from watching the forever lip-lock. "Thought you said Partyman usually hooked up with a local woman called Janean."

Moose turned to him. "He has in the past. This doesn't appear to be her based on his reaction and Janean being shorter with dark brown hair. Got nothing on this one."

When the kiss ended, Sam beamed at her as if someone had dropped that babe in his lap.

Angel asked, "What about her tag?"

Moose rewound the video to right before she pulled in. She hadn't gone straight in so even the second camera across the street in a different tree did not have a clear shot. "We may not get the tag number and location until daylight or when she leaves."

Nitro felt a twitch, the kind he got when something was off. Not that Sam didn't deserve to spend some time with a willing female, but ... something didn't feel right about this.

Logan had scrubbed Sam's existence from the point of Sam starting with the HAMR Brotherhood back to his birth certificate. There should be nothing about the woman he called his aunt, or her inn, tied to Sam.

Nitro wouldn't have dropped Sam at Angela's place and put her at risk. He'd felt Sam would heal in a safe place, somewhere he could think about his future. The cameras they'd installed were SOP for keeping an eye on any of their team during downtime.

Sam and Moose were tight, yet Moose knew nothing about this woman. Where had she come from if she wasn't on *his* radar?

Angel could have fifty women they'd never know about, and he'd likely forgotten half of them, but Sam's nickname of Partyman had been a poke at how he didn't hang out in bars. Sam had made it clear he had zero plans to ever get serious with any woman while he ran ops with the team because his background had scarred him.

He wasn't one to pick up a woman and take her home. Not after his sister left a party with the wrong man and didn't survive. That was the problem with stopping Sam from trying to save every female he perceived as being in trouble.

Nitro said, "Set up the third computer. I'll monitor it until Blade gets back. If anything pings in the wrong way for me, we'll make a visit."

CHAPTER 16

HALLENE WALKED PAST SAM, ENTERING his bedroom. She dropped her heavy shoulder bag on the chair next to a window.

The door snapped shut behind her and a lamp clicked on. "You could have given me a heads-up on this *plan* of yours."

She swung around. "You played it well. Had you known in advance, you might have overacted or tried to signal your team. I saved you from that mistake."

"How generous of you."

Was he going to snipe at her every minute? She felt bad enough for threatening Angela, who must be important to Sam based on the way he reacted. Hallene couldn't admit that Angela and this community would be safe and expect Sam to stick with her. "Would you prefer the alternative of this falling apart before we get started?"

Grumbling under his breath, he moved his hand in a rolling motion. "Moving along, what's your name or whatever you want me to call you?"

"Hailey." Close enough to her name to get a natural reaction when he said it. Even if he snarled when he called her, which seemed to be his only mood. They had to play this role completely or his team would be alerted and interfere.

She would not allow him or anyone else to put Phoebe in more danger than she was. "I am giving you a chance to find your kidnapped person. Can you not step up and work with me?"

His steel-blue eyes speared her with contempt.

Going to be tough to sell them as lovers.

He announced, "I'm getting a shower. Make yourself at home since you think you are." He pulled off his shirt and tossed it into the corner.

She'd seen him that night in the mansion, but she'd been pressed for time and had poor lighting.

Just that movement showed off cut muscles from his shoulders to his hard stomach. Arm muscles rippled when he moved. Then he turned and she got a heat-inducing look at his wide shoulders and strong back. Thick brown hair cut short on the sides and ruffled from the shirt gave him the look of a man just waking from a night of sex.

When he'd smiled that one time, she'd wanted to kiss him again. He'd tasted too good for her sanity that first time.

She hadn't kissed anyone in a long time. Really long time. She'd been on a mission to save children. Coop accused her of being too uptight to let a man get close to her.

She was not her mother to hand control over to a man.

Two years without dating seriously hadn't seemed like a big deal. She'd been content, or so she'd thought.

Her body picked a hell of a time to come out of retirement.

Sam turned to her as if eyes in the back of his head had caught her ogling him.

She jerked her attention away, but not before he noticed and made a smirky noise. She lifted the shoulder bag and took it to the bed, pausing to listen.

Water started running in the shower.

She glanced over to the open door. He clearly cared not if she'd watched him shed his clothes. Steam boiled over the top of the shower, filling the room.

Just to get him back, she should have watched and let him know being naked would not intimidate her.

Not even naked with water pouring down his slick skin while he soaped everything and paused to grab himself and start ...

Whoa!

She slapped a hand over her eyes as if that would hide the erotic image of him bathing. When this was done and she had Phoebe somewhere safe, it was time to get back into dating. She'd never had a problem keeping her mind on a mission in the past. Allowing her mind to stray with Grumpy would be stupid.

Emptying her bag on the bed, she sorted out the change of

clothes for this shower. They'd be leaving by daylight. They just needed to put on a quick show for the woman called Angela.

Her intel resource had found no blood connection between Sam and Angela. In fact, Angela's life had been well concealed behind a wall of attorneys. She clearly had money and liked her anonymity.

That alone reminded Hallene to be careful around Sam. Only while she held a threat over Angela's head would he play ball, but that didn't mean he wouldn't try to skew the rules.

She'd never put an innocent person in danger, but she made up her own rules when it came to saving Phoebe.

Kovac had better not be in league with the Collector or whomever the Collector might have as a partner. As of now, it sounded as if Kovac was caught in a blackmail scheme.

If Hallene found out differently, he'd discover just how dangerous she could be.

There had been no witness to Phoebe's kidnapping. When Hallene tracked her down to a party at a local bar, she'd asked around about Phoebe. No one saw who she left with. Phoebe had no close friends. Hallene couldn't hold that against the girl.

Hallene had found out just who her real friends were when her father died.

The people around her only wanted to hang out and have fun until her family scandal tainted her.

Phoebe ran with a money crowd who were just as shallow. Had someone lured Phoebe into the kidnapping? Or had someone taken advantage of Phoebe's naivete?

That wouldn't help right now but was something to keep in mind. Hallene dug around quickly through drawers in a high chest and came up with no weapon, but she found a phone. Opening it up, she found no tracker. This was a burner phone. She shoved that into her bag and glanced around for another place to keep a weapon. Her gaze lifted to the top of a tall bookcase. She slid her hand until her fingers touched a weapon she pulled down.

The Baretta M9 had no suppressor this time. She slipped it into her shoulder bag. Her weapon was hidden in her vehicle, but she had a knife inside a fake hairspray can in this bag.

The shower ended leaving the room in a hushed silence.

Gathering her bag along with a change of clothes, she walked over to the window facing the front where everything outside was still dark, but early morning light had begun leaking to highlight the bay.

"All yours," he muttered behind her.

She turned to find him wearing only boxer shorts and drying his hair with a towel.

He faced the door with his back to her. "Get your fill of ogling me. I'll be dressed when you come out."

Yep, Leclair was pissed.

So much better than a smiling Sam. She could better keep him at arm's length when he was angry.

Heat surged in her face. She ignored him and stepped into the bathroom, closing the door with a snap.

She needed sleep, which wouldn't happen until they reached their next point. She'd love hot tea but had found coffee easier to grab and suck down while traveling in this country. As soon as they left, coffee would keep her going until she could use her plan for sleeping when the time came.

Keeping Leclair on his toes constantly required thinking ahead of every move and avoiding any missteps.

After a quick shower, she used the blow-dryer to tame her hair and returned to the bedroom. As he'd said, he was dressed in jeans and a dark T-shirt. He stood with his arms crossed.

That was beginning to look like his normal pose.

She knew what had pissed him off this time but gave him a curious look. "Everything okay?"

"I'm sure that innocent act works on plenty of other men. What'd you do with my weapon and phone?"

"Both are safe." She'd dressed in a pale-pink blouse with a button-down collar and cuffs. She tucked that inside a pair of navy slacks, replacing her heels with running shoes. She wore little makeup and no lipstick to go with her hair pulled into a ponytail to finish off the casual look of someone on vacation.

He was not done fuming. "This isn't going to work if I can't trust you to leave my personal belongings alone."

She finished repacking the shoulder bag and dropped it by the chair. "Regardless of removing your gun and phone, you don't trust me any more than I trust you."

"Yet you think we're going to leave here, and everyone will believe you are someone I slept with in the past." His flat tone said he wasn't on board with that thought on any level.

Not that he didn't have a point, but she was too tired to schmooze him even if doing so would work.

Moving to the chair, she sat with her elbows on the arms and hands steepled. She lifted her gaze to him. "I agree with your point. We need some rules to make this work."

His eyebrow quirked up. "To make *what* work? You have yet to share what we're going to do, *Hailey*."

"We're going after both of our people. You may not care about my word, but it's solid in the intel community. I will help you so long as you help me and do not interfere with my goal. You should know I'm willing to stop at nothing to get this person back. That means anyone stepping in my way or slowing me down will face serious consequences. I can't be any clearer than that. In exchange for backing me up, I'll help you recover your missing person. Is that not fair?"

He stalked back and forth then paused. "I'll join you and we'll back *each other* up so long as you are not a criminal. If at any time I think you are, all bets are off."

She would break any law to get to Phoebe, but she would not kill an innocent or anyone who did not try to harm her first. "Laws may be badly bent, if need be, but I'm not a criminal wanted by any country."

"Yet," he said, throwing out his opinion of trusting her. His arms unfolded. With hands hooked on his hips, he made a little nod as if for himself only. "Then it's time to tell me the plan."

She stretched her arms along the chair arms, giving off a confident pose when her insides flipped around in chaos. This could go so badly for either of them or both. If that happened, it would be entirely her fault, but this was not the time to back out.

"We leave at nine after you convince the inn owner that we are a pair. That will give us both a chance for some sleep. Once we're on the road, I'll give you more details as we move toward the target. Feel better?"

"No. I want my weapon back."

She lifted her bag and pulled out his weapon, tossing it onto the bed.

He lifted it and checked the magazine, which was now empty. Cursing, he tossed it on the bed close to her. "Not much use without ammo. You might as well carry it."

"I gave you what you asked for. Be more specific next time." The fury in his gaze lifted hairs on her arms, but she showed only calm to him.

"Just remember that you set the rules for this mess, Hailey. Oh, and one more thing, I'm grabbing some sleep. You can have the chair since we don't have to put on a show in here."

This may be a worse idea than going after Phoebe alone the first time, but she was out of options and running out of time.

CHAPTER 17

———

S AM PULLED HIS BALL CAP on with a jerk and walked down the stairs. He carried his small duffel bag, glad to get moving. He managed zero solid sleep. His damn nose kept picking up the scent of Hailey with the sandalwood soap from his bathroom.

Like he needed a reminder *she* was in his bedroom?

He woke up twice, glanced at her curled up in the chair, told himself he was the worst shit in the world, then reminded himself that she was blackmailing him into helping her.

Oh, and putting his future with HAMR Brotherhood at risk even more than it was.

That would quiet his mind to fall asleep before another deep inhale started it all over again.

When Hailey woke him at eight to drill their details into his brain, he growled at her loud enough she jumped back. She recovered quickly and snarled at him that the longer it took him to do his part, the more time they'd be stuck together.

That had done it. He sat in fuming silence, repeating what she told him until she gave up.

He'd enjoyed the fact she hadn't seemed to notice her ponytail being jacked up the whole time. She'd clearly come awake ready to start tutoring him.

Waiting calmly for her to finish the rundown of how they met, how long they'd known each other, and way more information than he and Janean had ever exchanged, he smiled.

She'd gone quiet.

Then he pointed out that she looked like he'd banged her, and since that hadn't occurred, she should brush her hair before leaving.

That brought on livid cursing.

Miss Control Freak did not like having any shortcomings on her part pointed out.

Duly noted for use at a later time.

The smell of fresh bacon and coffee had him salivating as he descended the stairs, but they didn't have time.

They had a kidnapper to find.

Could she really have intel on W?

Hailey stepped off the stairs right behind him. Her voice rolled out sexy and refreshed. "That coffee smells wonderful."

He glanced over his shoulder. Who was that woman?

She beamed a killer smile, looking seriously happy. She'd pushed her sunglasses up to rest on her head as if they were headed for a day at the beach.

"Mahnin', yah two." Angie stepped out of the kitchen with one of her favorite aprons. This one read, "Made with Love, which means I licked the spoon ... and kept using it."

Sam suffered a moment of embarrassment, but not over the apron. He'd never brought a woman to Angie's home.

Never.

How was he going to smooth this over? He pecked a kiss on her cheek. "Morning."

Hailey moved up and offered her hand. Her voice would melt sugar. "I'm Hailey. I've heard so much about you. Please don't think badly of Sam for me being here unannounced. We hadn't spoken for a while when he called. He sounded lonely so I decided to surprise him."

Being the gracious woman Angie was when not irritated, she shook hands. "Nice tah meet yah." Angie glanced at Sam's duffel. "Yah leavin'?"

He shrugged. "I've got a week off and nothing to do. We're headed down the coast, but I'll be back before I return to work on Tuesday." He held his breath, fearing Angie would ask about the boat. He didn't want to mention it and give Hailey, if that was her freaking name, any more connection between him and Angie than she had.

The fact that Angie did not start asking questions indicated she wasn't sold on this relationship one bit. "I'm always sayin' yah should take some time tah have fun."

No, yesterday she was saying he should spend time working on the house so it would still be standing when he showed up unexpectedly again.

Had Nitro left her any way to contact them?

Probably not.

Sam hoped that was the case because Angie would be on the phone the minute he left to call and ask about Hailey.

"Want breakfast?" Angie asked. That was also not her standard MO. She'd normally tell him to set the table and fix coffee for him and her.

Hailey hooked her fingers around his arm. "I wish I'd thought about eating here, but I didn't want to put anyone out. We have brunch plans in Boston."

"That's so sweet." Angie gave Sam a smile that said she'd want answers as soon as he returned. Not to dare avoid her. "Run along and have a good time."

"Thank you, and it was lovely to meet you." Hailey started to move and tug him with her.

He patted her hand. "Give me a minute, baby, and I'll be out. Okay?"

She released her grip on him. "Of course." She leaned over and gave him a kiss on the cheek, then walked calmly out the screened door. The sunglasses were in place before she stepped out on the porch and stretched.

That was her letting him know she wanted him to get moving before the sun climbed higher over the eastern bay.

Angie stared at Sam. Her silence damning him for lying to her.

He sighed and leaned down, hugging her to him. He whispered, "I'm sorry. I'll explain when I get back. Try not to be angry with me while I'm gone. The boat is amazing. I love you for a lot of reasons and that's a new one."

She wrapped him up again and his muscles eased at not leaving her angry. "Be careful, Sammy."

No Sammy boy. She was worried, but showing him a strong front, she backed away and smiled. "Yah be good and dohn fahget tah bring me a gift."

"I won't forget."

She never wanted anything from him. Angie knew something was screwed up with all this but trusted him to deal with whatever was going on.

Angie had been the first strong woman in his life. He'd learned more than he realized just by being around her.

Her playing along reminded him of times in high school when she'd show up and rant about how he'd promised to mow her yard and trim the bushes. He'd apologize profusely until his dad would allow him to go. She'd then give him money to keep his dad content and take him to a movie and lunch.

He hated to leave this way but couldn't put it off any longer. Picking up his duffel, he walked out to join his unwanted partner. As the screen door closed behind him, he asked, "Ready, sweetheart?"

Hailey angled her head at him, a lover's glow on her face. "We need to get rolling if we're going to make brunch." She had a smile that would stop traffic.

Too bad it was as phony as her act.

"Let's go." When he reached her sedan, he made a point of walking around the back just to look at the tag. It was from Massachusetts, but the numbers had been splashed with mud. Probably belonged to a different vehicle.

He tossed his duffel in the back seat and would normally drive, but this one would not give up control. He rolled the window down to drape his arm outside.

"Put the window up." She gave that order with a grin in place.

"No. I usually drive. If I *have* to ride with you driving, I need fresh air."

"Am I going to have to warn you constantly about any games?"

He gritted his teeth as if he could barely tolerate her. Not far from the truth. "I'm pretty sure my team is keeping an eye on me. I'm trying to act naturally. I don't like riding in vehicles. I normally keep everything that runs operating and do the driving. On the few occasions I ride shotgun, I have the window down even in the winter. I ... don't—" He cut off his words.

"What? You don't what?"

"Hell. Might as well tell you and not fight over this again. I don't like being closed up in a small area with no fresh air." He wouldn't look at her, just kept his jaw rigid and stared ahead.

She put a hand on his arm. "I'm going to take you at your word until you prove me wrong for doing it. Leave it down, but at least smile when I back out."

He sighed a deep growling sound meant to give the impression he was not happy about any of this, which he wasn't. Then he scrubbed a hand over his face, took a deep breath, and smiled at her.

"Guess that will have to do."

"I'm smiling more than I ever do with others."

She muttered, "That I can believe. No wonder you don't have women breaking down your door."

He glared at her.

She didn't even look at him. "Backing out. Smile."

He did, but as she was busy turning the sedan around, he flicked his fingers quickly in sign language. Most of the team could read some sign language, but Moose was excellent at it. If he wasn't with the team, Nitro would send him the video.

Sam glanced at the trees across from the house and saw nothing. Where had they put cameras?

Had anyone seen his fingers?

CHAPTER 18

——◆——

"MR. KOVAC?"

Kovac smiled at his buxom date, a model he'd met recently at a cocktail party, then flicked his attention to the maître d' of his favorite Michelin restaurant in London. "Yes?"

"There is an urgent call for you."

Who could even know he was here? He'd made this reservation himself.

He excused himself from his dinner companion and followed the maître d' to a private room and waited for the door to close. He lifted the receiver on the landline. "This is Kovac."

"Everything is on schedule, yes?"

Kovac went from relaxed to stressed in seconds. This was the Russian who ruled his life until Sunday. "All done. I—"

"Cease speaking. Reply yes or no when I ask question." W's smooth voice could be a radio announcer if not for the underlying threat he lobbied.

Kovac opened his mouth to say he understood, but he'd learned by now to do exactly as told even if it infuriated him for anyone to speak to him this way. He questioned the safety of speaking on this phone but knew W would not have reached out to him here if the line was not safe.

W next instructed, "If your part is successful, Phoebe will be returned, and you will receive payment."

Kovac knew that. Why was W bringing it up again? He remained silent, which he decided was defiant at this point. Not subservient.

"If not, she will be used to point finger at your part in this exercise. Should that happen, the world's most elite forces will find you before you can use money you have been accumulating to escape."

What had happened?

Kovac struggled to keep his tongue still. When he'd first learned they'd kidnapped Phoebe, he'd hadn't cared. She'd been an unexpected birth and a future leech on his fortune. But he'd been looking for a big opportunity like this one for the past five years and made the appropriate concerned noises as her father. He'd wanted W to think he had the upper hand by holding Phoebe.

Kovac had considered offering to let W keep her as a token of his friendship once the job was done.

Now? She could turn into a deadly anchor capable of sinking his entire world.

Shit. What was the chance that bitch Hallene looking for Phoebe would be successful?

None. That meant he could not afford anyone in the chain between his shipping operation and that Chinese submarine to screw up.

Kovac gripped his phone hard enough for his hand to shake, but he waited for his chance to speak.

"I am sure you wonder why I bring up Phoebe. I believe Hallene Clarke is your stepdaughter, yes?"

Oh, shit. "Yes."

"She appeared during an operation in Venezuela where Phoebe was being kept for short time. Hallene interfered but managed to escape. I wonder at first if you are foolish enough to attempt to rescue Phoebe and cross me. You are not foolish, are you?"

"No, Sir." Kovac couldn't get that out fast enough. That damn Hallene!

"I thought not," W continued. "I will waste no resources on Hallene as she is your problem. Have I made myself clear, Mr. Kovac?"

"Yes."

"Will there be any delay in handling this?"

"No." Kovac had an insurance card he called Crusher who cost a buttload of money, but at this moment that insurance would be worth every penny.

The call ended.

Kovac pulled a phone out of his coat pocket. One with no navigational ability or apps. This was used only for Crusher, the one person he called for special jobs and who would be his personal bodyguard when the time came for Kovac to disappear.

Crusher answered on the second ring. "Yes."

Kovac explained his possible crisis.

"Can we track her?" Crusher had a mild voice for a man who could pass for a tall businessman or banker when suited up.

"I've tried. The phone listed for her has not left her London flat, but I know she was just in South America."

"Why?"

Kovac paused at that question. How had Hallene figured out about W's operation in South America? W had been communicating with Kovac via another mobile phone routed through Kovac's computer.

He had firewalls that no one should be able to breach.

Answering Crusher, Kovac said, "I think she might have lifted an electronic communication between myself and a client."

Crusher would understand it was not one of Kovac's legitimate shipping clients. "That's how we'll track her. Call me when you are at *that* electronic device. I'll tell you what to do."

Ha! Relief loosened the tight muscles in Kovac's neck. His man would deal with that annoying bitch.

As soon as Kovac cashed in on this last deal, it would be time to leave. He'd been dissolving investments to acquire enough to disappear comfortably. That W knew of his actions should worry him, but Kovac was safe so long as he did his part in W's secret plan. Kovac just had to work out how to fake his own death. Crusher could probably set that up.

Phoebe would inherit Kovac's money because her mother would be dead by then.

He'd blackmail Phoebe with his information of her having played a role in whatever W was doing. Kovac had no doubt he'd see it all on the news.

He straightened his tie and headed back to finish his meal. Then he'd return to his office where the building would be empty short of the night staff.

He'd call Crusher and get Hallene out of his hair.
Forever.

CHAPTER 19

———

HALLENE BLINKED HARD AND OPENED her eyes wide. She shook her head to stay awake. She'd been driving for seven hours, which wasn't long, but they'd stopped to dump this vehicle and drive a different one she'd stashed just in case Leclair's team had tagged the first one with a tracker.

After all that, it was closing in on early evening.

She hadn't slept enough in the last few days to keep going at this pace.

She should have gotten four hours this morning and felt better but sleeping in the chair had been difficult enough. She kept waking up every time she shifted her position. She'd glance around with her gaze stopping on Sam's body twisted up in the sheets. With so much exposed body, her weary mind would drift off into Fantasy Land, wondering how he'd look with the rest of the sheet and the boxers out of the way.

Exhaustion should have sent her back to sleep right then, but no. Her lusting mind used that first thought as a launching pad for Full Monty Sam.

She'd end up wide awake and longing to climb into the bed with him. A small part of her brain that still retained some sense wanted to slap her for finding Leclair desirable in any way. The guy had slept like a baby all alone in the bed while leaving her stuck in a chair with only her shoulder bag to snuggle.

Being dismissed to sleep in the chair put everything back into perspective.

He was here only because she forced him, not because he had been willing to join her voluntarily and help even with the chance to find the kidnapped person his team failed to extract in Venezuela.

Her method to motivate him might have been unorthodox, but would he not do the same in her shoes?

Who knew? His heart might be made of stone. Coop had been considerate to her, but he'd told her up front his duty and the missions *always* came first.

She yawned and shook her head again, keeping an eye on traffic. The one time she'd gone deep into sleep it had ended with a nightmare about Phoebe screaming as someone dragged her into a dark hole.

Hallene had watched the terrified girl disappear knowing that had been her last chance to save Phoebe. She'd jolted awake and stayed that way until she'd woke Leclair to coach him on their fake relationship.

Her head nodded. She snapped her chin up and pulled the car back to the center of her lane. It had started to stray.

This was dangerous. She couldn't drive much longer.

She tossed a glare at Leclair.

He'd dropped his head back as soon as they exchanged vehicles twenty minutes from Clercville and slept as if he had no care in the world about where she was taking him.

Maybe he didn't. Angry didn't cover his attitude.

Could she trust him to stay on course and not pull anything funny if they swapped seats?

Coop would be scowling at her. He'd admonished her time and again about running herself into the ground. "Every good soldier must rest."

At least he'd be happy she had backup this time, though he would think her choice a crazy one.

She had to let Leclair drive. With both of their phones in her shoulder bag, he shouldn't be able to get a message to his team. If he did, his team would grasp control and shove her aside. Their high-profile captive would take precedence over a teenage girl. Hallene would not risk her last chance to find Phoebe and bring her home.

She'd told Leclair she'd help find his missing person, but so long as Hallene remained in control, no one came before Phoebe.

She had considered the risk to Leclair, but he had gone into a high-risk line of work. To be honest, he had a better chance of surviving than her and she felt confident about her abilities.

That was her logic, and she was sticking to it.

Coop would not agree.

She gripped the steering wheel. Coop was not here, and he'd said more than once that no one was perfect at this game. He'd admitted even he and his men had made mistakes.

In fact, he'd probably tell her to stop listening to a dead man for advice.

That made her heart ache. They'd never been romantically involved, but he had become so important to her when she'd been alone for the longest time. Losing her best friend had broken something inside her.

After two years, she should be ready to let a man in, but what guy wanted to date a woman who thought about a ghost more than her date?

Had Phoebe felt abandoned by everyone after Hallene became more distant as the girl reached her teens?

Probably.

Add another brick of guilt for severing what little connection she'd had with Phoebe.

Noise from the tires running over rumble strips, which were installed to alert drivers of leaving their lane, jerked Hallene wide awake.

Had she closed her eyes?

"You gonna kill us before we reach this secret location or let me drive so you can sleep?" Sam asked in a gruff voice from sleeping.

She swung a peeved look his way, which had been wasted. The ball cap pushed down over his face had not moved.

He asked, "How much farther?"

"Three more hours then we'll have to stop." She wouldn't make it that long. "Let's change places."

Sitting up, he stretched his arms. The left one shot behind her head, but he didn't touch her. "How about stopping somewhere we can fuel up and I can get coffee?"

The tank was pretty low on fuel even with her conservative speed. She'd also like to get out and stretch. Flipping on her turn signal, she took the next off-ramp.

She pulled up to a pump in a large station and withdrew a credit card. "Use this to fill up. I'll get your coffee."

"You don't know how I like it."

"Black. Like your frame of mind." She got out, taking her shoulder bag with her. She couldn't trust him with their phones. The bag was heavy with his pistol. He'd given it back out of spite. If it wasn't loaded, he wouldn't tote it around.

She made a fast bathroom stop then paid for his coffee, a water for her, and two sandwiches.

When she walked out of the building into the muggy air, her white GMC Denali had been parked in front of the building.

Ah, hell. Where was he?

She spun around searching through the glass as he appeared exiting the men's room. He strode toward her.

Had he found someone in there to loan him a phone?

Leclair wouldn't tell her if she asked.

He'd been warned. She was not going to repeat the warning every few hours like a broken record. If a threat was sound, then it would work without reinforcing it continually.

Walking out, he seemed content. Too content.

"*Stop it!*" a high-pitched female voice cried from the end of the building.

Leclair turned at the sound, took a long look, then started for the corner of the building.

What was he doing?

She put the coffee, her water, and the sandwiches on the hood and followed. Looking past Leclair, she saw a young woman struggling with a middle-aged man who appeared in his late forties with deeply tanned arms muscled from working outside if that tow truck behind him was his.

"When I git you home, I'll teach you some manners," he growled in the young woman's face. She wore a wrinkled cotton shirt two sizes too large for her and baggy jeans only because she was skin and bones, not as a fashion statement. She was barefoot and her brown hair fell past her shoulders. Freckles and swollen red eyes stood out against her pale skin.

He yanked the girl to come with him and dragged her around the corner out of sight.

Leclair called out, "Hold up."

Hallene jogged to reach the corner as Leclair swung around to the side of the building.

The woman was maybe nineteen or twenty and crying. She dug in her heels, trying to pull away, clearly panicked at what the man threatened to do with her when there were no witnesses.

She whined, "I was not flirtin', Daddy. I was just bein' nice. Please, don't hit me. I didn't do nothin' wrong."

"You lyin' whore. You ain't no better than your sorry mama." He dragged her around the front of the tow truck.

Her terrified cries wrenched Hallene's heart. She'd like to kick this guy's ass into next year, but she held back, staying out of Leclair's way. What would he do?

"*Stop!*" Leclair shouted with force, still moving toward the pair.

Wiry hair the color of mud stuck out from the man's faded red ball cap. He had a stocky build and thick biceps. His massive hand had a tight grip on the girl's thin arm that would bruise for sure.

At Leclair ordering him to stop, the man turned his rage on someone new. "Make the mistake of takin' another fuckin' step this way and—"

Leclair closed the distance in one long stride, grabbed the guy's head, and slammed it down on the hood of his truck.

"What the fu—"

Leclair gripped the man's neck in a powerful hold and shoved his head down again.

The girl pulled free and backed up with her hand over her mouth. Angry red handprints already showed on her arm.

Holding the tow truck driver's head in place against the hood, Leclair lowered his face even with the jerk.

The man garbled out, "That's assault, you son of–"

"*Don't* make me slam your head again," Leclair warned in a gritty voice that gave Hallene chills. "I have your tag number. In five minutes, I'll know all there is to learn about your worthless hide."

"You a ... cop?" For the first time, the loudmouth sounded worried.

"Oh, no," Leclair chuckled with dark humor. "I'm way worse than a cop. I'm the one who shows up in the middle of the night and teaches monsters to change their ways or lose their right to play in this world." Leclair sounded feral with rage.

Loudmouth jerk started asking, "Who the—"

"Shut. Up. This is your only warning." Leclair took his time, giving every word power. "Lift a hand to hurt that child again and word will get back to me. You'll be watched from here on. Call the cops and convince them this happened if you want. There's no security camera on this side of the building, and even if you make the mistake of forcing her to tell the cops what happened, they can't find me. That will *also* bring me to visit you. I don't exist. Don't be stupid and make this mistake again. If you do and I come for you the second time, you won't have any hands to lift against another vulnerable woman when I leave. You'll be at the mercy of everyone, including her."

For a man with skin that dark from the sun, he lost two shades. His eyes bulged. "I ... uh ... won't." He sounded close to crying.

"I'm going to let you up. If you try to jump me, she'll have to call an ambulance ... or watch you bleed out. That will be her choice."

"I won't," came out in a weak and pleading voice.

Bullies were not so powerful when a bigger threat came along.

Leclair released his neck and stepped back.

Putting his hands on the hood, the guy groaned and lifted his head. He'd have a mega headache from his encounter with Leclair.

Hallene had no sympathy for him and quietly cheered Leclair for instilling fear in a man no one else in local law enforcement could intimidate. Not even the police could protect a woman at times even with a restraining order. Monsters ignored paper, often severely damaging or killing the women who dared to file a complaint.

Sure, the law had been broken once the monster came after her, but the female paid the ultimate price.

Leclair would not move yet. He stood with his arms crossed as the tow truck driver glanced over at the girl and quietly said, "Let's go."

She'd stopped crying and watched Leclair as if he had sprouted avenging angel wings. Probably no one had intervened to protect her from her father until now.

Leclair gave her an understanding nod. She got into the truck cab and kept her eyes locked on him until the truck drove out of the lot.

Hallene had been falling asleep until that. Her body buzzed with anger and ... admiration.

When Leclair turned to her, he paused.

Was he waiting on her to criticize him for drawing attention to them? No one had come around the building. Even if someone had, she still would never condemn him for what he'd given that girl.

She asked, "Do you want the turkey or ham sandwich? I got both."

The harsh lines on his face relaxed along with him letting his arms fall. "Ham." He walked over, waited for her to turn, and fell into step with her.

Who was this man? She was just realizing how much she did not know about him, but she respected the part he'd just revealed. Her insides flipped and churned in confusion.

She wanted to hug him for what he'd just done, but she couldn't allow herself to lower her guard. She had to keep this businesslike so he would respect her ability to see it through.

He tapped the key to unlock the doors and lifted the sandwiches to hand her. Then he grabbed the coffee and sipped it. "Perfect."

Once he had them on the interstate heading south again, she opened his sandwich and set it up on the console with extra napkins.

Before taking a bite, he said, "You're quiet."

Spending all day on the road alone had given her too much time to think. Guilt pounded her at forcing him to do this, but she could not back down now.

"I'm just tired." She opened her sandwich and took a bite.

He said, "Not going to ask me if I went into the store to call my team?"

She hadn't expected that question, but no point in lying. "I thought about it."

He ate more and sipped his coffee. "There is no point in me calling my people when I have nothing to tell them. I want to find our person as much as you want to find yours. If we can do that and return me to Clercville by Monday night, I might be able to talk my way around doing this without authorization."

More guilt. Would he be penalized for leaving with her?

She'd thought he was on leave of some sort. "My plan is to return you by Sunday. Will your team be mad at you if we find your missing person?"

For a guy who hadn't said a word in hours, he was on a roll. "I can't expose what is decided within the realm of my team. They're terrific. We work like a fine piece of machinery with everyone doing their part. The only way a team succeeds is if everyone is on the same page. Everyone trusts that the other members are going to do their part without question."

"Where are you going with this?" She hadn't meant to sound irritable, but she was. She hadn't even told him the plan yet. Was he questioning her skills?

He drove with one hand on the wheel, relaxed, but his gaze continually tracked around them.

"My point is that you and I have never worked together yet you think we're just going to mesh perfectly in a dangerous situation. I would prefer to survive this and get both packages out alive *if* you can really find them. That won't happen if you're unwilling to tell me what the hell you expect us to do."

She couldn't argue with his words. "We could reach our destination today, but we'd be exhausted and can't act until I receive a final piece of intel. We're headed south to get into the vicinity of where the kidnapper may be holding the captives. That location is loaded into the map system. My resource got me into the mansion in South America and located you, so his intel is solid. But as your team discovered, there is always the unknown factor. For that reason, I'd rather not say more until I have this next part confirmed."

He turned to her briefly, eyes taking stock of her.

Would he treat her as an equal or dismiss her as not being from an elite team like his?

Midnight Ferret had not found out who Sam worked for, but

from her experience, she recognized that this man appeared to walk the walk of an operator like Coop.

Leclair nodded. "I can work with that."

She did a double take at him, surprised he did not continue to argue. He kept his attention on the road where the traffic had been reasonable all day except for when she'd driven through Boston.

Her instincts were warning her that he was being too accommodating.

Had he called his team after all to have them follow?

The fact that Leclair addressed her concern about him calling his people did not prove he hadn't done just that. His team could be following them at this very minute.

If they interfered or tried to stop her, Leclair and his men would make a huge mistake. She didn't want to harm anyone, but that would not stop her from taking down anyone who stepped between her and finding Phoebe.

She might not trust Leclair but ... she liked him. Liked the man who had not hesitated to stop a man from abusing a young woman. Liked his smile when he showed a real one.

Closing her eyes, she tried to quiet her mind, but she feared Leclair would disappoint her.

If he did, she might have to face an ugly choice.

Allowing herself to be stopped or hurting Leclair.

CHAPTER 20

STREETLIGHTS LIT UP THE FOUR lanes of downtown Elizabeth, New York, a peaceful place with most of the business crowd gone by eight at night. Sam had two miles to go before they reached the hotel the navigation system squawked about being on the right ahead.

He'd had four hours to think of ways to fix this unauthorized action when he faced Nitro at some point. Four hours. He should have been able to come up with a plan for world peace with all the mental crunching he'd done in that much time.

How much longer could he go along without knowing all of Hailey's intel? At some point, he had to make a choice to stick this out or bail on her for any hope of a future with Logan and his teams.

Being here wasn't his fault.

That argument would not matter.

Just like everyone on his FALCA team, he could evade Hailey and get a message to Nitro. He could have talked someone out of their phone when he'd run into the large restroom at the gas station. He'd stood out of the heavy foot traffic while debating his decision to call or not before making a move.

Calling Nitro would mean his team coming in and taking over this operation. They'd expect Hailey to share all she knew.

She would fight them the whole way.

She would not listen to another word Sam said at that point or share one snippet of intel.

That woman would hold firm to get her way, not trusting his team to go after the senator first with Hallene's captive as second in significance.

She'd be right.

That was *the* duty of every team hunting for Senator Turner.

Sam faced making the wrong choice and destroying any cooperation between him and Hailey.

In the end, he'd reasoned that no one on the planet looking for the senator had Hailey's intel because she hunted someone unrelated to the senator.

Someone Sam believed was personal to her and worth Hailey risking everything to find that person.

What if he'd been searching for someone like *his* sister who had been kidnapped? No question he'd turn his back on any future to save her.

But if he could make this work with Hailey, they'd save her target and maybe even get the senator back as well.

That decision to not call Nitro hours ago might have sealed his fate with Logan and Nitro, but Sam believed he was doing the right thing. That he had the best chance to find the senator by staying with Hailey and hoping when things got down to the wire, she would agree to bring in his team for support.

Taking action was better than sitting around flagellating himself over Esteban's death and how close his team had come to being wiped out at the mansion.

He had to find out if that had all been his fault. Finding W would answer a lot of questions.

A sense of purpose settled him, the same one that had steadied him since entering the military and then joining the HAMR Brotherhood.

If that was his last mission, so be it.

The hotel sign came into view a few blocks away. He tapped Hailey on the shoulder. "Time to wake up."

She jerked upright, looking around in a moment of confusion, then blinked and rubbed her eyes. "I'm up."

Her hair had come undone from the ponytail again and parts were shoved up both sides.

He was starting to like that jacked-up style best. Gave her a softer look, a more human side than the one always in control.

He couldn't let her get out like that, though.

He'd never known a woman who wanted to be walking around with hair, makeup, or clothes messed up. "You might want to do a quick mirror check."

She stared at him as if she hadn't understood his words, then flipped down the mirror on the visor. "Good grief." Digging out a brush from that bag-o-everything she carried around, she undid her hairband and quickly brushed her blond mane all back into a tidy ponytail.

He parked under the arrival and departure canopy. She jumped out, informing the valet they'd prefer to self-park and gave the guy her name as Hailey Carlton for the reservation.

Was she using a credit card tied to that pseudonym because it sure as hell was fake?

"Be right back," she tossed over her shoulder at Sam. She walked into the lobby, fully in control and holding her back ironing-board straight.

The valet went back to his key stand.

Sam searched all around the hotel but saw nothing suspicious from this position.

Hailey returned with a numbered buff-colored card to lay on the dash.

He drove them to the underneath parking garage, then grabbed his duffel and followed her to the elevator.

Now she watched all around them. What about up on the street?

She was cute in spy mode. Not a fully trained operative after all, but she'd been tutored by someone with skills.

The elevator stopped on the fifth floor, and he strolled behind her to the door. She hadn't offered him a key. If he had his lockpick set, he could open any room on this floor.

The room was upscale nice. Two queen beds with fluffy white covers, a desk, and an office chair plus an upholstered chair in the corner. He hoped the food service still ran after nine in the evening.

Standing just inside the door with the bathroom at her back, she announced, "I'm showering. If you don't want to wait to order, I'll take a pizza, a pale ale, and fries, preferably with cheese."

He must have made a look.

"What?" She had that annoyed frown hanging on her face again.

"Nothing. I'll order."

A tendril of hair escaped her ponytail and fell along her neck, refusing to remain in order.

He liked the little rogue.

She kept staring at him then shook her head at herself, muttering something, and backed into the bathroom. The door snapped shut.

By the time she finished showering, he'd ordered food, including his steak with a baked potato, and had paced the room a few times. She still didn't come out.

The hair dryer hummed into action. Can't let her hair just dry naturally, huh? How would she function under duress when everything was not in her control?

He'd learned in boot camp that no plan survives contact with an enemy. It was more about being able to adjust on the run.

He'd just signed off on the food bill and moved the rolling table over between the beds so they could sit on each side.

When the bathroom door opened, he looked up, intending to ask her if she got every hair perfectly styled for eating in a hotel room, but he couldn't speak.

She wore a white hotel robe that reached her knees, leaving those sexy legs exposed all the way to her pink-and-white toenails. They had sparkles.

He'd missed that this morning, but she'd given him little chance to take a long look from head to toe. Her hair flowed to her shoulders in a silky gold waterfall. She wore no makeup and damn if she wasn't prettier without it.

Just her smooth skin, soft gray eyes, and rose-colored lips.

After the extended pause, she looked down at herself. "What's wrong?"

Not a freaking thing.

Always trying to make sure she was perfect.

"Nothing," he said as if he hadn't been dumbstruck by her. "Come eat."

She dropped the shoulder bag on the first bed she came to and slid in between the table and the bed. She started lifting silver covers and making hungry noises.

He swept another look at her. A pretty woman when he could get her to smile, but some man had drained her happiness.

He let her dive into her pizza and waited for her shoulders to relax before seeing how she'd answer his questions. "You have some impressive skills." Always start with a positive.

She slowed, watching him as she chewed. Those eyes hid all kinds of secrets.

He'd never tell Angel, but he'd like to have that one's gift as a silver-tongued devil. "You took out that guard at the mansion with moves I hadn't expected. Where did you train?"

"With some people who perform similar work as your team. Who is your team? US military Special Forces?" She put that question to him and attacked her fries.

"We come from different divisions of the military," he allowed. "Remember what I told you earlier about success depending upon us being able to function as a team?"

She kept eating and nodded.

"We can't save anyone if we're going to act like two dogs thrown into a pit and expected to make friends to keep from killing each other."

After drinking some of her beer, she put it down and turned the glass. "That's unfair. I've been considerate to you, and you've been fair with me. I think we're doing okay."

"That's not teamwork." He cut his steak, taking his time finishing it and the potato to let that sink in. When he had his empty plates covered, he drank his own beer, letting the silence do more to push her than his questions.

She finished her meal and emptied her glass. "I'm done."

He stood and moved the table outside the door then stepped back in to call for a pickup.

Hailey watched him do all that, her eyes full of questions. Was she not used to someone handling the menial tasks?

She walked over to the window and pulled the thick covering into place, then turned and sat in the chair in the corner. "I hear what you're saying, but the kind of teamwork you envision takes more time to develop than we have."

Sam wheeled the office chair out to where he could sit with his sock-covered feet on the bed he'd chosen. Pushing her to share control started with small decisions.

Impatience got to her. "No comment?"

"Yeah, I've got something to say," Sam said with his hands folded in his lap. "You're intelligent. You have skills, which means you've likely had enough conversations with people who do black ops to understand that wanting us to work like a team even though we're not putting in the time to make it happen is ridiculous. You don't hit me as a ridiculous person. That tells me you have a personal investment in this to push the limits, which has your mental wires crossed. That puts this mission at an even higher risk of failure."

Her face had relaxed when he'd called her intelligent, but any happy feelings scattered to the four walls after that. She started to speak and stopped.

Sam said, "Good. At least you aren't going to try to convince me this isn't personal for you. Why don't we start at that point?"

She huffed a sound of disgust. "You expect me to keep telling you things when you just said there is no hope for rescuing my person?"

"I didn't say that." He maintained a calm but serious expression. "I said it puts this mission at a higher risk of failure. Every mission has some risk of failure. The key is for a team to identify the weak spots and shore them up at any moment, which allows us to be fluid when things change so we can adjust on the run. I'm asking you to tell me why the person you're looking for is so important."

She propped her elbows on the chair arms and steepled her fingers again. "It's a seventeen-year-old girl who was kidnapped from a party in Clapham in south London."

Damn. It had to be a teenage girl. He asked, "Was there a ransom?"

"No. This was no standard kidnapping."

"How'd you learn she was missing?"

She yawned then scrubbed her face with her hands and dropped them to the chair arms. Drawing in a long breath, she said, "I'm looking for my half-sister, Phoebe. She missed a weekly meeting to visit our mother who is sick. Phoebe and

I know each other, but we don't have a close relationship. Still, I agreed to be present when she asked me to be there during visits with our mother. Phoebe is struggling with losing her. Like most teens, she has no idea what to say when facing a parent who is dying."

Her words reached into Sam's chest and squeezed his heart. Hailey sounded all business, but the sadness in her eyes gave away how difficult it was for her to face her mother's death. He asked, "Is your dad in the picture? Do you have any other brothers or sisters?"

She shook her head. "No to both questions."

Speaking gently, Sam asked, "What's wrong with your mother?"

"The doctors don't know, but I ..." Hailey started then stopped herself. She had an idea what was going on with her mother but did not want to share whatever she knew.

Why would she keep that a secret?

Did she fear giving voice to some misgiving?

Hailey said, "My mother asked me to watch out for Phoebe and help her through ... her passing."

"What about her father?"

"He doesn't care that she's missing."

"What?" Sam dropped his feet to the floor and sat forward. "Does he *know* she's missing?"

"I told him the minute I started hunting for her. He claims she's out spending his money somewhere and not answering his calls either." She covered her mouth to stifle another yawn. "He doesn't want a divorce. It would cost too much when marriage places no restrictions on him. He sends money to pay for their living expenses and my mother's medical costs. He'll send money so long as no one bothers him."

"Bastard," Sam murmured. He had the urge to comfort Hailey whose eyes were shiny, but no tear fell. She had probably ordered her tears to stand down.

She laughed at him.

He drew his eyebrows together, confused at that reaction. "What?"

"That's my personal nickname for him."

Even after what she'd pulled to get him here, Sam couldn't deny admiration building every time he gleaned a little more about this woman.

He knew how alone it felt to lose the one parent you cared about. He never stopped looking back and wondering if he could have saved his sister.

Part of him wanted desperately to keep his place with the HAMR Brotherhood, but another part buried deep understood Hailey's drive to save her half-sister even if it meant forcing Sam to come with her.

Hailey yawned again and said, "Sorry."

"It's late. Neither of us have had sleep. Let's call it a day."

She nodded and got up as Sam stood. When she reached him on the way to her bed, he caught her arm in a light grip. She'd normally stiffen and snap at him, but she must have been wiped out.

Her eyes latched onto his and her voice came out whisper soft. "What, Leclair?"

"Thanks for helping me understand. I promise you I will not put anything or anyone ahead of helping you rescue Phoebe."

Her face shifted with a mix of emotions and her lip trembled. She caught herself and said, "Thank you."

"You're welcome." He pecked a kiss on her cheek before she knew what he was doing. "Get some sleep."

Energy hung in the air between them.

She leaned a tiny bit forward.

Was she going to kiss him? He would stand here all night and wait for that.

Then her eyelashes flickered, and she mumbled something under her breath that sounded like, "Don't be stupid."

Please, be stupid, he wanted to argue.

She pulled away and he let her go but allowed his fingers to slide down her arm. Her skin pebbled.

The good news about having not showered yet was that she wouldn't know he had to take a cold one to kill his boner. He hadn't been this easily turned on before and never by someone he should be seeing as his enemy.

But she wasn't.

Not now that he'd made up his mind he was on her team even if the plan still had flawed parts.

CHAPTER 21

HALLENE WATCHED LECLAIR HANDLE THE SUV, maneuvering his way through traffic with ease. He'd taken the keys and brought the car upstairs so she could check out and meet him there.

They hadn't discussed who would drive.

She'd look like an uptight twit to argue that she should drive. To be honest, she was glad for the breather from trying to do everything on her own.

"Keep going south?" Leclair had surprisingly asked that without pressuring her for specifics.

"Yes. I don't have a location, but the kidnapper landed in Alexandria, Virginia after leaving Venezuela. He didn't go directly to that airport. He did some sly jockeying before he ended up there. Until I get another update, I'm heading there to be in the area."

He had his left elbow on the doorframe and his left hand against his cheek. He scoffed at something under his breath.

"What?" she asked nicely, not getting annoyed with him this time. She was beginning to realize his occasional mutters and grumbling were just part of his makeup.

"Your information is dangerous."

She lost her understanding smile.

He glanced her way. "Not criticizing. I'm saying it's a good thing we're working together so you have backup because I don't doubt for a minute you can find Phoebe."

Oh. He'd complimented her.

Her phone buzzed with a text. Only one person would be contacting her. She read the text and her heart leaped at the words Midnight had sent.

A proof of life meeting for P on north side of Wiggins Marina parking lot in PA. 11:20 local. Be careful.

Leclair had found a rock radio station and said, "You like that okay?"

Shocked, she lifted her gaze to his.

"What's going on?" His tone changed to serious.

She hesitated, thinking through how much of this to tell him.

Leclair sighed so loud it filled the car. "I'm trying, Hailey, but you have to ease up and loosen the death grip you have on control. I can't help if you keep me in the dark on anything."

She'd been called a control freak by an angry guy in the past. She didn't want Leclair thinking of her that way, but she did not share intel easily.

Still, he made a fair point, so she told him about the proof of life meeting.

He continued working his way to the interstate and taking the on-ramp while saying nothing.

"What are you thinking?" She could see him sorting through something.

"Why a proof of life meeting if her father doesn't care about her?"

This is why Leclair had to know more. "I found Phoebe the first time because my tech intercepted a communication between Kovac and the kidnapper when they let Kovac know they had Phoebe. My tech traced the call to that location in Venezuela. Kovac is being blackmailed to do something for the kidnapper. That's why there is no ransom. Phoebe is being used as a pawn."

"Holy crap, Hailey. That's information I need to help you."

"I know, I know. That's why I just shared it," she snapped defensively.

"Better late than never," he mumbled.

"What would you have done with that information yesterday?" She arched an eyebrow at him in challenge.

His gaze twitched her way. "Maybe nothing, but it might have been important then."

"In other words, nothing," she said, feeling vindicated. "I'm glad we've already eaten."

"Why?"

"Because the proof of life meeting is in Pennsylvania."

He sat up, his body tensing. She took that as him in mission mode. He asked, "What time?"

"11:20. We can make it without a problem if we don't hit a bad traffic jam." She leaned over and input the address into the map system.

Leclair drove for a bit before he asked, "Are you ready to see Phoebe and sit still?"

"No. We'll follow them."

"We'll try, but if I were doing a proof of life, I'd have two cars to keep anyone from following, plus a tracker to take out any car that did follow. Also, if we alert them to being there, whatever your techie is surveilling online will vanish. The first thing they'd do is change how they communicate."

She dropped her head back, sick at the idea of seeing Phoebe and not being able to get to her. This was where she had to prove she could hold her own. "I hear you. I'll sit tight."

His fingers covered her arm on the console, drawing her gaze to him. When he shifted his gaze to her before returning it to the traffic, she flinched at the pain burrowed deep in his blue eyes.

"I know how difficult this is, Hailey. I understand the desire to go running in there and fighting to get her back. If I thought we could do it without getting one of you killed, we would. I'm in this all the way. I just want you to not rush in and lose. You will never forgive yourself for making a mistake on this and losing Phoebe."

He squeezed her arm before letting go.

She had to work to breathe.

Emotion threatened to strangle her. That's why some people called her a control freak, but she had to push her feelings aside to keep her head on straight.

With one touch, Leclair brought all her fears to the surface. He knew she was terrified of screwing up and losing Phoebe. He'd spoken from the heart, which meant he'd lost someone too when he said he understood what she was feeling.

No one had offered her the comfort and understanding Leclair just had. She'd been alone for a long time and had forgotten what a simple touch or hug could mean.

She hadn't known Leclair when this started, but she'd had a peek inside the dangerous operative to the blood and flesh man.

Of the many things she had to worry about on this operation, any chance of Leclair walking away when things got tough was not one. She felt a blanket of calm drape over her, one she hadn't felt in a long time. Not since Coop would show up to support her with finding a child when he could.

But he'd never been on a mission like this with her.

He wouldn't agree to her even trying to do this.

Leclair had stated he would be side-by-side with her when it came to saving Phoebe. She believed him and believed they could do this together.

Now she felt even more convinced she'd made the right decision to keep his team out of this.

Strangers might put the high-profile captive above all else, but Leclair would not.

She let the music play to fill the quiet between them during the next two hours. It was a peaceful quiet because Leclair had many more questions, but he probably didn't want to push her for more until they saw the meeting.

For that reason, she didn't push him for more on his kidnapped victim either.

Two hours passed quicker than expected when Leclair began hunting the downtown marina.

"It's supposed to be across the street from the Freedom Mortgage Pavilion ... there! That building."

Leclair slowed and took the roundabout at Riverside Drive, exiting on the road to the marina.

He crept down the empty road.

Hallene's pulse jumped as they entered the curved parking lot with a division line down the middle.

Where was Phoebe?

Leclair took an empty spot facing the docks that allowed them to view the entire lot. He left the car running.

Two empty sedans were parked on the other side.

A Dodge pickup truck, also empty, sat between where they parked and the entrance.

Leclair studied it all.

Hallene waited for his assessment. She checked her watch again. 11:19

"This is an odd place for a meet," he finally said.

"Why?"

"This is pretty much a dead end. They can drive around and leave, but more than one exit point would normally be preferable."

At that moment, someone drove a white nondescript van into the parking lot on the opposite side from them.

Leclair said, "On the other hand, that van looks out of place here."

The van did not pull into a spot but parked right where it was short of them. A door on the side slid open.

"Shit."

The door slammed shut and the van drove off.

Hallene had seen nothing.

"What?" She panicked and reached for the handle.

"No." Leclair caught her around the shoulders and held her as the van drove past them and swung around on their left to drive out.

She jerked around to him. "I didn't even see her."

"Act natural, Hailey, or we'll be made."

She couldn't make sense of anything.

"Hell." He cupped her head and kissed her, making her brain stall even more. She wanted to scream and kick the doors of this SUV.

He whispered, "Calm down." Then he kissed her again and she understood finally. He was staying in his role so the kidnapper would not think they were sitting there spying, which they were.

As the van passed by behind them, Leclair stopped and held her, dropping his head to hers. "I hate this for you, Hailey. I absofuckingly hate it. But you stayed put, and we'll be able to continue on to get her back."

Hallene fought back tears. Stupid tears would do nothing to help. She reached up and grasped his forearms. Powerful man with a tender heart. He'd kept her from breaking apart.

She hadn't realized until the moment the van stopped, and

she couldn't see Phoebe, just how close to the edge she'd been living.

Sniffling, she said, "I'm okay. Thanks."

"You bet." He pulled away and it was as if part of her world went with him.

He drove the SUV out slowly again. The van was long gone. "I did look. There was no tag on the van."

She hadn't thought about that. She should have. This was why Coop warned her about jumping into something that was beyond her skill set. And to keep her emotions out of any mission.

Major fail on her part this time.

Leaning her arm against the window, she propped her head on her hand. "This was a bust."

"No, it wasn't."

"Why not?"

"Because now we know your tech is picking up solid intel."

She sat up and turned to him. "You're right. I need to get my mind back in the game."

"Your mind is fine. There are times our hearts overrule our minds and that's okay. If not, it would mean you had no soul." He looked over and winked at her. "And you, Hailey, have plenty of soul."

She hadn't realized how compromised she was by her emotions, but Leclair made her sound human instead of weak.

"Let's get farther down the road and find some food, okay?" he asked.

"Sure." She had to draw a couple deep breaths to calm down and think. "I've got a hotel in Fairfax, Virginia for tonight."

He nodded and drove without asking her for anything new. She'd thought he was short-tempered when she showed up in Clercville, which he had every right to be, but she changed her mind. Leclair was patient. She could see him sitting on a target for days until the right moment to act.

She would never have that level of patience, but she had to find some now or risk putting them in jeopardy. She hated to give up control of anything. In hindsight, Leclair had been generous in not trying to rip control from her.

"I'm getting seriously hungry," he announced, still a bit north of Baltimore.

She could eat and wanted out of this car for a break. "Looks like a restaurant at the next exit."

Leclair took the exit then noted, "This looks like the ghetto. Might as well eat gas station food."

"I bet you were fun on road trips," she cracked at him.

"We didn't do road trips."

It hadn't been the words, but the sadness in his voice that caused her to let it go.

In truth, this was a desolate area even for a small community. Older buildings peppered each side of the road, including a three-story rusting warehouse on the right. Probably the main employer at one time. But there were some active businesses. A local grocer, pawn shop, then a small shopping center that had been converted into an antique mall. She had seen the billboard for that a while back. Antique shops here were big draws.

As they neared the end of the city-block-long warehouse, a one-story restaurant advertising fried chicken and country vegetables sat in its shadow.

Two trucks were parked on the far side of the gravel lot.

Leclair pulled in next to those and climbed out.

She started to ask for the keys, but it felt ridiculous. He could have left her long before now. So many things had her looking at him differently, wondering how he could be so considerate and pleasant to her after she'd threatened Angela and Clercville.

Had he figured out the truth?

That she wouldn't harm an innocent person.

She wanted to admit as much, but just couldn't until they were done with this. Her only hope of getting Phoebe back alive was his skills and experience, which were way beyond hers.

She'd had to accept that after being captured in Venezuela and his wisdom in sitting still at the proof of life meeting. That still tore her heart apart.

Had Phoebe been sitting just inside the van gagged and tied up? Terrified?

Stepping out, she hoisted the shoulder bag strap into place and met Leclair at the back of the SUV.

"Let's sit outside." He hadn't demanded that, just put it to her in a reasonable tone.

"Sure. I need fresh air, too." She gave him a little smile. A part of her that still felt normal wanted him to see her as a nice person despite how she'd strong-armed him here.

She'd wanted to believe anyone else would do the same thing if they stood in her shoes, but she doubted Leclair would.

He would not have dragged someone else into his mess.

Reading the signs on the outside, he said, "Chicken and vegetables look to be their bestsellers. Can your palate handle that?"

She'd have taken fault with his question if he hadn't winked again and smiled, throwing her out of step. "What makes you think I don't eat that and pizza all the time?"

"'Cause you have a tiny British accent buried underneath your speech. It's why I'm thinking you might live in the UK and have been trained by someone in a British alphabet group."

Her jaw dropped. No one had ever caught any hint of a British accent when she was in this country. No one.

"Close your mouth unless you're catching flies." He chuckled and headed inside.

"Wait." She started digging into her purse. "I've got a credit card for this."

"You get the next one." He disappeared inside.

He was buying her food.

The man she'd coerced into joining her to rescue Phoebe was buying her a meal. She did not understand Leclair.

No man had bought her a meal since ... the last time Coop had. He'd treated her to meals as a friend would. They never dated.

Why did this ridiculous stop off the interstate feel like a date?

Because Leclair was treating her to a meal.

Incandescent bulbs strung around a roof over the ten-foot-deep porch offered a festive look to the brick building. The area was not a raised deck. Just a wooden platform with a picnic table on each side of a battered screened door entrance. The temperature had started to cool with the clouds coming in to dim the sunset.

She leaned on a picnic table reading what others had carved into the weathered wood.

Names of who had been there. Memories for people who lived an everyday life. They might have big families filled with love.

Sure, not everyone, but it made her happy to think of couples who sat here sharing their dreams.

Having tables out here was probably a sign of the business this restaurant did, meaning the food was good. They'd stopped just in time. It would close in thirty minutes.

She walked around, stretching her legs until Leclair came out carrying two trays and grinning.

Taking in a deep breath, she fought not to drool. "Smells delicious."

"Little dive like this has to be top-notch to make it out here." He sat her tray on the street side and his where his back would be to the wall of the restaurant like a gunslinger of the old days.

She smirked at the image of him dressed up in cowboy boots, a Stetson, and wearing a holster sporting twin six-shooters.

Busy pulling his plastic utensils out of a paper sleeve, he paused to stare at her.

"What?" She'd settled across from him and had the urge to look down and see if her blouse had come open. He had a habit of making her question herself every time he did that.

"You're damn pretty when you smile." He went back to attacking his meal and shrugged. "I mean you know you're good-looking and all but smiling really makes a woman memorable."

She had just poked her fork into green beans and forgot how to eat. He handed out that compliment as if she deserved it when they both knew she didn't. She might want to be a good person but blackmailing still hung over her head.

Not wasting a second, he picked up a chicken leg and started gnawing on it, making happy sounds.

Her stomach grumbled again. She lifted the beans to her mouth and forgot about her shortcomings, content to enjoy the simple cuisine. Leclair had bought her a fried chicken breast. She hadn't said a word, but that was her favorite part of a chicken. His was obviously the drumstick.

"What's that ring on your left hand?"

"I found it in a junk shop and liked the mount. It's not a diamond, just a cut glass insert." She started to tell him Coop had the ring made with a hidden LED for her, but that would open up a whole new set of questions.

She'd eaten most of her meal when he put the last bone down and devoured his vegetables.

"You like fried okra, huh?" She wrinkled her nose at the vegetable, but she enjoyed the sweet potato casserole he'd chosen for her.

"Love it. Angie would cook it fresh during the summer."

"You mean Angela?"

He seemed to catch himself and didn't answer as he wiped his mouth and wadded the napkin to put on the plate. "I never talk about her to strangers, but you found her even after I did all I could to keep her hidden."

That last bite she swallowed stuck halfway down. "I'm uh, well, I ..."

He crossed his arms, unwilling to help her out of this hole she'd dug.

She had to say it. "I apologize for doing this to you."

Giving it a minute, he nodded. "I'll accept that if you'll treat me like a partner. I can overlook the blackmail part but keep in mind you threatened someone I would do anything to protect. You found my soft spot. Be careful with it."

He could have yelled and cursed her, but he laid out how important Angela was to him like a gentleman.

Decision time.

She had a chance to win him over to her battle. He'd make a hell of a backup and dangerous enemy.

Taking her own time wiping her fingers and pushing the tray to the side, she leaned her elbows on the table and clasped her hands. "What would you like to know?"

Rigid lines in his face softened. He still frowned but he was listening. Coop used to tell her to assess a threat level.

Based on the number one being low and fifty being high, Leclair bursting into that basement had blown the top off a thousand. Right now, he was barely registering on the scale.

"Tell me more about Kovac. I want to know how he fits into this."

She laid out how Kovac had a shipping empire and her mother had met Kovac a year after Hallene's father had died. "After my father died, I encouraged my mother to get back out in the world and find something she'd like to do. She had been an administrative assistant when married to my father. He hadn't left her a decent insurance policy. She got a job at Kovac's company. He noticed her, wined, and dined her. For a woman who had been alone emotionally longer than the year as a widow, his attention had seemed like just what she needed. It all changed over time. He got tired of being a husband and father, so he returned to his bachelor days."

She would not give him a sob story about her father or her mother's troubles, just the truth.

Leaning forward on his forearms, Leclair said, "Your mom is sick. Where is she?"

"In hospice."

"Shit. Cancer?"

"No. They have no idea what is wrong."

"That's what you said, but I figured it was narrowed down to a possible disease."

Hallene gave it a beat then figured she had nothing to lose by being entirely honest. "I think she was poisoned."

That was the moment Leclair's attention sharpened as someone locked on a target.

"Who do you think poisoned her?" he asked in a rough voice, one holding back anger.

"The same person I believe who has put Phoebe in danger. Her father, Adam Kovac."

He grabbed his head. The lights above and behind him silhouetted his body. Moths flew in and out, taking kamikaze runs at the lights.

"Man, this is screwed up." He dropped his hands. "He's your stepfather? Why would he do that?"

Muscles in her neck tightened. "Kovac is *nothing* to me and *never* will be. He got my mother pregnant and married her, then basically ignored her after Phoebe reached six. He went back to his world of shipping and high finance while dating other women, most of them closer to my age. My mother had him served with divorce papers. She didn't ask for anything astronomical, just a reasonable amount to raise Phoebe. Kovac called, talking nice and telling her they'd work out the details. He asked that she wait until after October because he had so much traveling coming up."

"Sounds like it should have been an amicable divorce, but I get the feeling that wasn't the case," Leclair said.

"You'd be correct. A week after that call, Mother came down very sick and no one has been able to heal her. I can't prove Kovac poisoned her, not yet, but this is a man who will not willingly pay for a divorce. Now he's involved in something bad, and Phoebe is in the middle of it. I think Phoebe was taken to force Kovac to do what the kidnapper wants to happen, or Phoebe will be used to hurt Kovac."

"What do you think he's doing for his part?"

"Honestly, I have no idea. My first guess would be using his shipping lines, but in addition to doing business with the US, he has contacts all over Europe, India, and Asia."

Leclair's eyes moved back and forth while he stared at nothing. He sorted through every piece of information.

"How can anyone use a child in what sounds like international espionage of some sort?"

"I haven't been close with Phoebe, but I don't hate her like he does. In hindsight, I wish I'd taken more time with her and maybe I could have steered her away from the fast crowd she hung with. I think she confused them with friends." Hallene's eyes burned, but she would not cry. Her MO was to curse and go for the jugular when protecting someone.

"Damn," Leclair whispered. "There is bad in this world, then there's evil."

He got it. He understood every part of what happened to Phoebe was unfair on multiple levels.

"I've told you all I can about who I'm hunting," Hallene pointed out, ready for his side. "Who are *you* after?"

He washed a hand over his face and again leaned those muscular forearms on the table. He started to speak then became very still and whispered, "Don't move until I tell you. Then stand up slowly and lift your bag to hunt for something. Then laugh out loud and walk over to my side."

She was so disappointed he would not share what he had. "Have you lost your mind? I asked for—"

"Hush."

That had been a command as surely as a general giving an order. He wasn't playing a game.

Her training took over, warning her to pay attention. She looked closer at him. He'd dropped his chin, leaving the brim of his ball cap to shield his eyes, but his gaze stared past her with hawk-like intensity.

He saw a threat.

Her pulse jumped out of sight. She could see nothing in the reflection of the restaurant's small window slotted into a brick wall.

She felt vulnerable with her back exposed and no way to see what was coming, but she remained still.

Leclair continued in a serious monotone as he casually picked up his meal remnants and placed all of it on his tray. "Once you reach this side of the table and I tell you to go, walk into the restaurant. Turn left immediately and run to the back exit. Wait for me only thirty seconds. If I'm not there by then, find a place to hide long enough to load the gun in that bag with the ammo I heard jingle, then use your instincts and escape."

He was saying if he couldn't follow her, as in he would be injured too badly or ... dead. He was risking his life for her.

She'd pushed him to be her backup.

She never expected him to put his life between her and danger. "I'm not leaving you."

Eyes still fixed on something behind her, he said, "Don't, Hailey. Not now. This is important."

This was it, the moment she either believed him without question or not. This was no joke. He could have pulled something fast before now, but he hadn't.

He'd complained they weren't ready to operate as a team because she was holding onto control with an iron grip.

It was time for her to step up and become the person who

could follow instructions just like any of his team members who valued his assessment.

If not, she'd prove him right and get them both killed.

She lifted the bag from beside her and dug into it, pulling out lip balm. She swiped the balm over her lips and returned the tube to the bag then swung her legs around and pushed up to stand behind the seat.

Intentionally not allowing her gaze to stray in the direction he was staring, she cocked her head at him as if listening and burst out laughing. Looping the bag strap across her chest freed up both hands as she strolled around the table on shaky legs.

She dragged trembling fingers over the wood surface.

The need to touch him and make him come with her threatened to override her determination to be the partner he wanted.

The partner he needed.

Leclair reached out and squeezed her hand, gifting her with a smile that went nowhere near his dark gaze. "Got someone coming across the street and he's strapped. Ready?"

"Yes." Not really, but that was the right answer. She held his gaze when she wanted to look behind her, but that would give this charade away.

He patted her hand and firmly whispered, "*Go!*"

She strode into the restaurant.

The sound of the picnic table crashing came first then loud gunshots.

Leclair had no gun.

CHAPTER 22

———

SAM HAD MOVED HIS LEGS to the outside of the picnic table before Hailey came around. He said, "Go," waited two seconds, and dropped down to flip the picnic table up as he did and dove to the ground.

Bullets ripped large holes in the thick wood.

He scooted into the restaurant on his belly with wood and chips of the brick wall flying around him.

But the brick would block him as he jumped to his feet. Everyone who'd been in the restaurant was out of sight as he ran for the rear exit.

And almost bowled over Hailey who was facing him.

He caught her shoulders. "What the fuck are you doing?"

"Coming back for your ungrateful ass." She looked like a wild angel. God needed someone like her on the team, but not anytime soon.

More shots continued. Without Sam shooting back, the assassin would rush forward.

Sam spun Hailey around, grabbed her hand, and took off. She had no trouble keeping up with her long legs. He burst through the rear door into pitch-black and turned away from the parking lot. The shooter should go there first to ensure they did not escape in the car.

An explosion blew a fireball into the air.

Yep, he took out their wheels.

Moving fast, Sam and Hailey ran past the end of the warehouse. He paused to yank on the first door. Locked. Maybe this place wasn't entirely abandoned.

He raced ahead a hundred feet, taking in the tall windows that had yellowed with rusty frames. He stopped next to a window covered in spiderwebs that had a broken corner missing a triangle piece of glass.

Yanking his T-shirt off, he wrapped his hand. "Turn your face away," he hushed out. As soon as she did, he pulled hard on the glass to break off a larger piece.

Worked great.

Unfortunately, the rest of the glass fell in solidarity, making a loud noise.

Sam pushed Hailey against the wall to protect her body.

No shots yet.

They were being hunted. A professional who would wait for his best chance at getting them both.

Sam draped his shirt over the window ledge then cupped his hands next to his knees. "Step up."

No hesitation this time at his whispered order. She went up and inside faster than he expected. Good woman. He followed, snatching his dark shirt off the ledge as soon as his boots hit the floor. As he led the way, he shook the glass out of his shirt and pulled on the black covering again to hide the lighter shade of his body.

Sam dragged Hailey in a weaving pattern through metal shop machinery that appeared to be an active operation. He'd kill for a monocular to find the exit out the opposite side of this building. Probably in a front corner where offices were set up or had been at one time.

A tiny whine split the silence.

That had been the rear door being opened with lock picks.

Sam would have used them if he'd had his.

Time to play cat and mouse. He pulled Hailey close to whisper in her ear. "When we find a place, stay put. I can't see well enough to know which one of you is the threat if you move, too." Lie, but that would keep her out of harm's way.

She squeezed his hand, a quiet way to say she understood.

He was so proud of her for trusting him to lead them through this. No one was going to hurt her, not tonight.

He bent over to keep his upper body out of view as he moved. She did the same. He hoped to avoid throwing silhouettes someone using night vision would see from across the vast building.

He found a spot between a large piece of equipment and a stack of pallets. He said, "In there. Don't move."

"Wait." She dug his gun out of the bag, loaded the magazine, and handed it to him. "Stay alive."

Sam's adrenaline pulsed through him. He didn't like to leave her here without a gun, but he could go to the threat and keep any shots away from her.

He leaned in and kissed her. "You're amazing."

Then he slipped away on silent steps, slowly turning and twisting through the maze of equipment until he found a broom. He pulled his shirt back off and slid it over the broom then spun his cap around backward. Once he was far enough from Hailey to keep her clear of stray bullets, he pulled out a napkin he'd stuffed in his front jeans pocket and pried apart two small pieces. He jammed those into his ears.

Then he grabbed the handle of the broom with his left hand, tilting it with the shirt end at an upward angle.

He lifted his head just enough to see over large boxes stacked three wide, two deep, and four feet high. Gripping his gun in his right hand, he yanked the broom up and then quickly back down.

Shots zinged close to his left shoulder.

He returned fire. Heard a hiss of sound. He'd hit something but hadn't heard a body fall. He moved to a new location, closer to the shooter if the guy hadn't changed his position.

Something bumped metal way over on his left.

Sam would not go for the bait.

Then a noise in the area where he'd left Hailey yanked his head around.

Had that been her or the shooter?

Sam started back toward her. The broom handle tapped against the leg of a machine.

Shots pinged all around him. The killer was trying to herd them.

Sam lifted his weapon to return three shots and kept moving. The skin above his eyes burned. Hell. A shot must have ricocheted off equipment to skip across his forehead. He'd have blood running into his eyes soon.

Not slowing, he kept in the direction of where he'd left Hailey.

More shots rang out from straight back at the wall from where he squatted. Shooter was moving parallel with him. Sam had to get this guy before he closed in on Hailey's location. If she'd made that noise, hoping to help Sam, the killer knew where she was.

Warm liquid ran into Sam's eyes. The air filled with the smell of fresh blood. He swiped his forehead with the back of his hand.

Something skipped across the floor beyond where she hid.

Shots pounded that spot, tearing into the metal wall.

Sam took that opportunity to stand and unload five times where he'd seen muzzle flash. He heard a grunt then the sound of weight hitting the floor. Could be a trap to draw him in, but the fact the shooter went for what had to be Hailey's decoy sound probably meant Sam's first hit had done significant damage.

Sirens headed toward them from maybe a mile away.

They had no car, and this was not much of an urban area for finding a quick replacement.

Lifting the broom from where he'd left it, he moved it forward as he crouched. No shots. Lowering the broom, he pulled his shirt off, catching his fingers on holes shot through it. He rubbed his forehead and eyes then pulled on the shirt as he rushed to where he'd hidden Hailey.

Not there.

Keeping his voice down, he called out, "*Hailey!*"

"Here. On your right."

Relieved to hear her voice, he hurried to her.

She stood halfway. "Did you stop him?"

"Think so. Cops coming and the car is gone."

"We're left with escaping on foot."

He grabbed her hand. "Let's try something else first."

CHAPTER 23

———

NITRO REPLAYED THE VIDEO OF that woman kissing Sam again, looking for any shot of her face. She'd worn huge sunglasses and no lipstick the morning she walked outside Angela's inn. She kept her face turned down.

Never lifted it on the way to her car.

"I got nothing," Moose groused, slapping the desk next to his keyboard. He swung around in his chair. "She dumped the car ten miles from Clercville where another one had been hidden in dense woods. Our people went over the one she left. Other than Sam's fingerprints, nothing. Just give me a freakin' partial of her face to run. Anything."

"I wish I could, Cuz, but we don't have enough to match to anyone." Nitro rubbed his eyes. He could not sleep with one of his team in danger and Sam was in something deep. "What did you tell me the hand signs he made meant?"

"The angle sucked, but I doubt he knew where we'd placed a camera. Looked like he said 'okay.' Then he brushed his hand as if making space for a new word that looked like it could be 'fine' and then the word 'turn.' Can't figure it out."

Blade walked in mumbling, "Okay. Fine. Turn. Play the video again. I'm not on your level with ASL, but I've had to use it at times."

Clamping a big hand over his forehead and leaning his elbow on the table, Moose tapped a key, and the video came up. He ran it forward to the point where Sam dropped his hand out the window and played that part in slow motion.

Nitro watched the process, willing something new to come out of it even though Moose had run that section over and over for hours.

A microwave beep sounded, some banging around in the kitchen, then Angel came out with a frozen burrito he'd heated.

Moose shook his head, translating again. "Okay. Fine. Turn. That makes no sense."

Blade pointed over Moose's shoulder. "Go back to the second finger sign."

Angel sat in a recliner, eating his meal. Figuring out intel was not his forte. Performing impossible stunts and sniper shots were more his thing. Nitro never expected more than any of them could do.

Nitro ran the words in his mind again. Sam expected them to use what he'd shared. "Brainstorm anything, guys."

Blade said, "Okay finetune?"

Moose frowned, defeat hovering in his face.

Angel called out, "Where's your sense of humor, Nitro? Sam was probably screwing with us for dropping him in Clercville with his aunt."

That thought had crossed Nitro's mind once. He'd brushed it away. Sam would have sent them a message by now if that was the case. He knew they'd be keeping an eye on him.

Blade stared at the ceiling. "Okay. Fine. Turn. I feel stupid to keep trying the same thing and expecting different results."

Between bites, Angel suggested in a humorous tone, "Maybe the word is *find* instead of fine. Like he said, 'Okay, find me, suckers.'"

Find. Nitro stood. "Find. Okay, find *turn*."

Angel stopped laughing.

Blade and Moose spoke at the same time. "*Find Turner.*"

No longer joking, Angel said, "Sam is saying he's okay and going to find Turner."

Nitro had gotten that answer too, which meant Sam was on his way to get killed. "Get packed."

Every one of them knew that meant to load up weapons.

Moose had walked away then turned back to Nitro. "You callin' Logan?"

"Have to. I can live with Sam losing his place in HAMR but not with his death."

CHAPTER 24

———

SAM GAVE THANKS THAT THIS was a small community along the interstate. The two police cars and single fire department had their hands full figuring out what had happened at the little restaurant.

The fire department had the car fire snuffed out.

Where he and Hailey stood was dark as a tar pit compared to the restaurant where red and blue lights flashed.

A block away at the farthest end of the warehouse from the diner, Sam and Hailey crossed the road slowly to not draw any attention. The closest streetlight dimly lit was another block closer to the interstate.

He'd taken a moment to search the opposite side of the road from the warehouse to figure out what he'd believed the assassin had planned as his escape path.

One location made sense, but they didn't have a lot of time to get this right.

When he reached the opposite side of the two-lane road with Hailey, he glanced to his right to be sure no one had taken off from the restaurant to come this way.

All still stood. Two people were talking with their arms waving.

Sam let out a sigh. The bystanders had survived.

Moving faster through weeds growing knee-high in a strip of land beside the left side of the pawnshop, he kept track of Hailey behind him. She stayed step for step on his heels. She was savvy and could handle herself in a fight, but she was not trained for being shot at by an assassin.

If she had skills at his level, she would have just gone after her half-sister on her own.

The idea of her going up against W scared him bad and amped up his need to protect her.

He now felt justified for the night he'd slowed to make sure she'd gotten out of the mansion. He also didn't believe she was the kind of person who would harm someone like Angela. He would press her for the truth later.

When he could not see where he stepped, he slowed and had to catch her before her momentum sent her flying past him.

"What?" she snapped, breathing as if she'd just sprinted, but not out of breath.

"I'm looking for a vehicle by itself pointed toward us as an exit path to the interstate. Let your eyes adjust and tell me if you see anything."

"I have a better idea." She moved her hands then a light popped on with the beam pointed down from her palm.

"Where'd that come from?"

"My ring."

"The one you found in a junk shop?" He couldn't believe how smoothly she'd convinced him of that lie.

"No. It was made for me by the person who trained me."

Heh. She'd surprised him again. The tiny LED put out a stream of light without giving away their location. She wisely kept it away from his face to not blind him.

He let her take the lead as she swept it back and forth until the light flicked over a motorcycle. She asked, "Could that be it?"

"Maybe, if it runs and wasn't stuck back here just to get it out of the way."

When he reached the nondescript bike with faded black paint, the key was in the ignition. Hell, yes. This was their ride. While she gave him enough light to search, he found a helmet hanging on the handlebars and swung it to her.

"I don't think helmets are required here."

He groused, "*I* want you to wear it, but how do you know the helmet laws here?"

She muttered in an annoyed tone. "I research every unfamiliar place I visit so I know everything I can from vehicle laws to airport rules to anything that might make the difference in getting out alive."

"Sorry to sound surprised," he admitted. "I wasn't questioning your intelligence. I just don't think you live here."

That dialed back her defensive tone. "Fair enough. Should we get moving?"

"Waiting on the fire engine to leave first. That will leave the police to search for us and the shooter. Our exit shouldn't be noticed by then."

"Huh, good thinking. That's why I needed you to help me. I do have training but wouldn't have gotten away from that shooter on my own."

A huge admission for her.

He'd rather not be running from someone trying to kill them, but they were making progress. "I disagree. You would have found a way to escape. That's why I told you if I didn't show up in thirty seconds to trust your instincts."

Ambient light from her ring offered a soft glow over her face. A smile tilted her lips at his compliment. She whispered, "I wouldn't have left you. I had your gun and could have given you cover to get inside."

He didn't think she could get any hotter than moving step-for-step with him and maintaining her calm, but her declaration to protect him wrapped a warm glove around his heart.

This feeling for her was new and unexpected for him.

He stepped closer and brushed his hand over her hair then leaned in to kiss that mouth. The mouth that had snarled at him in the mansion basement, that had softened when he handed her a shirt to wear, that had smiled when he'd given her the chicken dinner, and the same mouth that had just said she would not have left him to bleed out.

She clutched his shoulder, leaning into the kiss and breathing faster than she had when they'd just run.

The sound of a heavy diesel engine groaned, picking up speed as it headed for the interstate.

He slowly finished the kiss and pulled away. "Life is not fair to give this up when you taste like a cross between heaven and the best fantasy, but we need to slide out of here."

She released his shoulder and complained, "Can't believe we were kissing right now. You make me crazy. You can't just do that whenever you want."

Once again, that mouth had gifted him. He liked making her control falter. "Then I'll do it when *you* want."

He didn't give her time to say another word as he grabbed the helmet to pull onto her head and snapped the strap into place. "Let me climb on first."

"I know that." She sounded miffed.

"You ride motorcycles, huh?"

"Yes, and horses. I've ridden a camel, too."

Sam threw a leg over the Suzuki Hayabusa and pushed hard forward to knock it off the center stand that kicked up out of the way, then placed his boots out to each side for support. Chuckling, he muttered, "Just keep gettin' hotter."

"What are you talking about?"

"I said to hop on."

"Liar." Her ring light disappeared.

He laughed and put his cap on backward, grimacing at scraping the dried blood. Thankfully, she hadn't noticed it in the low light.

When she was in place behind him with her arm around his middle, he cranked the engine, keeping the rumble low. He couldn't kill the headlight like on a vehicle, but the bike was positioned to leave with as little notice as possible. He eased on the accelerator and picked his way to the corner of the building then across the grassy lot.

Pausing at the end of the grass patch before driving into the open, he gave the restaurant one last check. A third police car had shown up and a dog was sniffing around.

Sam rolled on the accelerator slowly and eased the bike forward, leaning to send the motorcycle to the right toward the interstate. When he drove under the overpass, he took one last look behind him.

No sign of blaring law enforcement lights.

He patted her hand. She was getting better at understanding him and quickly wrapped both arms snugly around his middle. He took off slowly, gaining speed as he merged into traffic.

Someone was trying to kill her.

He didn't believe W had sent that shooter because the guy

failed. From all Sam had learned about W, that man would not send out one assassin without backup.

Regardless of who sent the killer, Sam had no idea how they'd located Hailey but suspected her intelligence system had been compromised. He had serious doubts that even Nitro and his team could find him after she'd switched vehicles on the way out.

Sam had a bad feeling about how this would end up with HAMR Brotherhood, especially with Logan who tolerated no one going rogue, unintentionally or otherwise.

They all knew Sam could have abandoned Hailey by now and gotten word to the team.

What they didn't know was Sam had made a commitment to stick with Hailey. He would not leave her to go it alone.

CHAPTER 25

HALLENE HAD CHECKED THE FUEL gauge over Leclair's shoulder a moment ago. Wind blew into her face harder when she didn't have his wide back blocking for her. They had enough fuel to go farther, and she enjoyed the cool temperature, but she had nodded off once already. Leclair had gripped her arms to keep her from falling back. That had awakened her.

He had enough to do handling the bike to keep them safe in the traffic without having to hold her in place.

She hoped he was headed to a hotel. They needed sleep and to regroup. What adrenaline had kept her going was long gone.

They'd driven around Washington, D.C. and were now in eastern Virginia.

If they still had a car, he could probably keep going but they really didn't have a reason to travel any farther south without more intel.

She feared Midnight's intel may no longer be of use.

Where would that leave her?

Sam slowed the bike and exited the interstate. A large fuel station lit up as bright as Christmas stood out on the right with a connecting hamburger joint. Beyond that, a bar appeared to be doing bang-up business for a Thursday night. She'd caught a look at the highway information sign before the exit, which had shown a hotel to the left.

Leclair took a long look in both directions at the bottom of the exit ramp, then puttered to the left.

The hotel sign was as tempting as a mirage of water in a desert. Her shoulders slumped with relief.

Leclair drove past the hotel.

What? She looked back then forward again, lifting to view

over his shoulder. What was he searching for? She wouldn't ask. She wanted his full attention on whatever he was doing.

A half mile down on the left side of the road was a long building with a large parking lot for a grocery store, seafood restaurant, thrift store, and hair salon. All were closed this late. She glanced at her watch. Just past midnight.

Slowing, he drove into the parking lot and made a U-turn, then jumped back on the dark highway heading toward the hotel again. When he pulled in at the hotel this time, he parked on the dark side of the manager's office. He had to have been watching for someone to follow them, then chose a place to stop where he could hide the bike.

She put her hands on his shoulders to climb off and stepped back to keep her balance. The helmet came off next. Her shoulder bag was still looped across her chest. Her eyes were gritty, and her hair had hit the point of ick.

Sam dropped the side stand and took her helmet to hook on the handlebars before climbing off. "How you doin'?"

She'd captured this man while minding his own business. He should hate her but had bought her food, saved her from an assassin, and kissed her. There had been more, but all she seemed able to recall was his kisses because it had been so bloody long since she'd felt desired.

That wasn't exactly right.

She hadn't desired a man like Sam who pinged all her female wants from being a partner to respecting her abilities to protecting her. Even Coop hadn't been around to protect her during some hair-raising situations while saving kids.

She ran her fingers back and forth through her hair that had lost the ponytail band, admitting, "I don't even want to know what I look like."

He stepped close, stared at her from head to neck, then kissed her sweetly. "You look like sex on a stick."

Her lips parted.

He laughed.

They'd been through hell, and he could still laugh.

She wanted that man. Bad.

When he went inside to get them a room, she didn't follow.

She wouldn't want the manager to think a sexy hunk like Sam couldn't do better.

Yawning again, she fought the urge to lay down on this asphalt and sleep. That would be too easy, so she kept walking in circles to stay awake.

"Got it." Sam came strolling out. "Let's walk around back and find a place to leave the bike. We'll have to ditch it at some point, but I want a set of wheels for now." He tapped the shifter to neutral with his boot, shoved the bike off the center stand, and rolled it forward.

Around the back of the freestanding office building were a vending machine and a shadowed spot where Sam parked the bike. He took the key and searched the tank bag before leaving.

Empty, just as expected.

She'd noted the bike tag but seriously doubted that belonged to this motorcycle. Even she had snatched a tag from a different sedan and stuck it on the vehicle she'd driven to the inn in Clercville.

Moving on autopilot at this point, she followed Sam through the breezeway where he tugged her closer to walk between him and the wall.

Yet again, he was protecting her.

Coop had taught her plenty of self-defense moves, but he'd kept her at arm's length even as a friend.

She hadn't realized how much she craved the touch of a man who looked at her as more than a friend until now.

In looking back, Coop had been right, though. She'd wanted someone to lean on if only for a short while. Instead, she learned how to depend upon herself, which meant she could now choose a man as someone to share life with.

Not a crutch.

No matter what her body was telling her, Hallene's brain pointed out Sam was not someone to get involved with. They would not see each other again if they survived this.

Sexy as hell, especially in combat mode, but he was not here by choice. Strangely, his attitude had changed during the first seven-hour drive. Instead of snarling every word at her, he'd become considerate and thoughtful. He'd made her laugh when she couldn't remember the last time she'd laughed.

He lived in the moment.

That's what the two of them had right now. A moment in time. This was only one moment in time.

Why did the thought of not seeing him again after make her chest ache?

She'd been running solo for so long she feared getting used to this feeling of being safe and cared for. She feared losing something she hadn't felt maybe ever.

You look like sex on a stick.

She could not get those words out of her mind. He just wanted to keep her feeling confident, but ... confidence wasn't heating her body up.

He opened the door to a large room, a cozy space. This wasn't a fleabag hotel, just an older hotel on the lower end of the price scale. Newer hotels wouldn't sell a room this big for so little, but back in the day, this was what people expected as standard size.

From what she could see and smell, the place appeared clean and neat.

A quilted spread covered the single queen bed and an upholstered peach-colored chair sat in the far corner. A chest of pine with a mirror stood to the right of the door.

She walked in and dropped the bag on the bed. It had begun to feel like an anchor.

Sam dropped the keys on the chest as well as the gun he pulled from beneath his shirt where it had been tucked inside his jeans. He stepped over to close the thick curtains on the window above the wall air conditioning unit, then flipped the air on.

He straightened and pulled off his cap, squinting in pain when he dropped it on the dresser.

"What the hell happened to you?" She went to him and put her fingers on his forehead. Dried blood had been smeared beneath his cap.

"Don't panic, babe. A bullet ricocheted and grazed my head. No real damage. Head wounds just bleed a lot."

She had no idea how close she had come to losing him in the warehouse. She could be just as dead had he not taken the gun and put himself in front of her. Once she had realized Sam was watching for muzzle flashes from the shooter, she'd found something to toss against the wall. That hadn't drawn fire, so she'd moved to a better spot.

"Hey," he said softly and drew her to him. "I'm really fine. No harm, no foul."

She had hit her limit for a day and shook hard against him, fighting back a sob.

Her limit for a week, to be honest.

She'd barely stopped since learning Phoebe had indeed been captured and was part of a nasty plan. That seemed forever ago. She was too tired to fight right now and hold herself apart from someone who offered her comfort.

Sam hugged her to him and shushed her with quiet words. He held her close and gave her so much more than she'd had maybe ever.

Wrapping her arms around Sam, she wanted to feel a deeper connection than friendship.

That was laughable. Two days ago, they were as far from being friends as two people could be.

His warmth spread around her. So nice. So ...

"Sweetheart? Want a shower?"

She blinked and lifted her head. Where was she?

A hotel.

"Are you awake enough to shower without falling asleep again?" he asked with a chuckle. "I can always stand behind you and hold you up."

Had she drifted off standing up? Forcing herself to pull away, she shot him a look. "You're selfless like that."

"I try." He grinned.

She stepped over to get her bag. "I'm good."

"I wouldn't say you're good," he started.

He was poking at her, but she refused to rise to the bait. Too tired.

Did that mean he would give up? No. "Good just doesn't cover a woman with your attributes. Sexy, badass, confident, and scary is more like it."

Yet again, he'd found a way to make her laugh. That right there made a man special. "I'll be out in a minute."

"Take your time. I think we covered our trail pretty good. I've got your back."

She knew he did. He was no longer Leclair, a man she'd kept at a distance just to rescue Phoebe. He was Sam, a man she now trusted when she had trusted so few over the years.

Dragging the strap off her shoulder, she put the bag on the bathroom counter and realized everything else they had was gone with the car. Sam had no duffel. She had no carry-on case.

But they were both alive.

Just to prove she could be fearless, she glanced at the mirror. And jerked back. No one could look at her and see sexy.

Sam's eyesight was going.

She turned on shower faucets and moaned when hot water hit her skin, loving it as much as any luxury hotel bath. She scrubbed the grime from her hair. To keep from using all the hot water when Sam needed a shower just as much, she reluctantly turned off the faucets and stepped out to drip on the bathmat.

Four towels. Bless the owners.

She used one to dry off with and the other on her hair. The room provided a hair dryer. She lifted it and shook her head, putting it back. She didn't have it in her to dry her hair.

Pulling out the black T-shirt she'd washed and kept in her bag, she held it against her like a lucky charm.

Would Sam realize it was the black shirt he'd given her in the basement of the mansion? Probably not.

Holding it to her nose, she inhaled, smelling the faint scent he'd worn into it. The same scent she knew from holding her face against his back on that motorcycle ride here.

She'd never met anyone like him.

Why would she? If not for having been captured trying to save Phoebe, Hallene wouldn't have ever found Sam.

Slipping the shirt on, she dug out a brush and detangled the mop of curls that fell around her face. Would he still say she looked like sex on a stick when he got a look at all this hair?

Leaving the brush for him since she had no comb, she packed up her shoulder bag and rinsed out her other clothes to hang on the towel bar. She could have worn her panties, but his black T-shirt fell past her bum.

They were adults. That meant they'd share the bed.

She'd be dead to the world the minute her head hit the pillow and trusted Sam not to touch her no matter how much she wanted him to hold her.

CHAPTER 26

SAM HAD BEEN RELAXING IN the chair when Hailey emerged from the bathroom with damp hair. She wore an oversized black T-shirt. He sat up.

That shirt looked suspiciously like the one he'd given her in Venezuela.

Huh. He liked seeing that on her. The little control freak had kept a dirty shirt from an unknown black operator. Had washed it even.

The more he learned about her, the more he wanted to know.

He'd like to see that shirt tossed across the room and all her pretty skin on display, proving he was a horndog after all she'd been through today.

Her hair naturally curled when wet. She hadn't used the hair dryer to straighten it. He liked the curls.

He'd say it made her seem less dangerous, but the opposite was true. That hair and body could tempt a monk.

He was no monk.

She yawned. "There are few things as wonderful as hot water regardless of the hotel rating when you crave a shower."

Standing up, he couldn't take his eyes off every move of her body. He liked seeing this not-as-controlled side of her. His gaze refused to move from that black shirt hugging her sexy curves. He'd like to know just what hid beneath *his* shirt, which was why he told himself to take a hot shower now or he'd need a cold one instead.

She opened her eyes wide and blinked, trying her best to stay awake.

Sam said, "A shower sounds great. I've locked the door and fixed the window covering so it doesn't fall open."

"Thanks." She headed to where he stood near the chair.

He caught her shoulders, and she lifted an exhausted gaze to his. "Go to bed," he ushered. "Don't wait for me." She was so close to falling asleep that he worried she'd face-plant.

Patting his hand, she assured him, "I can stay up a little longer. I'll watch *your* back." Then she gave him a sweet smile he would keep locked away in his heart for the days when she was gone, and he needed something bright to shove dark memories away.

She wanted to protect him while he was showering.

They'd started out adversaries, but little by little she'd proven to be a strong partner. He'd never had any woman determined to protect him besides Angie.

He had a special place in his heart for his aunt.

Hailey kept chiseling out her own spot in that petrified organ, opening the hole wider each time she smiled, and filling it with her own brand of warm happiness.

The sensation in his chest was more than protective.

It was a need to keep her close, something he had no business wanting. It was all he could do to keep Angie safe, and he hadn't managed to keep her hidden. How could he think to be with someone like Hailey in any form that resembled normal?

They had just lost their best hope of finding Phoebe.

Hell, he had to get his head straight in the shower.

After a scalding wash job, the rest of his cleanup didn't take long since he had no way to shave. He used her brush to comb his hair back from his face. He patted the damp rag over his forehead then rinsed out the blood. The wound would scab over by morning. He washed out his ravaged T-shirt along with his boxer shorts and hung them on the shower rack. The jeans could go another day.

Stepping out of the bathroom with a towel wrapped around his waist, he expected Hailey to talk a bit about her plan. That would pull his head out of his ass and put it on track to get this operation done.

She had curled up in the chair and done her best to stay awake, but she made a soft snoring sound.

Cute. Call her that and she'd probably use one of her martial art chops on him. He knew without question she had them.

She'd used her knees and legs on that guard in Venezuela and coldcocked him.

He turned down the bed, pulled the sheet back on one side, and clicked off the lamp on the nightstand, leaving only a nightlight glowing in the bathroom. Then he scooped her up.

She mumbled something that sounded irritated.

Giving him hell even in her sleep.

But she didn't wake as he put her to bed and covered her. He took it as a sign of her feeling comfortable with him, maybe trusting him more, for her to fall asleep.

When he walked back past the shoulder bag she'd dropped next to the bathroom door, he paused. Nitro would be chewing his ear off to search the bag for any information.

Trust was hard to earn and easy to destroy.

He would not lose the ground he'd gained with her.

He didn't want to sneak around and pilfer through her personal belongings like he would an enemy's. He wanted Hailey to keep opening up to him and handing details over voluntarily, to share with him as a partner even if they didn't have any idea where to go next.

He was not giving up on Phoebe.

He stretched out next to Hailey and smothered a groan. Having a bed when exhausted ran a close second to hot water. No telling what tomorrow would bring, but they'd made it this far by making some of it up as they went.

He'd worry about the future when the time came. His eyes drifted closed. His internal body clock would wake him before daylight.

Hours later, something slid across his neck, bringing him wide awake.

CHAPTER 27

—————

HALLENE STRUGGLED TO MOVE HER legs and fought the pressure holding her down.

"Wake the fuck up, Hailey!" whispered at her.

She heaved hard breaths. What was going on?

When her vision cleared, she could make out her surroundings from a nightlight in the bathroom. Her breath came out in rapid bursts.

She stared up into Sam's worried face.

He had her arms clamped down and his body holding her in place. What was happening? He wasn't trying to take advantage of her, just hold her in place. Her eyes tracked from wide shoulders and biceps pumped with muscle down his chest to where an impressive eight-pack then the rest of him was pinned against her.

And between her legs.

He was hard, too.

She needed her brain rattled to shake loose some survival skills. All she could think was that he held her down. Lifting her gaze to his, she warned. "Get. Off. Me."

He didn't move. "I will if you'll stop trying to kill me."

She blinked. *Kill* him? What was he talking about? She started to speak but nothing that made sense came to mind.

He watched her as one would a panicked animal. "I'm guessing you were in a nightmare, but you were choking me. When I tried to pry your fingers loose, you started fighting back. I was doing all I could to not hurt you. I just want to know for sure you're awake all the way."

Breathing slowly to calm down, she considered that she hadn't slept with a man in two years. She'd wakened more than once with the bed torn apart from nightmares of trying to save a child from a monster.

Her latest nightmare starring Phoebe had been repeated more than once this past week.

"I'm awake," she breathed out, feeling bad about snapping at him.

Sam's hands loosened on her wrists. He sat up and rolled away with a towel around his waist. Then he lifted her back and shoved a pillow behind her plus he pulled what he could tug loose of the sheet over her.

Once again, he'd shown her respect in a vulnerable situation.

While she scooted higher and reached under the sheet to pull the T-shirt down, he got out of bed and walked into the bathroom. When he came back, he had a plastic cup of water for her.

She took it and guzzled down a long swallow before handing the cup to him. He was giving her time to gather herself and she needed a minute to figure out what she was feeling besides embarrassed.

He climbed into bed and stacked pillows for himself.

Every move he made was slow and careful. He was trying to put her at ease. Who was this man that kept thinking of her needs?

The man who should have watched over and protected her from childhood had shirked his duty by turning his back on his wife and child.

She and Kovac had maintained a hate-hate relationship.

Coop had been a great friend and mentor, but she'd never leaned on him.

Sam had stepped up to protect her and be here for her.

His hand moved over to her cold one, threading their fingers. A warm grip, so full of power and ready for her at any moment. She closed her fingers tighter around his, thankful for a life ring in a turbulent ocean of emotions.

She swallowed hard and blinked back tears that would not fall. Not for herself. She was grown and strong. She had a powerful man standing by her side she'd have never expected.

Phoebe was alone somewhere with her terror.

The more days Hallene spent worrying about Phoebe, the harder time she had holding onto any annoyance.

After licking her dry lips, Hallene said, "I dreamed of Phoebe. Again." She took a breath and kept going. "Every time I find her, someone is dragging her away from me. The fear in her face is too horrific to describe and her screams rip my heart apart. Just when I get close and lunge for her hand, she's snatched away into a dark hole that closes over her and I know I'll ... never see her again."

Others would have tried to reassure her that they'd find Phoebe and not to worry.

Empty words that solved nothing.

Sam kept her hand safe in his. "We may face worse than that before it's over, but you'll have *me* by your side when we go after her. I will be with you every step of the way."

Muscles in her face relaxed and she smiled to herself at his confidence. From anyone else it would sound arrogant, but Sam wasn't bragging.

He was making a vow.

Just that support eased the tightness in her heart.

She wouldn't be alone after all.

But she had to admit the obvious. "I think my intelligence resource has been compromised. Either Kovac or the kidnapper realizes I know what they've been talking about."

"I've realized that, but we aren't defeated. Just delayed."

How long would Phoebe have? Looking around, she didn't spot an illuminated display on the digital clock. "What time is it?"

"I threw a towel over the clock so the light wouldn't wake you. It's just after two in the morning."

That's when she realized she had not gone to bed on her own. She'd gotten comfortable in the chair and had felt a wave of exhaustion hit her.

Sam had put her to bed.

She shoved both hands over her hair, pushing the mass back from her face. "We should talk about what to do next."

"You didn't sleep much. We can't do anything until closer to daylight. Why don't you try for a few more hours of sleep?"

Still taking care of her.

He would ruin her for another man even if they never did more than hold hands and kiss.

She couldn't fall asleep again after the nightmare and waking up to find Sam hovering over her. She might get past the nightmare, but not that formidable body so close to hers.

Half of it naked.

What would the bottom half look like?

No one would expect her to sleep with that mystery to solve.

She shrugged. "I can't sleep. I'm awake now."

"Don't give up so quickly." Sam pulled his hand away and her fingers curled, missing his touch. "Roll over on your stomach and let me loosen your neck and back muscles. Bet you'll be asleep before you know it."

He'd surprised her again when she would have expected him to say he could relax her if she'd shed her T-shirt. Would she have said yes? The fact that she questioned her answer meant her emotions were in a dangerous place right now.

"You're never going to relax if you don't stop thinking, babe," he grumbled. "It's just a back rub. I'm not going to attack you."

Sadly, he sounded firm on that.

"Thanks, I just—"

"Stop," he said gently. "Stop thinking. No explaining, just roll onto your stomach and let your mind unwind. Give up control for once."

That last comment was a challenge.

She'd prove she was not a control freak, dammit.

Shoving the pillow away, she cleared an area where she could lay her face against the soft sheet. The sheet on her back slid down, stopping at just before her bum. Then the T-shirt pushed up over her head.

Her tits came alive, but she still demanded, "Hey, what are you doing?"

"I don't want to massage a shirt. Chill out. I'm a pro at this shit."

"Says you," she chided him.

"You be the judge then."

Another challenge.

When he had the shirt above her with her arms contained, he smoothed his hands over her back from top to bottom. Now more parts woke with her tits.

Simple moves any masseuse would make but Sam had her skin tingling, anxious to feel his hands. Her nipples puckered more and ached.

The bed moved as he knelt with a leg on each side of her thighs.

What now? She worried he'd realized the danger in this. "You change your mind?" *Please say no.*

He chuckled. "No. I'm warming my hands by rubbing them together."

Before she could come up with another comment, those hands covered her shoulders again, hotter this time, and began working magic. She groaned from the feel of his fingers pressing deep into her tight muscles.

One hand went to her neck, gently but firmly massaging and searching for tight spots.

She had to admit she was relaxing like she hadn't in a long time. His hands pushed and smoothed down her back as he worked slowly inch by inch, heading for her lower back.

During a pause, he slid the sheet lower, exposing her rump.

Using a light touch, he began to softly massage there.

Tension coiled deep inside her. She had felt nothing before like the heat stroking through her womb. She shivered.

He paused then his touch changed from deep muscle dives to light as a feather. What had begun to feel relaxing turned needy.

Need to kiss him and feel his fingers everywhere.

Need to find out how he'd feel with her hands on him.

Her breathing picked up. She couldn't take this anymore. "Stop," she pleaded.

His touch vanished and she considered crying.

"What'd I do wrong?" He sounded hurt.

She pushed up on her elbows, ready to throw in the towel he was wearing. "You're spending too much time on my back."

Silence.

She owed him full disclosure. "I don't think I'm going to feel better until you ... touch me everywhere."

He didn't move.

This wasn't going to happen, and she'd made a fool of herself. "I'm ..."

His weight shifted forward, and his hands slid beneath her to cup her breasts. She gasped at the sensation shooting through her. His fingers began moving again, but with a new intention.

She gripped the sheets.

"Is that better?" he asked in a deep voice close to her ear.

"Uhm, huh. Like it."

He nosed her hair aside and kissed her neck. Her skin tingled everywhere he touched, but it wasn't enough. "More," she breathed out.

One hand abandoned a breast and moved lightly over her thigh. She shivered at the erotic feel. Her back arched up at the tension coiling inside her.

His knees moved inside her legs, easing them open for him to kneel there. Warm fingers brushed her folds.

Her arms shook from holding on to a jagged edge, fighting to stay there until she had to let go and fall. He held her between this second and the next, kept her safe, and drove her body closer to its limit.

"You're so responsive," he said in a rough voice. "I love the way you react to every touch." His whispers flowed around her, sometimes nothing more than a soothing sound. Kissing along her back, he played with both nipples that tightened hard.

His fingers brushed between her legs again and she squeezed out the words, "Stay there."

No. He stroked the inside her legs instead then moved at a snail's pace back to the spot that controlled her universe. The only place she cared about. She was breathing fast, waiting, waiting, waiting until ...

He barely touched her again with a finger then pressed inside her.

She made a crazy noise. "Please."

That must have been the magic word.

His deep voice pushed her. "Let go. I won't let you fall." He pulled the wet finger out and stroked her sensitive bud as if he owned the code to her body, driving her off the edge. She soared and fell into oblivion.

He would not let up until he'd wrung her dry and she slumped forward over his arm.

When she did, he pulled her back until she sat on his lap.

Where a major hard-on pressed the towel against her bottom.

He kissed her neck then her cheek, turning her to claim her mouth. She leaned around to give him all the access he wanted. Her boneless body was done. Finished.

She hadn't missed anything by not dating in the past two years because she hadn't known he existed. That this moment existed.

Using his mouth, he loved her slowly, keeping her lost in the high of an orgasm she would not forget. Ever.

Those mystical fingers started teasing her breasts again. Her heart pounded fiercely with her body coming alive once more. "Feels so good," she murmured. "What about you?"

"We're not in a hurry." He then backed that up by tuning her body all over again, bringing the tension back to a sharp level. Touching her everywhere, light fingertips across her skin and down between her legs.

Greedy woman that she was, she wanted it all again.

Like finding a dessert she had never tasted and unable to stop herself from gorging on it.

Fire raced from her womb to her breasts.

A second orgasm would be unlike any other time. She'd never thought it possible so soon in the past.

But Sam's hands switched from soft touches to serious strokes again, toying with her breasts then teasing her slick folds. Every touch gripped the reigns of her control, forcing her to wait, to hold on until her groin ached with begging for another release.

She would not allow him to be the only one to give. She gasped out, "I want you inside me."

"No condoms, babe."

"I'm on the pill and ..." She stopped breathing when he barely stroked her between her legs. She shook with need. "No ... uh ... sex in two years."

"Hell. Thought I was in a drought. A year for me. You sure about this?"

She'd trusted him with her life in that warehouse.

She'd trust him with her body.

He put both hands on her breasts, making it impossible to think. Her back bowed against him. She remembered what she had to say. "Yes."

"Drop down, babe," he told her in a voice getting deeper by the second.

She did, holding her body on her forearms.

He must have shed his towel because she felt him rub his hard dick against her wet folds.

Yes, she'd have all of him now.

Not yet. He had other plans, taking his time moving his gentle touch over her legs and up into the V of her legs. He'd pull his hands away, torturing her with the loss, then his fingers would move to her nipples, massaging the hard beads.

He kept it up, teasing her folds and breasts, brushing the back of his fingers over her abdomen, then kissing her neck. She shuddered at the unrelenting way he pushed her close then made her wait.

Leaning forward, he used both hands on her breasts, moving his thumbs over the tips.

She felt every flick, every kiss, every stroke deep in her womb. She couldn't do this any longer. "Hurry."

He pushed his dick between her legs, back and forth, then slowly fed himself into her.

She moaned at the feel of him deep inside, filling her.

Careful at first, he pulled out slowly and slid back in, now making her crazy in a new way. "I'm ready."

"Me, too. Fuck, you feel amazing." He began going faster and reached between her legs. His fingers stroked her again.

Her muscles clamped hard around him. His fingers moved faster, and she tensed then let go. Her orgasm rolled on and on because he would not let up.

He pumped hard twice then ground out a harsh groan, filling her.

Time fell away.

She lived in a world of her own with only him. Nothing else existed except feeling him inside her and holding her. He wrapped her in ecstasy and something much deeper. Something she couldn't put to words, or it would ruin everything.

She'd cherish the gift of this moment.

One she wished would last forever.

Her body had no bones left. It couldn't possibly with her this loose and relaxed.

Holding her with an arm around her waist, he rolled to the side, taking her with him.

Her arms flopped. Her muscles were noodles.

He chuckled.

Still inside her, he brushed the hair off her face and pecked soft kisses on her cheek and neck. "You blew my mind."

She smiled. He'd done all the work this time.

This time?

Were they going to do this again?

Her mind was wrung dry. Some days, she wanted to climb out of her skin and see what it felt like to live as other women lived. He'd managed to do the impossible and stop her racing thoughts.

He'd made her happy in her own skin.

She'd give him his due. "You were as good as you claimed. A *pro*."

"I was talking about my massage skills," he clarified. "Making love to you was ... no words to describe it. Never came that hard in my life." He smooched her again.

How was it he could make *her* feel like a superstar? "Mine was pretty bloody special, too."

He'd called it making love.

The few times she'd been intimate in the past, no one had made love to her. Not like this. She'd felt everything Sam did down to her center and not because he was an exceptional lover.

Sam cared for her on some level that scared her to think about. Why? She cared for him too. He put himself into lovemaking.

She felt his lips smile when he kissed the back of her neck and nuzzled her. Snuggling back closer to him cocooned her in his heat. He dragged the sheet over them, and his arm wrapped her up, once again keeping her safe.

How would she ever feel this way with anyone else?

She wouldn't. Sam had climbed inside her very being and set up camp, daring anyone to remove him.

It wouldn't be her.

She was replaying making love with him one minute and asleep the next.

CHAPTER 28

———◆———

KOVAC PACED HIS OFFICE, CHEWING on a nail. He hadn't done that since his teens when he started having manicures. Where was a message from Crusher?

His phone buzzed from his assistant.

Stabbing the button, Kovac said, "I do not want to be disturbed. Were you confused the first time I told you?"

In a shaky voice, his assistant said, "Someone is calling for you on my mobile phone. Says it's critical."

Who would call him on *her* phone? Then he knew. "Bring me your phone."

The twenty-three-year-old knock-out brunette hurried in and handed over her personal phone.

"Thank you." He had to maintain civility. "Sorry to snap at you. I have a lot going on right now."

"Of course." She gave him a brainless smile and scurried out, closing the door softly behind her.

He lifted the phone. "Kovac."

"Listen carefully," W started.

Kovac's skin chilled at the threat in this Ruskie's voice. At least, W's accent sounded Russian.

W asked, "Did you deal with stepdaughter?"

Kovac's voice shook. "Not yet."

"Unacceptable."

He had to do more than wait to give a one-word answer. "I'd like to tell you what I'm doing."

"I do not want loose threads running around. You have one chance to convince me bringing you into fold was not mistake on my part. I do not make mistakes. Speak quickly."

"Yes, Sir." Kovac quickly explained that he believed Hallene had someone hack his computer system even though he had exceptional layers of security. He set up a phony meeting for proof of life to draw her out of the shadows, which worked, then his man went to take care of her. He was waiting to hear back.

W said, "No confirmation from your man by now means he was terminated."

Breathing became difficult. "I'll do whatever you say, Sir. Everything I've agreed to have arranged by end of day Friday is on track. No hiccups."

"I will send someone to deal with this stepdaughter problem and deduct cost from your funds."

Kovac had never been so relieved to lose money. "Excellent idea."

"Here is what *you* will do immediately."

CHAPTER 29

———➤———

FRESHLY SHOWERED, SAM FELT DAMN happy for having almost died yesterday. They'd survived though.

Score.

A shower hadn't brought him out of his head where webs of dark memories captured him too often. Hailey had stomped into his life and demanded his attention.

After years of living with the guilt of not saving his mother or sister, of keeping women at arm's length to avoid destroying another woman's life, Hailey had wrecked him.

She'd obliterated any chance of another woman taking her place. He'd unfairly compare any future female to her.

He wanted only Hailey and no one else.

She had him thinking of what it would be like to have her in his life. How much he wanted to be the person who made her happy, kept her safe, and stood at her side.

He'd smile over outwitting that assassin but the idea of anyone harming Hailey dredged up his dark side. The side he'd done his best to keep tamped down so he could perform his duty for Logan and his team.

Being selected to join the FALCA team had been an honor and one he'd been determined to earn every minute.

But not this minute.

No one would fault him for taking a break with a woman, but his team were not fools. They at least suspected he had not left willingly at first.

Surveillance had been put into place to ensure no one came after him just because of what had happened in South America.

The minute he'd driven away with Hailey, Moose would have brought in Nitro. If Sam had sent a text alerting them that he was taking a few days with a friend, the team would accept his word.

Sam wouldn't have sent that text. He couldn't in good conscious intentionally lie to them.

He had no idea how all this would shake out, but he wanted a chance to explore what he and Hailey had once they saved everyone. He also wanted a chance to stay with HAMR.

Hell, he wanted everything, including saving her half-sister.

How the hell were they going to find Phoebe now?

The shower ran steadily. It sounded as if Hailey was singing. She'd woken during the night, gone to the bathroom, and returned with a warm rag.

Deep in sleep, a rarity for him, Sam came alert hard as stone from her cleaning him.

She'd found that funny.

She stopped smiling as soon as he'd flipped the rag away and gave her round two of a relaxing massage.

For the first time ever, he wanted time off.

That would blow Nitro's mind.

The shower noise ended, then a few minutes later Hailey emerged. "Good morning. Again."

He liked the happy in her voice and turned to lean back against the dresser. "It's a hell of a morning when I wake up to you. I like this picture."

Her blond hair curled as it dried naturally. She had no makeup on. When she dolled up, she could hang with any model. Without makeup, she had the kind of beauty that came from somewhere inside a person, the kind that bloomed on the outside from a good heart.

She lifted an eyebrow at him. "I look like a drowned rat again."

He crossed the room and slid his hands into her hair, drawing her in for a kiss. Man, he'd never get enough of that mouth. Even when it was snapping at him.

Her hands clutched his sides, holding tight.

When a woman touched a man that way, she made him feel like he was hers. That he could do anything.

Then he *wanted* to do anything for the woman holding his heart.

After a couple sips of her lips, he pressed his forehead to hers, hating to lose this moment. "We need a car."

"I'll just get another one and I'm not using my real ID, so we're fine."

"Did you use that ID on the last two cars?"

Her shoulders slumped. "Yes. I didn't think about that, but I don't think they found me that way."

"Look at me." He waited a beat because he wanted her to stay with him on this. "I think they knew where you were because of going to the meet at the marina."

"Me, too." She sounded gloomy. "If that's the case, my intelligence on the Collector just went out the window."

"The Collector?" Sam questioned.

She gave him an odd glance. "Yes. Who were you looking for in Venezuela?"

Well, damn. They weren't even looking for the same bad guy. "We have a missing senator and believe an international terrorist leader named W has him. The Collector might have been contracted to grab the senator, but he's never been known to be involved with terrorists."

Her eyes were distant for a second. "I have not heard of a US senator missing."

Sam had hammered her on sharing intel. He had to do the same for them to join forces. "No one can know that Senator Turner has been snatched. He must be present at a meeting that has been secretly in the works for months or a potential international conflict could arise if he fails to show. One side will take it as a sign that everything he has said up to now were lies to stall and mislead one party."

She opened her mouth then closed her lips.

"What?" Sam asked.

"I was going to ask which countries, but it does not matter. Not with Phoebe's life on the line, a senator to find, and time running out." She sat on the bed and frowned with a thoughtful expression. "I'm not familiar with W."

They had to put these pieces together. But how? Sam wished for Moose's ability to sort through intel.

She quietly suggested, "I know my resource hacking Kovac's

computer is compromised, but if I contact my techie with this information, he might come up with something useful on the senator. That Russian guy might be W."

Sam scratched the beginning of a beard on his cheek. "I think you're right based on what you told me because I thought we were talking about the same person. Still do. We don't have a visual on the Collector either. No one in our business is going to be happy to learn the Collector could be working with W."

She dropped her hand to the bed, tapping her fingers. "I've paid large amounts of money to reveal the identity of that scumbag kidnapper, but no luck so far."

"Did you get your intel resources from the person who trained you?" Sam was fishing and waited for her to snap at him, but she didn't.

"No. I have a computer whiz I met in college. We were nerd friends and studied together to get decent grades. He struggled with some subjects and never wanted anyone to know how brilliant he was with a computer and keyboard. He liked hacking. He accessed Kovac's computer and has been capturing messages from Kovac's phone that show up on his computer."

"Kovac was stupid to do that."

"He's not stupid so much as arrogant and overconfident. He pays a small fortune to keep his computers secure. My techie is just better."

Her phone buzzed. She stepped over and dug it out of her bag. "This is my contact and I'm going to ruin his day by telling him we've been caught."

She opened the text and read the message out loud. "R u okay? Just picked up convo. Bastard xchgd msgs w/someone called Crusher. C tagged van carrying P, but informed Bastard stepdaughter showed up at the meet. Bastard lost his shit over that news. C reported he sent someone to eliminate you but failed (so glad). New orders for C. Grab P before you get to her. C is tracking van and will go after P when van stops for longer than an hour. He'll contact Bastard to confirm when he can make the snatch. Said he would extract P by ten ET no matter what. Don't freak. I found area C is in. Map attached."

She opened the next image and said, "We have a location."

"You think this is legit?"

Her voice shook with excitement. "Yes! The shooter didn't find us because of sweeping Kovac's messages. He was sent to track the vehicle bringing Phoebe for the proof of life meeting. He tagged the van. Evidently, Kovac has had this guy called Crusher hunting me and he told Kovac he saw me at the meet. Said he'd sent someone to eliminate me."

Black anger burned Sam's brain. He hoped he'd killed the assassin.

Hallene hurried to fill Sam in on everything as she saw it. "Crusher tracked the van that is circling the Alexandria area of Virginia. That fits with what we know so far. He's going to contact Kovac when it stops for the night and snatch Phoebe. Those were Kovac's new orders for him. We just need to get close and be ready for when my tech sends the final location."

"That's great," he murmured.

"You don't sound entirely convinced, Sam." The hope shining in her eyes said she needed him on board.

He had to be honest. "I'm not, but I'm going to go with what we have unless anything changes. I just don't trust easy intel and I'm not discounting your tech."

"I understand, but I can't sit still and lose this opportunity. Ready to make a plan?"

"Yes, of course," he assured her and gave her a kiss to settle her fears. "Let's grab clothes from the thrift store and change here then I'll rent us a car with an ID Kovac would have no knowledge of. We'll get something to eat and figure out our next step."

"Unless I hear back with the location for the van first, I can think better after we eat."

"Let's dress and make a run to the store." He didn't want to leave anything since things could change at any moment for them.

It didn't take long to finish dressing and packing when Sam could hold all they possessed in his hands. "Got your bag, hon?"

She lifted it from the chair and turned to him. She chewed on the corner of her lip, deep in thought on something.

"What's wrong, Hailey?"

"That." She pointed at him and walked over to where he held the door open.

Mr. Grumbly said, "I'm gonna need a few more words to figure out what you're talking about."

"Calling me Hailey. My name is Hallene." She started to walk past him to leave, but he stopped her with a touch on her arm. She had a spark of the devil in her today. "Something bothering you ... *Sam*?"

"Yep. It's named Hallene, and I like being bothered." Grinning now, he gave her a kiss that turned fiery and had him ready to drag her back to bed.

She bit his lip and laughed, walking out.

CHAPTER 30

A LL SAM COULD DO WAS shake his head at the surreal world he was living in and follow *Hallene's* swaying hips. He'd never felt blessed, not until today.

Once they hit the road, he found the rental company she'd located and parked. She dismounted as he started telling her where to rendezvous. "There was a huge parking lot at that outlet center we passed."

"I saw it." She checked the chin strap on her helmet and made a move toward the bike. It would have been too tall for a woman of average height but no problem for a woman with her inseam.

He frowned. "You need eye protection."

"Got it." She pulled a pair of sunglasses out of the bag hanging across her body.

"Be careful, babe." He had a hard time letting her leave, but he wanted her to find a safe place to wait in the parking lot. He doubted anyone could know they were here, but if someone followed him out, he wanted to unass the tail without her being involved.

"I will." She climbed on and rocked the 'Busa off its center stand.

"If you see anything suspicious—"

"Stop, Sam. I'll park in a low-profile spot where I can watch for you, then I'll pull out when I see you."

"Your brain is turning me on, *Hallene*." He liked saying her name. He'd muttered it to himself the whole way here.

She'd given him her real name. Another gift his heart tucked away.

"Too bad you don't have time for the rest of me, *Sam*."

"Keep torturing me, babe. We'll never get this done. Just scout

out a safe spot. Don't grab the first one."

"You remind me of the guy who trained me. He was MI6."

Sam became very still. "Was he your *lover*?"

Was he jealous? Well, hell yes.

Hallene lifted her hand. "Stop. We became close as *friends*. I admit I wanted more at one point. He told me there was no life with someone like him. He couldn't function if his attention was divided between his duty and someone waiting at home for him because he never knew when he might not come back from a mission. He said my friendship meant the world to him. That sort of hurt my feelings at first, but I got past it and now realize he was right. I needed a friend more than a lover at that moment. Then he died fourteen months later."

Sam couldn't be angry at the guy who trained her, especially with him dead.

If anything, he felt selfish for wanting what that guy had passed on. Sam would like to think he had honor and would make the noble decision, but he was having a hard time weighing duty against never seeing Hallene again.

That made him a liability to his team.

But who was he without HAMR Brotherhood? He wanted to rid the world of vermin like W and Phoebe's dad, wanted to ensure Angie and her friends lived in peace where Clercville could be a sanctuary for others as it had been for him.

While he was making a life wish list, he also wanted Hallene with every fiber of his being. He'd never said the L word to a woman, never intended to, but his brain kept pushing that four-letter word forward.

Nothing about their lives meshed. She clearly lived in the UK and his team was stationed here in the US.

What was he going to do? Marry her? She'd get the short end of that arrangement, just as the MI6 guy pointed out, damn him.

Sam gave her a half-smile, keeping his screwed-up thoughts to himself.

She cranked the engine then backed away and took off fast, dragging his heart behind her.

He'd carried one of his second sets of ID when he left Angie's inn. No way he'd have brought his real ID on an op. After a quick discussion with the rental agent, he drove out in a pewter-colored Ford Expedition with less than a thousand miles on it.

He always took the insurance in his line of work but hoped he could return the car without a scratch. That would mean he and Hallene hadn't faced another firefight or had their car blown to pieces.

At the shopping center, he slowly made two passes down the same aisle where there were plenty of spaces then parked all by himself.

Where was she?

He'd looked everywhere for that motorcycle.

From between a van and truck parked next to each other a parking aisle over, Hallene drove the motorcycle through an opening with barely enough room for the handlebars.

His jacked-up pulse began to slow.

She pulled up next to the passenger side of his vehicle. Parked the bike and used a dirty towel to wipe down everywhere they had touched, including the key before putting it back in.

Smart woman.

Someone would boost that bike in no time.

Tossing the rag in the back of the SUV, she settled into the passenger seat, explaining, "Found the towel in the parking lot and was just coming back to squeeze into that spot to watch for you."

He leaned over. "That deserves a kiss."

"You think everything deserves a kiss." But she met him over the console and licked his lips before sliding her tongue between his.

Aggressive female. So damn hot. He could kiss her for hours, just spend a lazy day holding her and smooching. He loved being inside her, loved her response to his touch, and had a scary feeling he'd never get enough of her.

She shifted back to her seat. "Nothing new from my techie. Feed me."

"Yes, ma'am." As soon as they found a restaurant, Sam faced a new hurdle. He could no longer hope he was right about Angie and Clercville's safety.

Would Hallene trust him enough to tell him the truth?

He'd made it clear that he wouldn't leave her, but he wanted her to wipe away any chance of someone going after Angie and her cove should he and Hallene not survive their next move.

The only way Hallene would die is if someone took Sam out first.

CHAPTER 31

———◆———

INSIDE THE CHAIN STEAKHOUSE THEY'D chosen, Hallene kept glancing around, waiting for someone to pop out
from behind a booth to attack them.

Everyone else in this place was enjoying their meals. They
didn't watch for assassins.

"Eat your meal, babe. I'll know if anyone shows up." Sam was
busy cutting and eating his thick steak.

The man was a true meat eater.

"I'm almost done," she admitted. She brushed crumbs from
the long-sleeved red T-shirt with the logo of an ice hockey
team she didn't know. Sam had approved. He'd also given a
big thumbs-up to her cargo pants. This was so not what she
normally wore back home, no more than leaving her hair to dry
curly.

He liked it, more than liked it. He'd given her a hungry glance
that had her breasts perking up, ready for him.

She'd enjoyed shopping at the thrift store down from the hotel
where they'd gone hunting clothes.

Sam shopped like a man. Short-sleeved shirt with Hawaiian
print and baggy shorts. He found another cap that was just as
worn out as the one he'd gotten blood on.

They looked like any other couple in this restaurant.

She'd never fit in so easily before. Never felt like she fit it. She'd
dressed for business meetings while running her organization
because that's what it took to get people involved. The only time
she didn't wear a suit was when she went with her people to
rescue kids.

Even then, she was never this casual, always trying to keep
up appearances. Why? For strangers who cared nothing for her?

Being with Sam had shown her a middle ground of how to be comfortable doing everyday things. It was a healthy mindset and hers had been set wrong for a long time.

In the next few minutes, he finished his meal, took a drink of water, and leaned forward on his crossed arms. "Let's talk."

That hadn't sounded casual or teasing.

Warning signals flared in her head. She pushed her plate aside and propped her elbows on the table to keep their conversation private.

He asked, "How much danger are Angie and Clercville in?"

She'd expected him to ask about finding Phoebe, not that. He wanted to know the truth she believed he suspected. If she failed to admit it, he would look at her differently.

Deep breath. She gave up her only card to keep his team out of their hair and to ensure they continued as partners. "They'll be fine."

"Even if neither of us shows up again?" he pressed.

She covered her eyes for a minute then lowered her hands. "No one is going to come looking for me or hurt anyone in Clercville." The fact that he asked her should be okay, but she worried she was making a mistake. She narrowed her eyes at him. "Is that what you wanted to hear?"

"To be honest, I did not think you had it in you to harm any innocent people, but we ran into something bad yesterday. I don't intend to let anyone hurt you. They'll have to come through me. I just needed to be sure there was no trip wire we might accidentally cross if you didn't contact someone on time."

His words were woven with truth and commitment.

Again, he was determined to keep her safe. She had to let go of suspicions that jumped up and clouded her vision. Sam said he wouldn't contact his team and he would stay with her to find Phoebe.

Hallene had to show him she could be trusted, too. "I do have a sort of safety button, but that would only send someone to track me to the last location I was at based upon what I know of finding Phoebe. My techie is funneling information to me as often as possible. He knows I'm in Virginia right now and would have no reason to send anyone to Clercville. If he doesn't get a reply to one of his messages in six hours, he'll contact someone I know in the UK."

"Someone connected to your MI6 friend?"

"Yes."

"But that would mean you were likely no longer alive."

"Exactly. Phoebe would probably not be alive either. At the point I stopped replying to my techie, he would know to alert an elite contractor, tell him I was dead, and activate him to track down the people responsible. Even if it took years to find and annihilate them, that contractor would not stop until taking down the killers. I funded an account for my techie years ago to cover that type of cost. But my resource guy knows about you. He would make it clear you were helping me."

Sam studied her a moment while that sharp mind of his did some calculating. "Speaking of this techie, he helped you find me, right? I need to know how that happened so I can plug holes when we finish this."

She could understand Sam's concern for Angela down the road. "He started with an image I gave him for facial recognition."

"*Where'd you get that?*" He tilted his head toward her when he'd whisper shouted.

"When you took your mask off and followed me as I backed up in the basement."

"Son of a bitch," he murmured. "That would only get him to where I went to school and entering the military."

Even she had been shocked at Midnight Ferret's ability to find Sam. "Right. He's truly a ferret when it comes to any electronic detail. He did a lot of searches and found an old picture of you and a boat in your backyard. Someone had painted the name *Le Jolly Clerc* on it. He pulled crumbs together and came up with Clercville. What's with the boat?"

Sam leaned back with a distant look in his eyes. "I bought that just to piss off my old man. I'd worked every odd job you could imagine and fixed cars for people I knew to earn money. Bought the boat from a hurricane sale. Engine was trashed and it had holes in the hull." His gaze came back to her. "Old man beat the shit out of me for holding out on money he said belonged to him for keeping me fed and a roof over my head. What I had for food and shelter was the same as tossing a rotten apple to a rat and throwing a ripped-up sack over its head."

He didn't whine or make it sound as if he wanted sympathy, just again stating facts about what his life growing up had been like.

That deep-blue gaze swept away, missing nothing, then back to her. "That damn boat." He let out a sad laugh. "Angie must have had it hauled away from that shack after I had to go into the military. She shocked the hell out of me when I saw it in Clercville."

Hallene caught something in his speech. "You *had* to go into the military?"

"Yeah. I put my old man in the hospital. I was seventeen and came home from working three days straight on two demanding labor jobs to find my mother unconscious. She was strung out on drugs. She'd done pot before that but never hard drugs. She was in constant pain from the times he'd hit her when I wasn't around. She found a stash of hard stuff the old man had hidden."

Hallene had no words to ease his misery. Listening was the best she could offer, which Sam seemed to need.

"I should have known the old man was dealing, but I was gone a lot that month. Any minute I was not working or at school, I tried to be there to keep him from beating on her and my little sister. I *should* have been there all the time. He walked in while I was trying to wake her up. He kicked her."

Sam's chest rose and fell with fast breaths as if he relived the moment all over again. "I lost it. Must have grown stronger than I realized from the hard labor I'd been doing. I broke his jaw, his arm, and two ribs. I left him bleeding when I carried her to the hospital. She died that night. Angie sent a lawyer who negotiated a deal to put my father in prison for my mother's death and cut a deal that I went into the military. He died a year later."

Pain stabbed Hallene just hearing his words. "What about your sister?"

Sam's eyes lowered and the life drained from his face. "Angie did her best to help us growing up, but my dad hated her. Thought she filled my head with stupid ideas. My sister, Sissy, had been living in a dysfunctional nightmare for so long, she was beyond help. She'd been making bad choices the last year leading up to our mom dying. Me constantly telling her she was putting herself in danger did little good. I had no idea what to do. I just did not want her to get hurt. Then I barely sidestep going to jail for taking my dad down and got shipped out. The day after I finished basic training, they sent me home for Sissy's funeral. She'd left a bar with some scumbag who raped and gutted her."

Hallene covered her mouth. A tear spilled down her cheek. She could see how so much of what happened had shaped Sam. He could have turned out to be a monster like his dad but took the opposite path of protecting others.

Easing back, she lowered her hand and gave him space to talk or not.

The low hum of dialogue in the restaurant filled the vacuum when Sam stopped talking. He scrubbed his hands over his face. "I've never talked about that. Don't know why I did now. Angie pokes at me sometimes to talk, but I avoid opening that mental box. My fault my mom died and that I wasn't there to watch out for Sissy."

"That's not true, Sam."

"Has to be someone's fault."

"It was. Your dad caused all of that. If he'd been a strong man inside like you are your family could have been happy."

Sam didn't show much on the outside. It took someone watching closely to see the tiny slips on his stoic face.

He carried their deaths on his shoulders, and the guilt he couldn't let go of had to be a terrible burden. He'd done the best he could with what he had as a teen.

She pointed out something to him. "I'm guessing your fierce need to protect Angie is because she's special to you."

That brought up a smile. "I call her my aunt. She was in the same orphanage as my mom. When Angie got adopted, she still treated my mom like her sister when my old man didn't get in the way."

Now Hallene understood why it had been so hard to find anything on Angela. Midnight might be a mastermind in the computer underworld, but Angela had built a fortress around herself no one had broken through until Hallene hunted for Sam.

She made a vow to him. "When we are done, I'll give you everything we found on Angela. Although it is not much, my tech will send me a document on how she can better secure her identity ... and you can close holes in yours. To be honest, I can't see how an intelligence agency would have found you without us meeting and my guy's obsession with finding anything. Also, Angela has a wall of attorneys circling her."

Sam smiled. "That's good to know. Angie is more than financially comfortable. She was adopted by wealthy parents who left her their fortune. There's not a snobby bone in her body. She lives a normal life and uses her funds to help others ... like me. I had no idea she'd found the boat." Any lingering emotions slid off his face. He clapped his hands together. "We need to talk about our next move."

She forced a smile for him when her stomach flipped over at all she'd learned. Sam would not appreciate sympathy.

He deserved her respect.

She said, "Still no word yet from my tech."

"Oh well, we can sit here a bit." He drummed his fingers on the table. Sam couldn't sit still for long.

"Let's get out of here and get some ice cream."

Sam got the check, paid it, then took her arm on the way out.

Her head was clear. Her heart was happy.

The man at her side would be there for however long she needed him.

Leaves in trees next to the parking lot ruffled with a swirling breeze. Dark clouds hung in the east and would likely be here soon.

A feeling of impending doom swept over her.

She wanted to slap herself. That was no way to think positively. Midnight Ferret would send a text. She had no doubt.

Sliding into the passenger seat as Sam dropped into the driver seat, her gaze stopped on a mobile phone sitting on the console.

She hadn't left one and Sam's phone was still on airplane mode in her purse. Please tell her that was not connected to his team, but she knew better.

Who else would have put the phone there?

Disappointment iced over her earlier warm feelings. "You contacted your team. How did you do it?"

"Hold up, Hallene. I've been with you," he said calmly.

"Don't play word games with me, Sam." Her heart began cracking into pieces. She'd trusted him and he'd lied to her.

He'd waited until he knew Angela and Clercville were safe, then he'd signaled his team.

CHAPTER 32

———◆———

SAM STARED AT THE PHONE with the same apprehension he'd feel for a coiled rattlesnake. He hated the disappointment in Hallene's voice, hated it, but the time had come to face the consequence of his decision.

He started by explaining how his people were here now. "I told you my team would be watching Angie's house. They have probably been hunting me since you took me from Clercville and dumped the first car."

She flinched at that, and he wanted to kick himself. He hadn't meant for his words to come out angry, but this might drive an unfixable wedge in their relationship.

"That's why you wanted to rent the car with your ID." She sounded as if she were putting together the pieces of how he'd done all this on the sly.

"You make it sound like I had this covert plan to trick you. That's not true."

"Oh Sam, stop."

The finality in her voice was killing him.

No point in tiptoeing when he had to contact Nitro. The phone had been left as an order. *Call immediately.*

Sam tried to get her to understand. "I have to call my people. The fact that they didn't blow in here and pull me out means they'll listen." He had no idea if that was the case for sure since he'd never been in this spot. When Hallene said nothing more, he tossed out a possible upside to this. "I'll be honest. They could help us."

She pulled the shoulder bag strap off and shoved the bag down by her feet. "The minute someone else shows up, all my hard work to find Phoebe and save her will be destroyed."

"That's not how it is." He hoped to avert a disaster. "Keep in mind that you pulled me out of Clercville with no time to cover that extraction. I'm not complaining or giving you a hard time about that, just saying to think of it from my side. I did not call them in. Did I expect contact after renting a car with one of my IDs? Yes, but not this quickly. They're giving me a chance to discuss what's going on."

She looked away, a bad sign. Not open to what he was trying to say.

The air ran out of his hope balloon that he could fix this. "I need a chance to explain why I'm on an unauthorized mission." He'd tried not to think about the consequences waiting for him.

Fury still overrode every other emotion in Hallene's face when she turned back to him. "I'll make this easy for you. I was clear with you about any interference. Now that your team is involved, we part ways."

Pain stabbed his chest. How could she want to break apart now?

"Don't do this, Hallene," he pleaded because he could not handle her racing into a death trap unprotected. He'd never find her again if she did survive. "Give me a chance to talk to them."

"Talk all you want. I'm not changing my mind."

Sam would like to have a private conversation with Nitro, but he couldn't step outside if he wanted her to still trust him.

One number had been inserted with the ID of the letter N. Sam's throat tightened with guilt over being at odds with his team.

Sam spoke first. "I'm here."

Nitro spoke in that quiet voice again, the one that came naturally when he wanted to rip someone apart. "Want to explain what the fuck is going on, Sam?"

Hell, Nitro wasn't even calling him Cuz. Sam said, "I'm on a lead about the senator's kidnapping."

"We figured out your hand signals. Why haven't you unassed that female and contacted us?"

"That would terminate our agreement and jeopardize success of finding the senator." Sam closed his eyes against what was coming.

"Logan wants me to pull you in."

Shit, that can't happen. Sam sent a look to Hallene when he spoke to her. "I have to tell them what is going on."

Her jaw couldn't get any more rigid.

Nitro asked, "Let me get this clear. Not only are you acting on intel from an unknown source, but you're asking permission from the blonde who showed up at your aunt's place and tried to swallow your tongue?"

"That one."

"*Who* is she?" Nitro could be furious and would still dig for any bit of intel.

"The one I met in the basement of the mansion." Sam struggled to get a deep breath. His world was circling the commode and he had nothing to grab hold of to save his future. "Her intel put her in the mansion before us and she was the reason we got out ahead of the blast. She's looking for someone else, an innocent girl being used as a pawn. We're both looking for the same kidnapper. I just want the time to follow through on what I've agreed to. If nothing comes of it in the next twenty-four hours, I'll call to meet you. Fair enough?"

Her eyes widened and her mouth dropped open. Betrayal flooded her face.

"Did you think we were negotiating, Sam? How'd she even locate you in Clercville?"

No one was happy with Sam right now. "I'm only asking for a little time to confirm this intel. That's all. As for how she found me, I'm not entirely sure yet."

Nitro went silent for a few seconds. "You're telling me this woman has a lead on W and the senator."

"Yes. Until I learn differently, I believe she's found him from a different avenue that was unavailable to us because of the kidnapped girl she's looking for."

He flicked a look at her, hoping she'd realize he had not shared Phoebe's name or hers.

The blank stare she gave him could be positive or negative. Only time would tell once he ended this call.

At the rate he was sinking in everyone's opinion, he'd bet on negative.

Sam kept selling his plan to Nitro. "This may be our only chance to extract our target, and from what I've learned, it has to happen soon."

"Why?"

Sam leaned back, wishing for once in his life to be an average Joe again. He lived for his life with the FALCA team, but the walls were closing in on him. "I don't have this firmed up yet, but it sounds like the kidnapper does have an event planned for his usual date."

"We know about the last Saturday in August."

"But we don't know where. It may be on US soil. That's what I'm hoping to pin down before Saturday morning, which would give us around seventeen hours if he sticks to his standard time of ten in the morning." Sam released an exhausted sigh. "I think it's going to be on the upper northeast coast."

Nitro cursed. "You can't keep going forward with just the two of you. Not dealing with W."

"We can," Sam argued, sitting up with a renewed sense of swinging this conversation in his favor. "She's got skills and we're just now on the same page. Please, give me until tomorrow morning. I'm not leaving her to face this alone and I don't see us getting any closer without her intel."

Nitro took his time responding then reluctantly said, "I'll explain this to Logan but no promises, Cuz."

Using the brotherly name Sam's team utilized gave him hope for not severing every tie with them. Nitro regretted having to do his duty, but Sam would not blame him.

In Nitro's place, Sam would do the same.

"Don't think I'm not appreciative," Sam told him in a gruff voice. "I know what I'm facing when this is done. I just can't walk away."

A soft curse came next before Nitro said, "You're one of our very best, but women have been a chink in your armor since day one. You've avoided any serious issues until South America. I don't know why this woman deserves your commitment, but she better be worth what it may cost you. Logan will have to make a tough decision when this is all done, and he won't like it. None of us are willing to give you up."

Sam swallowed against the lump of misery clogging his throat. He thought he was ready to accept what he had to face until talking to Nitro, which made it real. He had to put that loss into a compartment in his mind so he could function, or it would destroy him.

"I understand," Sam said quietly. "I'm not excusing my actions and I won't blame anyone for the consequences, but I'm telling you straight up she's trained and has intel we haven't found, or you would have all gotten to this point ahead of us."

"There's money in the trunk and a weapon," Nitro said in a resigned voice Sam had never heard before. "I'll call if Logan sends us to pick you up, so it isn't a surprise. I know you won't run."

"I would never do that." Sam ended the call and placed the phone on the seat beside him. He would tell her what he believed to be true at this minute. If it changed, he would tell her then. "My team is not going to crowd us. You heard the rest from my side."

Turning back to him slowly, she shook her head. "Their presence will alert the kidnapper."

His voice came out harsh, but he was at the end of his rope with all of this. "You didn't even know they were here and had probably followed us for a while." He slapped a hand on the steering wheel. "Give me a break. We've built a bridge of trust. I did not throw you under the bus with my team and I won't, but you gotta back up and let me out of this corner. I'm doing my best to prove I'm still trustworthy. If I thought you were willing to meet my team and join efforts, I would have suggested that because we'd have more support. But you're so sure you can get in and out of the kidnapper's secure facility you won't consider it. Even knowing Angie and Clercville will be safe if I walked, I'm still in on our original terms."

Her face fell.

How could he hurt someone he'd just been loving only hours ago? He'd never experienced this powerful draw to a woman. Maybe it was love, but this proved he didn't deserve anyone.

He would not wreck her life.

Was she listening to him? Would she slow down and give him

a chance to stay with her on this mission?

He was sticking with her any way he could. He couldn't bring himself to let her go ahead alone.

She nibbled on her thumbnail, clinging to the top of the emotional fence she straddled.

Taking a moment to calm down, he gave one more shot at pushing her to choose a side. "I've been playing catch-up the entire time while trying to support you in an op where I'm running blind. My people have every reason to question my sanity. I have not tried to take control and I won't, but I need you to meet me part way for any of this to succeed." He drew another deep breath, telling himself this was not over. "If you can't do that and speak freely about what you get from your techie, then I'm no more help in this mission than a chair in that restaurant. I thought you were willing to do whatever it took to get Phoebe back because I am."

She covered her eyes with her hand, sitting there at a mental crossroad that had only one smart choice.

Her hand dropped. Her eyes glistened. "We continue together."

Relief spread through him, allowing him to breathe easy again.

She added, "Before you think all is okay again, let me be clear. We do this mission. I get Phoebe. You get your guy. We say goodbye."

He felt that jagged blade slash deep into his chest. They'd made no plans for after, but only because time hadn't allowed any conversation beyond rescuing two people.

Screw it. Finish the mission first.

Convince her to give him one minute when they were done ... if they both survived. He needed to tuck that hope away and let this chaos in his head go to keep his mind on the mission.

He cleared his throat. "Understood." If only that word didn't sound like an agreement to walk away.

CHAPTER 33

———

WHY DID HER HEART ACHE so much?

Hallene had never been a slave to her emotions, but she'd handed Sam her full trust.

Should she believe Sam when he said he never thought his team would just show up? The timing of him asking her about Angela and Clercville being safe then his team sticking a phone in the car had shattered her easy faith.

Sam started the engine.

Her phone made a little two-tone noise that had her heart jumping around. "Wait a minute. I need to read this and don't want to jockey connections if I end up having to call someone." She opened the phone to a text.

Midnight Ferret had sent:

Van stopped for 2 hrs. C snatching P at 21:00. Location attached.

Midnight must have been shaken by her informing him someone might know he was hacking Kovac's system, or he'd have sent a map.

The image attached was of a mocked-up news article about a butcher and included the word pound eight times in the text. Different numbers had been placed before each use of pound as if the weight had been in dispute.

Those numbers were latitude entered first and longitude listed second. She knew to take the second set.

Her hand shook. She looked up at Sam. "We have a location on the van."

"Hey, that's great news." He tried his best to sound happy, but she heard the sadness rolling under his words.

She gave voice to what he avoided saying. "But that doesn't

mean we'll find your high-value target."

He shrugged as if that was only a small bubble when it was so much bigger. "One thing at a time. Let's rescue Phoebe, then let me bring in my people to go after our guy. Fair enough?"

That was more than fair, but now she stood to get what she desperately wanted, and Sam might lose out. How quickly the table just turned. "I'll help you any way I can, Sam."

"I know you will, hon."

And he did, but she'd destroyed something important between them earlier. She'd been so panicked over losing this chance to save Phoebe that she'd lunged for her tight-fisted control and crushed his feelings in the process.

She'd never had someone like Sam because she had never let anyone close enough for her to experience true happiness. She had no idea how to nurture that kind of caring when falling back into her work came so much more naturally.

"Where to?" Sam asked, reaching to put the car in gear.

She punched the coordinates into her phone and studied the map. "Looks like the van is maybe parked at a resort. If it's in the parking lot, would that possibly mean W is inside the hotel?" She looked up at him.

"Doubtful, but let's start with getting to the van first. We'll have to scout the area once we find the van. After Kovac's failed first attempt, I'd expect him to send more armed backup this time. How long should it take us to get there?"

Her insides were having a boxing match with the tension between her and Sam, but she calculated time while punching in the coordinates for the distance. They'd eaten a late breakfast this morning then driven around for a bit, just staying in this area before deciding to grab a late lunch.

It was now close to four in the afternoon. "The drive takes a little over three hours if we don't hit a bad traffic jam. I'm thinking we need to get there early ahead of the 21:00 time mark."

"Agreed."

His calm acceptance battered her conscience. Now she'd drag Sam into another firefight. As if putting him in trouble with his team hadn't been bad enough?

Did she have to keep destroying his life? "Sam, maybe you shouldn't—"

He'd started backing up the vehicle again and stopped, putting the car into park. Worry ghosted over his face before he brought up a smile, a sad one, and moved his hand to her cheek. "I'm gonna be just fine when this is done. We'll get there early, find a place to observe, then you create a diversion while I get into the van."

He had a way of making everything sound reasonable. She knew none of this was reasonable or even safe, but she would not turn into the weak link for him at this point. "What would your team do?"

"The same thing they're going to do. Follow at a distance even I won't see and be available if things don't go the way we hope. I'm gonna tell you the truth because that's what I'd do in their shoes."

"I'm more than good with that." She had to lean on her trust of Sam again. If his people had a listening device in the car, they'd know exactly where she and Sam were headed.

That Sam had told her his team would follow gave her a bit of relief. If the situation became too risky, she'd give him the thumbs-up to call in these unknown operators.

He had only nodded, not made some joke about her agreeing, and squeezed her arm with reassurance.

Her heart whimpered. She'd lost something special. Sam was the one person who had become her sanctuary. She should have let her guard down all the way and brought him inside her world. He was the man she had fallen so hard for she would never be able to climb out of the emotional hole she'd dug for herself.

The man she had always wanted in her life, but never realized it until meeting Sam.

Once he was on the interstate again, she asked, "How bad is all this for you with your people? Tell me the truth, please."

Where he'd been agitated earlier while talking to someone on the phone, Sam now had a calm about him that worried her.

The kind of calm that meant he'd accepted what he had coming.

Keeping his eyes on the rearview mirror as much as the road

ahead, he explained, "I didn't try to find a way to contact my team after you picked me up. All of us follow orders without question. Without that, we can't trust each other in dangerous situations. Our team answers to the man who oversees all the teams. He's the one who will make any final decision on my place in his operations."

"Are you with Special Forces of the US military?"

"I was at one time. All of us have mixed military backgrounds. I'm now with a highly skilled group that, when authorized, protects national security for the US and other countries who are allied with the US. Sort of like Special Forces with no borders," he joked, but sounding too quiet. "Our teams are hand-picked, and this organization goes back many generations." He sent her a half-smile of apology. "That's all I feel comfortable saying about them, okay?"

"Sure."

Losing his place with an organization like that would be unforgivable.

She didn't deserve forgiveness. "I really am sorry for what I dragged you into, Sam." She could barely get the words out. Her throat hurt from squeezing regretful words past the pain.

His hand found hers and pulled her fingers to his lips. That small touch gave her encouragement, but she was a realist. None of this would end with a chance to see him again. She'd accept that if he survived and his team kept him.

That would be enough.

The hurt balling in her chest could be blamed on no one except her. Maybe if she'd come up with a better idea to convince him to partner with her instead of pushing him into it, this might have turned out differently.

She had no idea she'd end up trusting this man so much, but that first meeting in the basement should have clued her in.

If she had been willing to relinquish some control and lower her emotional walls, she might have ended up saving Phoebe and ... herself. She found the man she could love and may have destroyed his life in the process.

Her heart would never want another man.

After he kissed her fingers, he rubbed the back of her hand

with his thumb. "I don't regret being with you. I feel like I finally understand who I am. If I'm not meant to continue with my team, then I'm the one who made that decision. It's not on you. I could have pulled away and called them at any point."

In other words, he'd chosen her over his team.

Her shoulders drooped under lead weights of guilt. He'd kept his word the whole time. He'd gone above and beyond when he could have called in the cavalry he trusted.

She'd accused him of alerting his team as soon as he knew Angie and her town were safe. He hadn't.

Her fear had paralyzed her ability to think clearly. She'd been so scared to think what would happen to Phoebe if the Collector discovered that not just Hallene was coming for him, but also the black ops team from Venezuela he'd believed was dead.

The minute they found Phoebe, Hallene would have Sam call in his team so they could follow the Collector to hopefully find the senator and save both captives.

Like Sam said, one thing at a time.

Find Phoebe then call in his people.

"What does W stand for?" she asked, anything to get them back on even footing.

"No one knows. I promise you many searches to do with W have been performed. You didn't get a look at him before they took you to the basement?"

"No, and I had my back to the stairs immediately. Also, the lipstick camera that got your face ..." She paused to send him an apologetic glance, which he answered with a shrug. "... was not angled to reach the top of the stairs. It's just a good thing I understood enough Russian to figure out the place was going to explode. Cyclops was so stupid and clueless about the flashing green light."

"Cyclops?"

"I had to give him a name in my mind to make cursing him easier."

"He died too easily." Sam's eyes turned dark at the reminder of what that guard had been doing to her. "Knowing W is Russian is more than we've had before now."

"What do you think W has planned?"

Sounding more himself, Sam began sharing details of what had brought them to the mansion in South America. "Many special operations have focused on this elusive W. You said you believe Kovac is being pressured to do something for an upcoming event. That fits W's MO based on past events. To be honest, I don't think the Collector is still involved, especially at this point if he's delivered the kidnapped victims. Finding out he's been in the same location as W is new intel as well."

Sam paused to jockey their position and get out of a slow pack of cars. "W has been rumored to drop barrels of money on something he wants badly. The Collector grabbing the senator would make sense."

"What does W want with the senator?"

Sighing heavily, Sam sounded tired. "This senator has sworn to stop W. He's pushed money to the military in this country just to locate and take down W. We believe W's going to use the senator at his next terrorist attack this Saturday. Based on your information, it sounds like he's planning it somewhere near the northeastern coast for the meeting with Phoebe to be the night before a terrorist attack."

"Whoa, wait a minute." Hallene waved her hand trying to slow down what Sam was saying. "Terrorist? I don't understand. I thought you were just trying to extract a kidnapped victim."

"We are. Keeping the senator safe is our first mission, but the man who captured him has been behind five attacks in as many different countries. For the last five years, he has toyed with every military in the world by executing an attack on the last Saturday of August at ten in the morning local time. You recall what happened in Baghdad at the end of August last year?"

"Yes. It was horrible. Thirty-eight people were killed, including two children."

Nodding and deftly weaving the SUV through traffic, Sam said, "Hundreds more were wounded and maimed. We think he executed that attack as vengeance for a powerful man whose home was destroyed by a drone bomb. I can't give more details. It's classified and like following a chess game with pieces that are not visible until it's time to make a move."

Those were the monsters Sam hunted.

She dealt with monsters too, but on a different scale and in the civilian world. Hers weren't after international fame, just innocent children.

The silence brought her back to what they'd been discussing. "I didn't realize those annual attacks were related other than the media trying to show them as copycat acts."

"That's because we keep the details quiet just to avoid a real copycat causing even more harm and muddying our investigations. But this time, we were hoping to find the senator and maybe learn the identity of the man behind all this."

"You never said why the intelligence community knows him as W."

"Oh, there's a barely alive victim hung near every attack and photos taken in case the media doesn't see it before the big event. The body is stripped of clothes and a W is carved into the abdomen. That's why intelligence has named the perpetrator W."

No wonder Sam went along with her pushing him to join her. He was willing to put his life and his future on the line to find W.

Sam had stopped talking, but not because he was holding back. She'd come to understand that intense look meant he chewed on a thought.

"What are you thinking, Sam?"

"Not something specific. I'm just trying to make all these pieces fit. The senator. Phoebe. Kovac. The Collector. W. An arms dealer."

"What arms dealer?"

"A guy I knew as Esteban. He and I escaped an enemy camp then went our separate ways, but he'd told me how to find him in the future through a cryptic message in a Miami newspaper. I watched for three months until I found it. He had set up shop again in Venezuela, South America, but he only sold to those of us protecting sovereignty for the US and their allies."

She kept quiet as Sam made up his mind on what he'd say next.

"When we got a lead on the senator, we believed W was behind it. We had little time to plan. I suggested Esteban for our in-country arms supplier. I would never have doubted him. He had no family when I first knew him and said he avoided being close to people because of his line of work, but he must have had a change of heart during the last two years. The team who tortured and killed him left a picture of a woman and a small boy. The kid looked like Esteban. I'm not going to condemn him for trying to save a woman and his child, but the bottom line is that one is on me. They wanted our team, and the connection was someone I knew."

She wouldn't downplay what happened by saying it wasn't his fault. Sam would not see it any other way. "Why were they after your team?"

"See, that's a piece that doesn't make sense." He flipped his turn signal on, changing lanes and constantly watching his rearview mirror. "We moved so fast on that operation no one could have known. Someone had to be sitting on top of Esteban to know we'd been there. They left a note on him saying, *One down then the final delivery.* I keep turning that note over in my head and can't make sense of it, not in context of the senator's kidnapping."

She sat back thinking on all he'd said and turned the information over in her head since she'd had no personal connection to Sam, his team, or Esteban at that time. "What if the note wasn't about your team finding the senator?"

He scratched his scruffy chin again and stretched his shoulders. "I don't know what you mean. What other reason would they have had to come after my team?"

"You said that you and Esteban escaped a prison camp. Could Esteban have been a loose thread of some kind?"

No quick reply followed.

Sam was back in his intense mode of sorting through facts and information. He had a contemplative expression on his face and started speaking as if thinking out loud. "The camp we escaped was a drug-running operation in Libya. I ran into them by accident while trying to find a missing female journalist. Esteban had already been captured because they knew he sold arms to the US allies and wanted his contacts for weapons and clients. They tortured him. He was in bad shape when I showed up, but he hadn't given up one name. Not seeing how this could be connected to our team hitting that mansion."

She had to agree with Sam. That didn't sound connected.

The drive passed quickly because Sam kept her talking. She knew what he was doing by keeping her mind off worrying about how this would end. He wanted to save Phoebe, the senator, and protect the world. When he moved the conversation to what she did back in London, she told him story after story of families and the children her organization had rescued.

It surprised her to realize how she'd needed to share some of the heartbreaking missions with someone. Giving him a shrug, she said, "Basically, I hunt monsters too, but not like the deadly ones you track down."

"Don't discount the danger you face. Saving children is a righteous career decision," Sam said, sounding proud of her.

In a different time and place, they could have been so great together. She would have supported him any way she could, and he'd have done the same.

Life was one screwed-up goat rope some days. She'd picked up the term goat rope from two businessmen talking during her flight here. She was keeping it.

"Thank you, Sam." Many parents had hugged her when she returned children to loving families, but it wasn't always a happy ending. "I hate when I have to hand the recovered children over to family services."

He angled his head at her with his eyebrows drawn tight. "They didn't have the names of families for the kids?"

"That wasn't the problem. Some parents sold their children for drug money or just to turn a useless eater into a gain."

"Man. Guess I have no reason to complain."

She hadn't thought of his life compared to those children, but he'd managed to become an honorable man after a tough life. She searched for words to tell him so, but he spoke quickly as if to fill the void by changing the subject.

"We're getting close to the exit for the resort. Time to fuel up." He pulled into a huge automobile service area with a line of pumps longer than the building. She had to make a bathroom stop. "Where will you be when I come back?"

Pointing at parking spots near the road, he said, "Out there. I'm not pulling up into that madhouse. This would be a terrible choice for a hit but watch your back."

Just like that, she was hyper-aware of everyone around her, but the bathroom visit was fast and without incident. Sam was right. There were families everywhere hunting snacks and looking at toys. This would be a bad choice for a sniper.

That didn't give her a lot of comfort if a new one was on their trail.

Sam came up and put a hand on her lower back.

She smiled at him, hoping to lift his spirits that had taken a beating this morning, mostly her fault.

He stared over her head at the television she'd noticed in her peripheral vision on the way in. What caused his grim expression? She started to ask just as the cashier finished ringing up Hallene's snacks and bagged them.

She paid in cash while Sam grabbed the bag then led her to the door. "What were you looking at back there, Sam?"

"The news station talking about *the* senator."

Hallene hadn't thought about the senator as more than a captive until now or his family waiting for any word of him being found. "What does his family know?"

"Wife and kids are in a safe house under armed guard. They know he's been captured." He heaved a long sigh. "I think about them every day, knowing what it will be like if they get news we failed."

Hallene felt the weight of what Sam had been juggling the whole time with her. If W succeeded, that family would lose a husband and father, the country would lose a senator fighting deadly criminals, and an international conflict might erupt.

She'd only wanted to find Phoebe when this started.

CHAPTER 34

HALLENE HAD THOUGHT THE STORM would miss them, but clouds joined forces overhead, turning day to night as Sam drove them down a two-lane paved road to the resort. The four-star rated place sounded as if it offered everything but came up lacking on one point.

This dead-end location had only one way in and out.

Even she knew that was not desirable on an operation like this. Coop had said how he hated caves for the lack of a decent exit strategy.

She kept twisting the ring around her finger.

Sam reached over and took her hand, pulling her out of the torment spinning through her head. So many things could go wrong. They could fail to save Phoebe. Sam could die.

Sure, that sounded selfish when compared to losing a senator whose presence affected so many others beyond his own family, but she was feeling selfish. She wanted all her chicks tucked in close and safe.

"Get out of your head for a bit," Sam said gently.

Smiling, she draped her arm on the console. "Thanks. I'm fine. You need both hands in this wind."

He shrugged, handling the SUV with no trouble in a driving wind that bucked his side over and over. "It's not so bad. You said you and Phoebe weren't close. Is she expecting her dad to come in and save her?"

Hallene appreciated Sam talking about Phoebe with them so close to seeing her. "Sadly, I'm thinking she's feeling alone and abandoned. I'm not sure how much our mother has told Phoebe about what I do. My mother constantly tries to get us to connect. If not for seeing me in that bedroom on my first attempt, she would have no idea I was hunting for her. She probably thinks I'm dead and is hoping Kovac will pay a ransom. I doubt she knows money is not the currency for this deal."

A silence passed slowly.

Sam prodded, "What kind of girl is Phoebe?"

"She's not bad, just annoying sometimes. In fairness to her, I've kept my distance when I could. She's the product of a wealthy father who doesn't care and believes she and our mother are only financial burdens. She's close to our mother so I sometimes feel Phoebe sees me as a threat—the older daughter whom my mother admires." Hallene chuffed a sad laugh. "I've had a lot of time to think about all this. Phoebe and I have more in common than I realized when it came to fathers."

"That's messed up about Kovac." Sam shook his head.

"True. Our mother was very pretty before she got sick. She leaned too heavily on her looks to get by and never chose well when it came to men. My father was an investment broker, but in truth, he gambled. He came from old money. My grandmother would not feed her son's gambling addiction. When he got deep into trouble, his mother made him go into rehab in exchange for bailing him out of bad debts. He did that, then came out and acted normal for two weeks. Then with no warning, he withdrew large amounts of money and flew to Monaco where he spent a stupid amount of cash on an escort and gambling. Our mother had to live through the media pictures and videos, including the one of him smashing a Lamborghini into a church. Death mattered little to the media when they could run with a headline of his betrayal to my mother and grandmother."

"Man, what a piece of work. You didn't like him much, huh?"

"That's putting it mildly," Hallene admitted. "I had what I needed financially growing up, and my mother loved me, so I didn't struggle compared to so many others."

Sam's fingers wrapped around her arm and gave her a little squeeze. His way of saying he understood her life hadn't been a cakewalk either.

The wind shoved them again and he two-handed the steering wheel, always keeping everything under control.

"How'd your mom end up with Kovac?"

Having Sam interested so much in her life shouldn't surprise her. He was that person who wanted to know as much as he could, but he wasn't asking for any benefit of the mission.

Sharing some of the painful parts gave them less power over her and allowed her to breathe a little easier.

"My mom went into hiding for a year."

Sam gently interrupted. "How old were you then?"

Hallene rarely thought about that time. She had grown up quickly. "I was twelve when my father died. I told you I encouraged my mother to get back out of the house and find something that would make her happy." Hallene released a stream of air like a boiling tea kettle. "That's how she ended up with Kovac. I give her credit for not capitulating easily. She'd been burned the first time and did not make it easy for Kovac to woo her, which probably just motivated him to work harder. The thrill of the hunt and all that. When he'd beaten down her walls, he convinced her to marry him."

Sam slowed as sheets of rain blasted across the road, but he kept going. They had plenty of time to reach the resort. "Then Phoebe was born?" he prompted.

"Yep. My mother and Kovac lasted two years, during which I decided to live with my paternal grandmother. She was strict but fair. I learned a lot from her. I skipped my first year of college to stay with her when she got sick with terminal cancer. She passed right after I turned twenty and left me her fortune, which I had not expected. I knew my father had come from money, but ... not that much. She never allowed us to go hungry when he failed as a provider, but she kept a tight grip on her purse strings."

"Money hasn't affected you, has it?"

She hesitated to reply. "I'm no saint, Sam, but money has been the root of all bad things in my family, and now Phoebe's. As my grandmother was failing, she told me what I'd inherit and that she wanted me to spend it doing good for the world. That was a big responsibility. I always want to use the funds in a way my grandmother would have approved."

"Any grandmother would be damned proud of what you're doing, Hallene."

This man kept finding new ways to twist her heart in knots that only he would know how to unwind. "I've kept my fortune secret even from my mother. She doesn't make healthy choices when it comes to men and money. I'm pretty sure she found Kovac's wealth as attractive as him and believed she would have a partner to enjoy spending that on a fun life with. I will always take care of her, but she's better when she's earning money than sitting around trying to figure out how to spend it."

"Then Phoebe doesn't know about your fortune either, right?"

Hallene replied in a decisive, "No. Phoebe would have become my new best friend." It was laughable, but the sad truth. Hallene had come to learn she became far more attractive when a man realized she had to be financially independent to spend her time tracking down children.

Those same men immediately lost *her* interest.

Thinking back now, she might have been unfair grouping Phoebe in with people trying to get close to Hallene for her money. In truth, Hallene had never spent enough time with the teen to make that claim.

She felt the need to speak up for Phoebe since she wasn't here to defend herself. "I still regret having avoided Phoebe so much. If I had at least been friendly with her, she might not have been vulnerable to what happened. She might have listened to advice from a female with experience of growing up in a similar world. I might have gotten her to understand how dangerous this world can be."

"You don't know that for sure, Hallene. Some kids are well informed and still rush into trouble."

"I know, but I've been running so many things about her through my mind. I feel I may have judged her unfairly at times. I looked at Phoebe and saw her father. That's just wrong. I wouldn't want anyone to judge me based on *my* father."

"Of all people, I get that." Sam smirked.

Funny how they came from two different worlds with similarities at times. Just thinking about Sam's world reminded her of his team following them.

They should call his team now so there would be no chance of them losing track of Sam. What was the difference in calling them in now or later?

She could take one stress off him by doing a better job of meeting him halfway on all of this.

Maybe bringing in his team now would help Sam later when he had to face his superior.

Just thinking this through felt freeing. Sam had not been trying to change her but being with him was showing her the true meaning of being a partner.

No one person should hold all the control between two people.

Happy to do something for him, she said, "Sam, I think you should—"

Sam shouted, *"Hold on!"*

Bright lights blasted the inside of the SUV from behind.

He stomped the accelerator, but whoever was behind them caught up to their SUV and hit the back corner at an angle.

They went spinning on the wet road, blowing up a wall of water.

He handled the car like a pro, but as they spun across the road, their attacker hit them broadside.

Airbags exploded. Hers hit her in the face.

The SUV dropped off the road, tilted, and rolled. Her head hit the window.

She saw stars.

The world continued spinning.

"Hallene!" Sam kept shouting her name. His hand grabbed her shoulder, then fell away when they suddenly hit hard.

They should be stopped.

The car was on its side and moving.

Floating.

No. They were sinking.

CHAPTER 35

———

SAM BLINKED, TRYING TO CLEAR his vision. They'd hit the river. Fast moving current. He felt water coming in around his feet.

He punched his airbag to hurry the deflation. "*Hallene!*" Why hadn't she answered? There was still enough light from outside to see her.

She was slumped forward over the airbag.

"Talk to me, baby." He gently tugged on her shoulder.

"I'm ... I'm okay," she breathed out as she lifted her head. Blood ran from her nose. "We're in water."

"Got that. Don't move." He punched her bag and it flattened beneath his fist. Then he found her seat belt latch and released it while holding her upright with his arm. She was free.

He hit his seat belt release, but it wouldn't unsnap.

Why couldn't he be lucky twice?

Something pinged the roof. Shots hitting them.

The back window broke. That round must have burrowed into a seat.

He kept his voice calm, but nothing would slow his racing heart. "We gotta get out. They're shooting and will follow the car to confirm we're dead. Can you breathe through your nose?"

She wiped her nose, flinched, but said, "I can breathe." She reached around her legs and dragged her wet bag up to the seat. The car was half submerged. She pulled out a switchblade and cut him free.

"Thanks."

Bullets struck the water around them.

No way to get to the weapon Nitro had put in the vehicle. Sam pulled his gun from the console now loaded with ammo he'd found before they stopped for lunch. "Put this in your bag."

"We have to wait to get out of range," she warned, taking the gun to shove in her bag with the knife. She sat her bag on the airbag, deflating it more.

Sam wouldn't tell her they wouldn't be out of range soon if their attackers included a sniper. That wouldn't be an issue if they drowned. One problem at a time.

He took in the river they would have crossed if he'd made it over the bridge.

Bullets kept zinging around them, but the river was curving.

Water rushed around his knees and kept creeping up. He wished he'd left a window open, but he'd closed it to shut out road noise. He tried the window button. Not working, as he expected since the lights had shorted out.

She used the bottom of her shirt to wipe blood from under her nose and sounded congested when she spoke. "Have you escaped a sinking vehicle before?"

He admired her for staying calm, but her voice shook. "No, but I've spent a lot of time in water, and I know what to do to free us. I'm gonna climb over to your side to tilt the car more so it fills faster, then we'll exit on your side."

She didn't appear to have much faith in that suggestion, but she didn't argue. "This is probably a laminated window, which won't break easily, right?"

"Most likely. Have you got anything like a rescue hammer in that bag?"

"No. What about a gun?"

"Shooting that will blow out our eardrums."

"I meant will it break the window?"

He gave it a second before saying, "Never tried that. I don't want to risk not breaking the whole window at one time and flooding us too quickly." He could get out on his own.

Sending her out quickly would be a challenge but getting her out of here first was the escape plan.

Doing his best to sound confident so she would trust him to follow his instructions, he said, "We have to let the door completely submerge. Once that happens, the pressure inside and outside will have equalized so we can easily open the door to swim out. We have to grab a big lung full of air at the last second."

He'd caught himself before saying they *should* be able to do this. If it didn't work, failing to disclose everything was the least of his concerns.

Rain began coming down faster, slapping the still exposed roof so hard it was difficult to tell if any of the strikes were from bullets.

The SUV floated around a bend in the river. This was their chance.

"Ready, babe?"

A sign of this woman's strength came in her unhesitating answer. "Yes. Tell me what to do."

"Take your shoes off then just stay still and I'll work my way over." Shoes might hamper her ability to kick her way up to the surface.

She reached down and moved her legs then said, "Done." Water swirled around her breasts.

He was terrified of losing her. "Give me the bag."

"No."

"We were doing so well," he deadpanned. "I'll give it back as soon as we reach the surface."

She rolled her eyes at him. "I know you will, but you'll be busy making everything else work."

"I'm a strong swimmer. I can handle it." The sound of sloshing water stirred.

"Don't drown. Nothing in that bag is worth losing you." She handed the shoulder bag over.

He swallowed down his fear and hoped he was worthy of her faith. He slipped the long strap around his neck to let the bag hang in front of him and kicked off his shoes. Then he rolled over the console, pulling his legs through the water dragging at him and shoved his airbag aside. Twisting to get his right knee on the console for support, he stretched his arm past her and clamped the armrest on her door. He flailed his right hand in the water until he felt the driver seat and clutched it.

It was imperative for him to be as close as possible to open the door and push her out first.

Now he was face-to-face with her, inches apart. They had maybe thirty or forty seconds to wait. Her gray eyes were wide but filled with trust.

So different than when they'd first met in the basement of that mansion.

A thought hit him. "You can swim, right?"

"Are you serious?" Her eyebrows tucked together over the bridge of her nose. That pretty gaze narrowed with insult. "I may not have experience escaping sinking cars, but I *do* have basic abilities."

He grinned at her confidence. So damn hot.

Water climbed up to his neck.

"What is so funny, Sam?"

"You." He leaned in and kissed her quickly, just enough to get her mind off drowning. Her lips parted and met his, kissing him with the same determination she did everything else.

Hallene did nothing halfway.

Water splashed his chin. He said, "Get ready, babe. When I bump your left arm, take the deepest breath you've ever drawn in your life."

Her eyes blinked fast with renewed awareness. She looked around, but she gave him a quick nod as she pushed her body up to keep her mouth and nose above the water closing in on the ceiling.

His heart battered his chest.

He couldn't fuck this up. Couldn't lose this woman.

The second he went to draw his last breath, he bumped her arm and waited.

Nitro would be screaming at him to keep moving.

Not until Hallene drew in that deep breath.

She sucked air and her face disappeared into the water.

Sam inhaled, then shoved his knee on the console, reached for the door handle, and opened the door. He kicked it open, using his knee to hold him in place.

Hallene had moved to leave but not fast enough for him.

He grabbed her around the waist and pushed her out.

One of her kicking feet caught him high in the chest.

He spewed a blast of bubbles, losing some of his air, then

shoved out behind her but the damn bag got caught and held him up. He yanked but it would not come free with the car dragging it down. He ducked his head out from the strap, then shoved off hard to drive upward.

He hadn't told her to head toward the light, but she knew what she was doing.

Her silhouette blurred in the murky water.

Where was she?

He paddled his legs and dug in with deep strokes to pull himself up, thanking Angie for the summers at her place when she'd only had a three-bedroom house in Clerc's Cove.

He'd swam constantly.

Reaching the surface was taking more effort with the current. His lungs screamed for oxygen. Hold on.

He broke through the surface, gasping for air. On his first breath, he croaked, "*Hallene!*"

Spinning as he treaded water, he searched the dark smothering where any remnant of light touched. The rain-bloated river moved fast. "*Hallene!*"

The wind ripped his voice away.

He fought panic. He had to find her.

Lightning flashed. She bobbed upstream behind him.

He took deep breaths and kept yelling her name until he heard her.

"Stop yelling. People are hunting us."

Crazy man that he was, he found that funny.

He must have been pulled farther downstream as he'd paddled for the surface. He swam against the current. Stupid to do that when it drained a person's energy, but he had to remain in place and wait on her.

In another bright flash, he saw her floating wide of him and moving downstream quickly.

He lunged over and caught her arm before she could pass, pulling her to him. She'd have a bruise from his grip, but he was not losing her out here.

Her arms came around his shoulders while he moved his legs holding them in place so they could catch their breaths.

The storm began to let up.

That would help, but they still had to swim across a ferocious current to reach the other bank where the ground rose gradually from the river. The terrain on this side shot up a sharp hill, meaning the water over here was deeper with no place to get a foothold.

Bringing his gaze back to her, he asked, "Are you okay?"

"Yes. What about you?"

He soaked in the sound of caring in her voice. "I'm good. We have to reach the far shore. Ready to swim?"

She twisted, sized up the task of getting across the rapidly moving river, and said, "I may not get there as fast as you, but I *will* get there."

"You'll be there at the *same* time. We're going together."

She pulled her face back to him, her soaked hair hanging to her shoulders. "Let's do this."

He smiled and said, "I know you can swim, but I'm probably stronger against this current and it's testing me. Grab my shirt and hang on."

"I can take the bag."

"Lost it. The strap got caught on my way out. Sorry."

"I'm not so long as you are here. We'll figure out the rest."

That was so unlike the woman he'd met who had to know what was going to happen every minute to hold her control.

Even accepting that they had no chance for a relationship after this did nothing to lessen what she meant to him. He had never experienced the fear gripping him at the thought of losing her.

Was that love? In his mind, yes.

He'd feared losing his mother. Losing his sister had broken him.

Losing Hallene would destroy him completely. Game over.

He begged her, "Promise you won't let go of my shirt."

She stilled and said, "I won't let go and I'll paddle my feet, too."

As soon as her grip tugged on his shirt, he lunged forward and started digging in with one long stroke after another. Swimming against this current was brutal, especially with extra weight, but he would not stop.

He gave her a silent kudo for hanging on plus using her free arm to stroke the water in sync with him.

Smart woman. Tough woman.

He liked a fighter—someone who wouldn't quit.

Even with him being the more powerful swimmer of the two, the current demanded every bit of endurance he could muster to cross the river with her.

An arm's length from shore, his feet hit the bottom. He turned and cupped an arm around her waist to haul her with him when he pushed against the mud to reach the shore. Lowering her to the ground first, he dropped to his knees then fell onto his back, sucking air in fast gasps.

She wheezed just as much and tried to talk. "I swim ... every week ... but that was ... insane."

He breathed out, "That last fifteen feet was a test I don't want to repeat."

Her hand flopped onto his chest.

Smiling at her need for his touch, he gripped her fingers. Drawing in another deep breath, he said, "You were amazing. Not everyone trained for an escape like that remains calm, which is more important than being the top swimmer." He gave her hand a squeeze. "Thanks. Neither of us would have made it if you hadn't held up your end."

She made a pfft sound. "You would have reached the surface no matter what."

"Not without you there first," he declared.

She said nothing in reply but gave his hand a squeeze.

That had become their silent dialogue of love.

Now he just had to figure out how to keep them alive, but she had to be informed of what they were up against. "This is different than a single hired gun. This is a team contracted for the hit. They won't quit until they find us and there will be more than one vehicle full of them."

"I shouldn't have waited so long," she muttered.

"Waited for what?"

"Right before we went spinning and rolled off the road, I was saying to call your team."

He remembered her saying, "I think you should—" That she'd been willing to bring in his team before they reached the resort meant she trusted them because she trusted him.

"I'm sorry I've been bullheaded, Sam."

"Hey, I'm just glad you're ready to work with my people."

"It's a little late after we've lost our phones. We don't even have a gun."

He rolled over to face her. "No, but my team will find us. They're amazing. We just have to stay alive until they get to us."

Hallene grabbed his arms. "What about the meeting? I know I sound like a broken record—"

He placed a finger on her lips. "You aren't wrong. We might as well go and observe the meet. You up for hiking?"

"Wouldn't your team find us more quickly here?"

"Possibly, but so would the group trying to kill us." Sam pushed up to his feet and gave her a hand up.

She hugged him and his arms automatically wrapped her close. He whispered, "This will be okay, babe."

"In case it isn't, I want you to know how much everything you've done to get us here means to me." She lifted her head and kissed him. "How much you mean to me. I have never met anyone like you. I don't want you to die here. If you know where we can go to wait for your team, that's what we'll do."

Proud of her for being open to making a change in plans, he kissed her forehead and lifted her chin. "We're still on the mission to save Phoebe. We'll be careful and get any intel we can so when my team shows up, we can catch up to her that much quicker."

The faith she had in him filled her voice. "You lead the way. I will never forgive Kovac if anything happens to Phoebe. He's not trying to save anyone but himself."

"We'll worry about him later. Let's take one step at a time and try not to make any bad moves."

She put her hand on his cheek. "You always have my back, but I have yours, too."

He kissed her hand and hugged her, holding on a little extra because he had no idea how this would all play out. He did trust his team to find them if they survived, but he would not let anything happen to Hallene no matter what he had to do.

"You still got your super spy ring?" he asked.
She flipped her ring on and he laughed.

CHAPTER 36

———◆———

HALLENE WOULD NEVER COMPLAIN ABOUT dress shoes again after walking through a forest barefoot. She'd flinched when stepping on a rock and tree debris. Tough guy next to her could probably walk a mile on gravel and be fine.

She had hoped they'd find Phoebe by now just to rescue the terrified teen as quickly as possible. But now that she knew Phoebe was in the hands of a terrorist using her as insurance to make Kovac perform, Hallene shuddered at how little time Phoebe had left.

"This the resort?" Sam asked, drawing her head up.

She followed his gaze to a sprawling hotel built in the style of Cape Cod manors. "That's got to be it. Should we go in and try to call your team?"

"No."

"Why not?" She sounded crabby, but it was more that she was tired of feeling behind the curve yet again and ready to make something happen.

Sam's voice took on a consoling tone. "You're trained and a cool operator under stress, but now you aren't thinking like someone executing a mission. You want to fix not calling my team. Let that go. We'll be okay until we find them." He waited a breath and asked, "Do you still trust me?"

Those five words were leaning toward disappointment.

She'd disappointed him enough. "Of course, I trust you. I just fear seeing Phoebe for a moment and maybe never seeing her again."

"I understand that. I do, but we didn't drown, and even though my team hasn't found us yet, neither has that hit squad."

"You're right." She shoved wet hair off her face and searched the grounds beyond where they stood among trees where undergrowth had been cleared away. Ornate light fixtures on tall metal poles lined the drive to the main building offering enough ambient glow for them to finally see their way without her LED ring.

The silly thing had survived the river when her expensive phone would not have even if Sam had managed to drag that bag to the surface.

Lights inside the elegant structure and shining up at it from outside gave the hotel a magical image for someone arriving at night.

She hadn't trusted anyone to this level since being around Coop, but she'd been through more with Sam in the last few hours than she had ever experienced with Coop.

Maybe she was done listening to a dead guy and ready to embrace the very alive one at her side. If she had loved Coop, she would never have accepted friendship.

She knew without question she loved Sam and losing him would rip her heart into more pieces than she'd ever put back together again.

He suggested, "Let's make a wide arc around the front of the building and look for a parking lot. Somewhere that would make sense to meet."

"Okay." Hallene followed Sam as he angled them around the three-story structure. Wide steps led to an inviting veranda entrance where some guests sat outside with drinks to enjoy the rainy night by candlelight.

On each side, tiered gardens stepped down and spread out for a stunning view. "Why would anyone meet in a location that had only one way in and out, Sam?"

"Because they have an alternate escape route."

He'd figured that out before now.

"What would it be?"

"I don't know for sure without surveilling this location, but if I had to make a meet in a place like this, I would have another way to leave. I'd probably have an ATV plus a helicopter waiting nearby."

An all-terrain vehicle made perfect sense. She wished they had one.

Sam grabbed her hand and angled his stride more to the right. "This way."

She had never allowed anyone to lead her around. It had been so long since she'd dated, she couldn't remember anyone holding her hand. Probably because she would not let them. She'd seen her mother led around by powerful men as nothing more than arm candy.

Sam had not treated her as a tagalong woman. He respected her skills and ability. When he took her hand, his strong fingers reminded her she had a badass partner in this, one who would stick with her to the end.

She only hoped the end would be with him still alive.

Stepping carefully since her ring was now turned off, she kept an eye out for any threat coming at them.

No parking lot had appeared on the left side of the building or beyond the circular entrance where a private tour bus had parked to the side.

Sam kept moving like he knew exactly where he was going.

She had to train harder and learn to look at a situation the way he did. Train her people who hunted children so they would be sharper and safer. Thinking back on what Sam had said about a new threat chasing her, she whispered, "How did this hit squad find us?"

He didn't answer at first, warning her she would not like what he was thinking.

"Tell me, Sam. I need to understand what is happening."

"Remember when I was hesitant about the last intel drop you got?"

"Yes, I could tell you didn't trust my guy."

"Wrong. I believe you have an enviable resource, but I think we were right the first time when we believed Kovac had figured out that someone had hacked his system and was feeding you information. I believe Kovac set us up to be seen at the marina meet. Then when he lost his guy, Crusher, Kovac came up with a new plan."

"I was played twice." She shook her head, disgusted with

herself. "I never gave him that much credit."

"I don't think Kovac came up with this second scenario. Based on what you've told me and him sending that first lone shooter, I think W must be involved now. That hit squad fits W more than Kovac."

"I still got played and need to tell my techie to close up shop in case they can find him."

"Maybe, but I don't see W expending resources for so small a threat in his mind, but it still wouldn't hurt to give your tech guy a heads-up when the time comes."

All of this weighed her down. How many people had she put in danger? She'd never been one to quit or get beat down but trying to save Phoebe might be her greatest challenge.

If she failed, she'd live with the horror forever.

Sam stepped on something, hopped, then kept going. His voice remained low, a steady reassurance they were still safe. "Our team went to the arms dealer's place to start tracking down the leak. Didn't take long to figure out that was a dead end for us. Then we had to fight our way out. We were ambushed. Whoever sent killers to take out Esteban stayed to wait for us. That has to be W's people. I haven't figured out how W would know to send someone to stake out Esteban's place. But that group would have gone back to the mansion and discovered just the three bodies of the guards."

She could see that, but not exactly. "No one would have known I was there. They thought if they killed me that would be the end of anyone coming for Phoebe."

"If W is doing business with Kovac and discovered your identity, which is easier than finding mine if they had cameras in the main house, which they likely did, he would have contacted Kovac to threaten him over sending you."

"Kovac would deny it and tell them to do as they wished with me," she replied, looking at his point logically.

"That could mean Kovac was trying to kill you to please W then needed help when his assassin failed."

She'd been so careful, sure that she'd been written off as dead after that explosion in Venezuela.

Sam's thinking was right. Kovac knew nothing about her or

her life, but he'd have enough information to give a killer to find her. She used a second set of ID and credit cards she'd had Coop's team create for her a long time ago.

The fastest way for an assassin to track her down had to be by using facial recognition to capture her in the airport.

She sighed and stopped.

"What?"

"If Kovac sent that killer, would he know by now the guy had failed?"

"Sure. The killer would have had to contact Kovac to deliver confirmation. So Kovac is pissing in his pants about you still being alive."

She grinned. "That's a lovely thought."

"Come on, badass." He took her hand again and moved around the far end of the building where pieces of light flicked in and out between trees. Sam whispered close to her, "Think we've found a parking lot. May not be the spot, but we'll give it a look. We have to be silent the closer we get."

Hallene moved carefully to keep from making noise. Sam could be a shadow with as quietly as he navigated unfamiliar grounds in the dark.

They covered another hundred feet and reached the edge of the parking lot. It was large enough for a couple hundred cars plus a row of long lanes for tour buses. Most vehicles had been parked neatly in rows starting nearest the resort building, meaning valets likely handled the parking.

Probably no one coming or going this late at night. Her watch was not working. Evidently not waterproof. She tugged Sam's neck close to her lips. "Did your watch survive? How much time is left?"

Sam turned his head and barely whispered, "A little over fifteen minutes until the meet. I can see no other place for it to happen."

Still speaking softer than the forest noises, she pecked a kiss on his cheek and said, "I understand. Let's hope this is it."

"I'll let you know when we're five minutes out, then four, and so on."

"Okay." She sat on her knees.

He eased down close to her but clearly with enough room to move if they were attacked.

When Sam's finger tapped five times on her arm, she tensed for a moment and took a breath to loosen up.

Four-finger tap.

No vehicle had arrived.

Three-finger tap.

Lights bounced through the trees on the far side of the parking lot, heading toward the empty spots.

An electric ATV making little noise emerged with two people. One was Phoebe with her mouth covered.

Tears burned Hallene's eyes. Her heart thumped wildly at seeing Phoebe.

Sam's fingers curled around Hallene's arm as if worried he'd have to restrain her. She'd be lying if she tried to convince anyone she didn't want to run out there and kick the driver's butt.

She could.

A gun would stop her.

The ATV driver didn't look around. Phoebe did with terror-filled eyes, searching for anyone to save her. Poor kid.

Hallene turned to Sam who glanced at her with a light shrug. He had no idea why someone would be late for this meeting either.

Five minutes passed slowly.

Every second pushed Hallene's heart rate faster.

The ATV driver moved his hands on the steering wheel then the vehicle made a slow circle.

"No." Hallene squeezed that out. "*Please.*"

Sam held her firm. "Shh. We can't. He'll be armed."

Hallene had endured losses in her life but this one would gut her if she never saw Phoebe again. In a low voice out of the side of her mouth as she watched the parking lot, she asked, "What now, Sam?"

He made a grunting sound and his hand fell away.

She turned in time to catch a fist across her jaw and blacked out.

CHAPTER 37

KOVAC HAD BEEN SO NERVOUS since his last conversation with W, he'd stayed in his office waiting on word of Hallene's death.

Had the text messages on his computer reached whatever hacker that bitch had used to get inside his computer? He felt violated by someone not worth wiping his feet on.

His assistant buzzed him. W had used her phone to call Kovac the last time. For that reason alone, he replied to her promptly whenever she contacted him.

"Yes?"

"A package for you has arrived, Sir, and you are the only one who can sign for it. I tried, but—"

"Not a problem. I'll be right out." He hurried to the door and paused to smooth his hair. He would not appear as some scared rabbit.

Stepping out of his office, the first thing he noticed was how the delivery guy was not some Joe waiting to get a signature and leave.

This one had a bulge under his loose uniform shirt.

Kovac smiled and signed quickly, accepting a box no larger than the one a custom set of sunglasses had arrived in weeks ago.

When the delivery guy didn't scan the label, Kovac's assistant said, "Don't you need to—"

The man's eyes darkened.

Kovac quickly said, "It's fine. Thank you."

When the guard left, Kovac hurried back into his office and ripped the package open to find a nondescript black mobile phone. He'd just lifted it out of the box when it rang. "Kovac."

"This is last check. You are certain all is ready, yes?"

Kovac had requested updates on his ship every thirty minutes until it had stopped three hundred miles off the US coast. He'd warned the ship's captain to alert him if anything like a typhoon came up. Otherwise, stay put.

"Yes," Kovac replied.

"You sound confident."

"I am. There is no way I'd let you down."

W said, "I require one more thing from you."

Hesitating only because he did not want to commit to a job that he wasn't absolutely sure he could perform, Kovac said, "Yes?"

"You are hesitant. Is there problem?"

"Not if I have enough time left to deliver, none at all."

"Time is of no worry. I intend to keep Phoebe."

Kovac wouldn't care if not for having a loose end floating around that could strangle him. "You agreed to return her if I met my commitments. I have."

"I will not use her to point finger at you this time but keep her for future motivation. I find her interesting."

Feeling relieved, Kovac waved a hand W couldn't see, he hoped. "She's yours with my blessings. I intend to be your best supplier."

W allowed silence to build before he said, "As comforting as that might sound to others, I am only one who can make such a determination, which is based upon performance."

Kovac cursed himself for becoming comfortable too quickly. "I understand, Sir. Just wanted you to know I'm in all the way."

"Once this project is successful, I will contact you to confirm money has been sent."

Excitement sparked in Kovac. He couldn't wait. Phoebe would be reported as a runaway and he wouldn't have to give up his lucrative operation just yet.

Nothing happening Saturday would tie to him.

CHAPTER 38

S AM CAME TO WITH PAIN shooting through his skull. They'd hit him with something hard like the butt of a gun. He blinked his eyes and shook off the fog clouding his brain.

He was in a room with fifteen-foot ceilings and four six-foot-tall windows spaced out around the top on one side. The curved walls were built of radial bricks against a metal structure.

Still dark outside the windows. A red light glowed over the room. He rasped out, "Hallene?"

"She's not awake yet."

He turned quickly at the British accent and regretted the movement. "Shit."

When his eyes cleared again, he saw Hallene lying on the floor with her head in the lap of a teenage girl with pink and blond hair sticking out in corkscrew curls. No makeup, but mascara had run from the corner of her eyes, probably from crying. She had dirty tan pants that stopped at the knees. One side had a tie and the other had been ripped. Her black short-sleeved top hit her short of her bellybutton. Her nails had been painted black at one time but were chewed into the quick.

Phoebe.

The girl scowled at him. "Wot'd you think bringin' 'er 'ere? She tried to get to me once in some mansion. I was gobsmacked to see 'er. Then that sod 'urt 'er. Thought she'd died. Now you get 'er captured."

Sam pushed himself into a sitting position and turned to lean against a wall with his knees bent. "I'm Sam. You must be Phoebe."

"Yeh. Still don't know wot's goin' on."

"Hallene clearly made it out of the place in South America

where she found you then came to get me to help her in a second attempt." No reason to mention how Hallene had convinced him to join her.

"Why you?"

"Just lucky I guess." He tried to smile.

Phoebe was not impressed. She continued to drill holes through him with angry eyes similar to the shape of Hallene's.

Sam thought about how much to tell her, but the girl was up to her neck in a mess that was not of her own doing. "I was with a team inserting into the mansion where you were held. I—"

"Why?"

Just his luck to get a teenager who questioned every word. Come to think of it, his sister had been like that as a teen.

"We are hunting a different kidnapped person." Damn, he might get usable intel from this girl. "Did you see a man who has also been captured?"

"No. They've kept me alone in a bedroom everywhere I've been moved to before 'ere. Alone except for the creep guardin' me in that mansion. That's who smacked Hallene when she found me." She looked down at Hallene and brushed hair behind her ear. Her harsh tone softened. "Soon as I realized was me 'alf-sister walkin' into me bedroom, I tried to warn 'er but ..." She sniffled. "The buggah knocked 'er out and dragged 'er away. I knew if she died, I would too. I lost it and threw a wobbly. They taped me mouth shut to plug me screams."

Hallene had made it sound as if she and Phoebe were estranged, but maybe Phoebe didn't feel that way. Or maybe realizing her half-sister had tried to rescue her softened Phoebe's side of the relationship. Being a teenager, she probably kept her feelings to herself, but seeing Hallene back again to find her might have touched a place no one else had been able to reach.

Sam said, "When I found Hallene in the basement of that mansion, everyone was gone except her and three guards. My team would have rescued you had we found you there."

Phoebe gave him a thousand-yard stare. "Wot were the bloody guards doin' to Hallene?"

He didn't want to freak Phoebe out more, but he also didn't want her to not trust him because of lying to her. He needed her to listen to him for any hope of escaping. "A guard was torturing her when I walked in."

Phoebe's face crumpled. A tear slid down her cheek.

Sam quickly added, "But I freed her before he could do more."

The girl sniffled and swallowed. "Wot about the bloody fucker who 'urt 'er?"

"He's dead."

She nodded. "Yeh."

Sam could understand that blood-thirsty feeling after what Phoebe had been through. He felt she needed to appreciate her half-sister's skills. "To be honest, Hallene had neutralized him before I reached her. She's one heck of a badass."

Surprise lit Phoebe's face.

She didn't know much about Hallene, huh?

He didn't know why he felt the need to help those two be closer when he'd never figured out how to bond with his own sister, but he didn't want Hallene to ever regret missed opportunities the way he had.

Said badass moaned and moved her head.

Phoebe murmured, "Hallene? You awake?"

Mumbling something that made no sense, Hallene lifted her hand to her cheek where a bruise was forming.

Sam felt a renewed blood-thirsty lusting seeing Hallene hurt.

Eyes blinking, Hallene looked up at Phoebe. "*We found you!*"

The thrill in her voice made Phoebe happy. She smiled through tears. "You are one determined bird."

"Sam?" Hallene called out.

"Here." He jumped up and moved closer to Phoebe, hoping the girl now realized he was not the enemy. He and Phoebe helped Hallene sit up.

"Got any water in here?" he asked Phoebe.

"Yeh." Phoebe navigated the room lit only by a red light and bent over to lift a plastic jug of water from next to the door. The door had a six-inch-tall slot in the bottom and was half as wide as the door, probably for sliding food through.

She hurried back with the water.

Sam slid around behind Hallene with her back against his chest. Phoebe helped Hallene hold the jug as she drank. Then

Phoebe handed it to Sam to take a slug before she put it aside.

"I'm doing better," Hallene said, moving a hand to her face. "I can sit up on my own. I want to see you."

Sam reluctantly moved to where he could also see the two of them.

Phoebe sat with crossed legs, shifting her gaze to Sam then back to Hallene. "I'm chuffed to see you, but now *you're* caught."

Hallene seemed unsure of how to respond. Her throat moved with a hard swallow. "Sam and I are here to get you out of this place. I won't let anyone hurt you again."

Eyes bulging with tears, Phoebe nodded. She gulped down a swallow and sobbed, "I'm sorry."

Hallene said, "You didn't do this, Phoebe. There are bad people in this world, and you just got caught in their web."

Sam let them talk. This was not the Phoebe that Hallene had told him about and expected to see again. The teen had been through a horrific situation to this point and still had no promise of being freed.

When that happened to anyone who didn't function in his world, it often broke them. Phoebe wasn't broken yet, but she had long forgotten whatever trivial things had been important to her before being captured.

She wanted to feel hope she would escape and for someone to care about her.

"Yeh," said Phoebe, as she sniffled and coughed, "but you told me to be careful to not trust any blokes." Phoebe looked down at hands she twisted and clenched. "I think one of 'em set me up."

"What do you mean?" Hallene asked, hands fisted. That one was back in badass mode and ready to kick some idiot's butt.

"'E was a 'ottie and talkin' all nice. I'd never seen 'im before and ... I was crushin' on 'im. Thought 'e was so much nicer than the other blokes." She snorted out a derogative sound and wiped her nose with the back of her hand. Looking up with regret bleeding from her eyes, Phoebe explained, "The place was packed. Asked me to go somewhere to eat with 'im. Like an idiot, I said sure. Told me 'is car was parked way back in the lot and to wait for 'im by the side exit."

"Oh, Phoebe."

Tears spilled again. Phoebe took a minute to pull herself together. "I stepped out in the dark and someone grabbed me then shoved a stinkin' rag over me nose and mouth."

Hallene had been holding herself erect, the distant half-sister. But when Phoebe covered her face and began crying in earnest, Hallene shot a glance at Sam then scooted over to pull Phoebe into her arms.

She rubbed Phoebe's back. "It wasn't your fault. I made mistakes at your age, too."

Phoebe mumbled in a watery voice, "But you didn't get kidnapped."

Sam didn't say anything, but Phoebe did have a point. He lifted the bottom of his Hawaiian design shirt and ripped off a swatch of cloth he tossed to Hallene.

She sent him a smile of thanks.

When the emotional storm passed, Hallene gave Phoebe the cloth to clean her face.

"Thanks." Phoebe wiped her eyes and nose, then folded up the cloth and shoved it into the front pocket of her jeans.

That simple action showed how she'd lost everything in this kidnapping and would not let go of even a rag.

Hallene had a thoughtful expression. "Maybe now you and I can communicate better to keep you safe in the future, Phoebe."

"Keep you safe, too, yeh?" Phoebe's gaze drifted to Sam and then to Hallene. "Who's this bloke?"

"I told you," Sam pointed out, annoyed at being called a bloke like the ones who kidnapped her.

"You gave me a name and 'ow you met Hallene, but not *who* you are."

Sending him a frown, Hallene said, "You told her about the mansion basement?"

"I had to tell her how—"

"She doesn't need to be terrorized any more, Sam."

"For the love of ... I didn't describe it. Just told her what happened to you after they dragged you away. She wanted to know how you escaped."

"Let's avoid the gritty details, okay?"

How could Hallene be annoyed at him? He sent her a look he

hoped asked that specific question.

Phoebe started laughing, which broke the staring contest between Sam and Hallene.

"What's so funny, Phoebe?" Hallene looked down at her with tenderness.

"Never seen you with a bloke. You two sound like you been knockin' 'ips."

"Phoebe!" Hallene sighed then said, "Sam was in Special Forces and trained for dangerous operations. I have skills I gained while hunting missing children. He's been a godsend in finding you."

"Wot skills?" Phoebe asked, seriously interested in Hallene's every word now. "Mum said you 'elp people with their kids."

"Tell her, Hallene," Sam pressed before Hallene's modesty sugarcoated what she really did.

Sighing in his direction, she clearly gave his words consideration and nodded. "I started an organization eight years back, which hunts for missing children of all ages, but we seem to search more often for the young ones. I trained with an elite operative because it was only me at first. I have a much larger staff of people in the field now. I also have intel connections, which is how I found you the first time."

Phoebe's lips parted. Her eyes rounded in surprise, but it was her softly spoken, "Wow," that captured Sam's heart. In that one word, he heard admiration for Hallene that would be a big block in building their new relationship.

Being the kind woman Hallene was, she would remain humble and use this opening to close the distance between them.

Sam just had to get them both out of here first.

"Was Sam the one who trained you? Thought you two met at the mansion." Phoebe frowned. "Wot's the deal with you two?"

"Oh, no," Hallene replied. "It was another person. Sam and I joined forces to save you and someone his people are hunting. That's all."

Why did that hurt his heart?

Was that all they were?

Did he have any right to expect more?

"Keep tellin' yourself that," Phoebe said, returning to the

mouthy teenager Hallene had alluded to when describing her.

"Let's talk about how to get out of here," Hallene suggested.

Phoebe's face fell. "There's a guard outside somewhere nearby."

"What can you tell us about this building?" Sam asked.

"Looks like a smokestack from outside and someone converted the inside for an office or place to live." Phoebe lifted a shoulder.

"How high up do you think we are?" Sam wanted her to say fifteen feet or less.

"I climbed four levels of stairs. Maybe sixty feet off the ground."

Sam's hope crashed. At sixty feet, they'd need a rope even if he could reach the windows inside this room.

Hallene didn't look any more encouraged than him and switched topics. "Phoebe, did you see an older man who was also captured?"

Phoebe lifted her chin in Sam's direction. "'E asked me about that, too. No. They gagged me and put a sack over me 'ead before I was moved. Another bloke could 'ave been around, but I couldn't tell."

Sam suggested, "They're probably holding that captive in a different place." He asked Phoebe, "Is there anything you can tell us about this bunch, the man in charge, maybe any discussion you might have heard?"

The girl finally realized she had value in this situation. She could share what she'd learned about the group. She shifted to sit taller. "There's a big guy wot runs everythin'. That one 'as an accent."

"Russian sounding?" Hallene asked.

"Yeh, like that. I've seen up to five guards, but I don't think they're all 'ere now. One brought me into the tower and tossed me in this room."

Sam rubbed his jaw, which rasped with the sound of his beard coming in. "If we could trick the guard to come in here, we might be able to escape."

"Mebbe," Phoebe allowed. "But when they brought in you two, a guard further up the food chain ordered the one stayin' 'ere to not come back in this room even if it caught fire."

Sam got up to pace. He had to think.

"Why 'asn't me dad paid the ransom money yet?" The longing in Phoebe's voice hurt Sam. He could only imagine what it did to Hallene.

Would she tell Phoebe the truth?

"He's not paying a ransom but doing a job for the big guy you mentioned." While Phoebe chewed on that, Hallene asked, "Did you hear about whatever this group is planning? Any details."

"Not exactly. I 'eard the Russian say everythin' 'ad to be ready by Saturday mornin'." She sounded small when she asked, "Saturday is ... tomorrow, yeh?"

Hugging an arm around Phoebe, Hallene said, "Yes."

Continuing to walk around the room where everything had a red cast, Sam asked, "Did anyone say what would happen at that point?"

"No, but the Russian did say they were movin' me out of 'ere at daylight." She described how they'd moved her from place to place and she had sensed the time between each stop getting shorter.

Damn. That narrowed the time for an escape. He looked at his watch. Almost three in the morning. He and Hallene had been out for a while.

He scanned the room and Hallene.

How could he get a signal out to his team? There was no way he'd reach any of the windows on each side of the room. His team had to be in the area. They likely had a tracking device on the vehicle, which Sam hadn't mentioned to avoid arguing with Hallene.

Good news? She'd been willing to call his team before they went into the river.

Nitro would have sent everyone to search the resort.

Had they seen Sam and Hallene being captured or at least the ATV with Phoebe?

Even so, this place was like a fortress where the guard could hold them off on his own so long as he had ammo. Nitro wouldn't risk hitting the entrance with a hand grenade or C4 without knowing where Sam, Hallene, and the captives were.

He looked at the windows again, glancing to his left then his right.

It was dark enough in here for a light to reach that glass. He swung around. "Hallene, is your ring still working?"

She gave him a confused look. "It should be." She fingered her ring. It came on then went off.

"Whoa," Phoebe breathed out. "I wondered why you always wore that ring. Thought it was from a boyfriend."

Standing, Hallene glanced at Sam as she said, "A male friend had it made for me, but he was *not* someone I dated."

Now that Sam knew more about Hallene and her friendship with the MI6 operator, he had nothing but admiration for everything she'd been taught. He lifted his eyebrows at her then winked.

If it wasn't so red in here, he'd probably see a blush in her cute cheeks.

Phoebe began to watch her half-sister with respect.

"Here." Hallene handed her ring to him. "Do you have a plan?"

"More like an idea at this point. I'm hoping my team has reached this area to search. If so, they'll notice the light. He asked Phoebe, "Any chance you know which way the sun rises and sets here?"

Pointing at a high window to the right of Sam, she said, "Was dark over there when I got 'ere but some light in the windows behind me."

"Excellent." He caught her surprised smile at his compliment and aimed the LED for the window he designated as east, turning it off and on in a series of Morse Code flashes.

"How will they know to watch that window?" Hallene asked.

"I'm doing this in the window facing east then also in the one facing west. We're always brainstorming different scenarios for escaping somewhere and for finding a captured team member. The rule is that when hunting someone at night in an urban area, we pick those windows if more than one faces a different way." He flipped around, sending the same message to the west-facing windows.

After a pause, he repeated the process.

Hallene followed his head turns. "Is it Morse Code?"

Sam answered, "Yes. I'm keeping it short. SOS and the number one."

"One what?"

"One guard, but they won't blow the door without knowing where we are and if any other captives are at risk."

After repeating the message five times, something hit the west-facing window. Sam stopped and watched.

A light flashed from outside the window.

Hell, yeah. He grinned. "That's my people."

"Was that light a drone?" Phoebe asked, sounding surprised at what was happening.

"Yep. They're letting me know they found me."

His team would rescue them, which meant Phoebe and Hallene would be safe. That was enough for him in the face of potentially no one leaving here alive.

"How long?" Hallene whispered.

"Can't say. It could be twenty minutes at the soonest or an hour or two. I don't know what they're going to do and how difficult getting to us will be."

Noises outside the door caused Phoebe to jump up and run to Hallene who pushed the girl behind her.

Sam stepped in front of both females.

That rescue might come too late.

CHAPTER 39

HALLENE STEPPED UP BESIDE SAM, glaring at him for standing in front of her. He knew she could hold her own.

He pecked her cheek. "Old habits die hard, plus I'm gonna kill the next one that hurts you so I'm technically saving a life even if it is a worthless one."

Phoebe whispered, "Don't argue. I like 'is logic when it means no one is goin' to kill us."

Twisting to face Phoebe, Hallene gave her a sincere vow in a soft voice. "We will both stand between you and them. Sam's got a team hunting us and we now know they found us and are coming soon."

Hope had never looked as endearing as when it filled Phoebe's face.

Hallene just needed to stop Sam from going up against men with weapons. He stood with his feet shoulder width apart and his arms crossed, not the least bit concerned.

The voices got louder as if approaching.

Hallene stilled. She hissed in Sam's direction, "The Russian is out there."

Sam cut a look her way. "What's he saying?"

"He's giving orders to pack up here in an hour. Will that be enough time?" She didn't have to spell it out for Sam that she was talking about his team showing up.

"Maybe."

The door swung open fast with two AK-47s pointing inside. "*Raise hands!*"

Sam lifted his as did Hallene. Phoebe tucked herself even tighter behind Hallene.

"Where is girl?" one guard ordered in a guttural Russian accent.

"Behind me," Hallene replied in an even tone.

The guard demanded, "Tell her move so I can see."

Hallene said, "Step up next to me, Phoebe. It'll be okay."

When the girl moved between her and Sam, she was shaking worse than a leaf in a hurricane.

Both guards entered, keeping their AKs pointed at Hallene and Sam. But either weapon could sweep the room and mow all three of them down.

Then the boss walked in.

Sam cursed.

Hallene looked between him and the Russian. "What?"

Instead of answering her directly, Sam lifted his voice. "Hello, Senator Turner, or should I call you W?"

Blood rushed from her face.

W stepped forward while still flanked by his guards on each side. He lost his Russian accent, speaking perfect English with no accent. "What a shame for you to survive South America and escape being killed at Esteban's, Leclair. I would say you are part cat with nine lives, but this one shall be your last."

"If that's the case, answer a dying man's wish."

"What, Leclair?"

Hallene's heart hit her feet. This man knew exactly who Sam was.

"Why did you send a team after Esteban? Were you after me or my team?"

W brushed at his suit as if the air carried dirt. "There is quite a price on your head. On Esteban's too, but you were the one reported as shooting the leader of the Libyan drug-smuggling group."

Sam seemed seriously confused. "You're telling me a drug-running bunch has the kind of money to have us tracked down?"

That amused W. He laughed, a wicked sound. "That would be absurd. You killed the only son of the top bomb maker in our world. S'abe offered his newest design in exchange for the person who brought him evidence of your deaths. He offered a bonus for your head alone." His mean gaze moved to Hallene.

"Thank you for helping me connect the last dots to find him."

Hallene was going to be sick.

She'd put Sam in the crosshairs of this maniac.

"As much as I would enjoy more conversation, I need Phoebe. Her association with her father is now of value."

Phoebe started whimpering.

Sam said, "You must have better intel than to expect a child to fill in the blanks for you."

Hallene loved Sam for what he was doing to protect Phoebe, but she could see in W's face that his words had little effect.

She did love Sam.

She would protect him to live and fight another day.

W said, "You misunderstand me. I don't need intel. Her father has caused me undo stress. He will pay a price by being linked to my operation."

"No, please, no." Phoebe crushed her body against Hallene.

"*Enough!*" Hallene ordered.

Everyone went silent. W studied her as he would an odd insect. "You clearly do not value your life, Hallene."

She couldn't look at Sam. "You want someone who will be an unquestioned tie to Kovac? I'm your girl."

"Don't do this, Hallene," Sam pleaded in a heartbroken voice.

She finally turned to him with all the love she felt in her heart for him. "It's me or Phoebe. I spoke to Kovac twice in the past week. That is the simplest way to link him to W's plan."

Sam tried to speak.

She shook her head, begging him to not say a word.

What could he say? They would not take him because they had an equally disgusting plan for him, but she was betting on his team to save Sam and Phoebe if she could buy them time.

Betting her life on it.

She fought back tears. She'd just found Sam. None of this was fair. "Protect her for me, Sam."

He struggled to breathe. "I'll find you."

She smiled, unable to say another word.

W sighed loudly. "Very touching, but you have convinced me you will be a suitable connection. I had not decided how to pay you back for escaping the explosion. This will work perfectly.

Then I'll find something fun for little Phoebe."

Phoebe's body shook harder as she clutched Hallene. "I don't want you to go either. This is awful."

"Let's go, Hallene. I am a busy man."

"One moment, *please*, then I will come quietly," she implored him.

"When did people start thinking I was a generous person or one who negotiated?" He waved her off. "Go ahead. I don't want to hear any whining once we leave."

W began speaking to one of his guards, but she could not waste a second to find out what he was saying. She turned to Phoebe and hugged her. She whispered in the girl's ear, "Trust Sam and do as he says. He has a team coming and will get you out of here."

"Wot about you?" Phoebe blubbered.

"We have a plan," Hallene lied, trying to leave this child with as much hope as she could. Phoebe could mourn her when she was free and far away from here.

Nodding her head, Phoebe said in a broken voice, "Okay, I can do this. Be careful ... Sis."

That word clutched Hallene's heart in a tight fist. She held Phoebe close one last time and swallowed back her tears. "I will, *Sis*."

When she turned for the door, Sam pulled her to him and kissed her. "I love you more than life. Do whatever it takes to stay alive. I *will* find you."

Hallene laid her fingers over Sam's hand on her arm. Pain lashed her face. "I love you too and trust only you to keep her safe. Let me go."

Unable to watch the agony in his face any longer, Hallene turned to go.

A guard grabbed her.

She yanked her arm from his grasp and snarled, "I said I would come willingly."

"Then do so," W ordered, no longer sounding amused.

Following W, she glanced back before the door closed. Sam and Phoebe had matching grim expressions.

CHAPTER 40

———

LET ME GO.
Those three words had broken Sam. They were the last words his mother had said as she died in his arms.

As Hallene had walked out with W, his heart tried to crawl out of his chest and cling to her ankle.

How was Sam going to function with his heart shattered? He had to get out of here. Scaling Mount Everest with one hand tied behind his back would be more realistic than climbing the wall to the windows.

Where was W taking Hallene?

He listened as all the footsteps trailed away.

Phoebe hiccupped between sniffles. "She told me."

He realized he still had someone else to protect. He lowered his voice. "Talk softly so they won't hear us. She told you what?"

Pulling out the colorful scrap of material, Phoebe dabbed at her eyes before putting it back. She stood a little taller and dropped her voice to conspiratorial level. "Hallene said you 'ave a team comin' to save us then you two 'ad a plan to save 'er."

Of course, Hallene would say that, so this child did not live with the guilt of Hallene taking her place.

Sam would kill for that to be the truth, but he didn't know for sure when his team would insert into this building or if their rescue would be successful.

Anything could go wrong.

Just like it had a minute ago with Hallene walking out of here.

Phoebe waited patiently for him to reinforce her belief that Hallene would live.

"She's right," Sam said, backing up Hallene's lie. "But I'm going to need your help."

"Mine? What can I do? I'm no Hallene." Her moment of confidence fell apart.

He gently clutched her arm and leaned down until he had her full attention. He needed her strong and ready. "You don't have to be anyone but yourself. Hallene is her own person, and you'll never have a better role model than her. I won't let anyone harm you, but it will take both of us to save her."

Fear banked Phoebe's gaze, but she nodded fervently. "Yeh." Then she took a deep breath and seemed to stand a little taller as resolve crossed her face. "I'm ready."

"Good girl."

"Wot do we do first?"

"My team should be here soon. Once we get out of here, I have a plan." He could lie with the best of them.

"Wot is it?"

Of course, she asked that.

Something tapped the window. He looked up at the window where the drone had flashed him.

Sam caught Phoebe by the arm. "Let's move over to this side."

"Why?" She followed Sam's gaze to the window. "Wot's goin' on?"

"I'm not sure yet, but if that window breaks, I don't want you close to it." He put her as far from the window as he could and placed himself in front of her.

The sound of a glass cutter was followed by a circular line in the glass two feet in diameter. With a pluck sound, that section of glass pulled out and probably fell to the ground.

Black boots entered, followed by black leather pants, which would protect his legs against the glass edge, and a matching long-sleeved shirt.

Phoebe asked, "Who is it?"

"The freakin' cavalry." He walked over as his team member used a rope to walk his way down the wall.

Rushing up beside him, Phoebe said, "You know 'im?"

"Yep, that's Angel the Magnificent, master of impossible stunts."

Turning and taking a bow, Angel said, "At your service." He pulled his mask down but left his NVG monocular in place.

"'Ow'd you get to that bloody window?" Phoebe asked, completely awed by Angel.

Sam saved everyone time by saying, "He rarely gives up his secrets, sort of like magicians." Sam extended his hand, which Angel shook hard. "Good to see you, Cuz."

"You as well, my friend. I was outside the window when the guards came in. I could not see all of them but enough to know they were armed. I had to wait for your company to leave." He gave Sam a sad glance. "If I had come sooner, I would not have watched your lady walk out."

His lady? Sam liked that idea.

More than anything, Sam now had a plan. "No apologies. Damn glad you're here now. I need to get out of here and find her."

"The team is following the vehicle that took her."

That was encouraging, but Sam doubted following W would be that simple. He had a sick feeling. "I'll explain why later, but I have a backup plan for finding her. I need you to get Phoebe to safety."

"Not me, but we have others on the team."

Shaking his head, Sam made one thing clear. "W is not to be underestimated. I feel certain the inside of the door to this tower is wired with explosives. We have to escape this room and open that exit door safely for our guys. The minute I'm free, I'm going after Hallene. Phoebe has to be kept safe no matter what."

"I'm sure Nitro can handle that." Angel took any high-risk task in a mission, but he avoided dealing with hostages unless he had no option. "Have you found W?"

"Oh, yes. No time to share everything, but Senator Turner *is* W." Sam could count on less than one hand the times anything surprised Angel, but that news did it.

Angel dropped his voice. "Logan picked up rumors that the Chinese have lost a special submarine and believes the US has it."

Holy crap. Sam said, "That's got to somehow be connected but I don't see it yet."

"Us either." Angel's gaze danced over to Phoebe. "We open the door then Blade will show up."

Sam was not passing Phoebe off to any more unknown people even if he trusted his team without question. The girl had been through enough.

He glanced at Phoebe and raised his eyebrows as in it was time for her to help.

She lifted her chin and begged, "Don't let them kill me sister. I'll go with you. If Sam says you're safe, I believe 'im."

After a curse in Spanish, Angel sighed, "You will owe me, *Primo*."

"Agreed, Cuz. First, we need a plan to get out of here and neutralize the guard at the same time, so he doesn't alert anyone."

Angel began digging into his tactical vest. "Hand grenade or C4?"

"Shock grenade."

Sam ignored Angel's look of disbelief and quickly explained, "The guard is downstairs, but I'm betting he's close enough to reach this cell as soon as his boss tells him to take us to the next location. Phoebe explained W's MO since leaving Venezuela was to move often and every change of location seemed faster than the last."

"What are you thinking?"

Sam felt the first surge of adrenaline as his body powered up for action. "We draw the guard in close then you roll the flashbang through the opening in the bottom of the door. That should send him backward and disorient him enough for us to blow the door with the grenade."

"Why not just blow the door and him at one time?"

"I need his phone," Sam explained. "I'm hoping he doesn't fall on it."

Angel put away the C4 and dug out the flashbang. "How will you lure him up the stairs?"

Sam slid his gaze to Phoebe then pointed behind her. "She's going to back up to that wall and start screaming bloody murder on my signal."

Phoebe backpedaled to the wall and gave him a thumbs-up.

Tough young woman who would only get stronger if he could save her role model. "That a girl. As soon as you see Angel roll the flashbang, squat down and face the wall with your fingers in your ears. The light is blinding, and the noise will render you deaf for a while. Got it?"

"*Yeh!*" No hesitation when Phoebe snapped out her reply.

Hallene would be so proud of Phoebe.

Angel knelt on the left side of the door with two grenades beneath where his hand hovered. He gave Sam the okay nod.

Sam pointed at Phoebe. "Go."

She opened her mouth and good grief what a pair of lungs. It sounded like someone was butchering her. If she'd yelled for help, the guard would have ignored her, but he was responsible to deliver both captives alive until W said otherwise.

He would have to investigate or face W's wrath.

Heavy footsteps pounded up the stairs and hit the top landing.

Sam signaled Angel who pulled the pin.

Phoebe kept screaming.

As the guard stomped across what Sam had estimated to be a twelve-foot-long walkway, Sam counted down on his fingers three, two, one.

Angel rolled the grenade through the opening, flipped away, and covered his ears.

Sam had moved to shield Phoebe and mimicked Angel's actions.

A deep voice yelled, "What is prob—"

Sam felt the concussive energy in his chest from the exploding grenade sounding like a bomb. Even with his eyes shut tight, bright light had glowed.

Angel quickly returned to the hand grenade he'd placed by the door, pulled the pin, and left it in front of the door. Then he raced across the room and rolled into a ball.

Sam swung around to cover Phoebe. She stayed tucked with her hands over her ears. He covered his, loving how working with FALCA team meant not having to spell out every detail.

That blast sent splintered wood flying everywhere. Pieces battered Sam's back. No wooden spike drove into his body. He checked on Angel to find his team member knocking debris off his back and standing.

Sam hooked his hands on Phoebe's shoulders and lifted her

to a standing position. She opened her eyes and uncovered her ears. "Did it work?"

He turned her to see the blown door.

She gasped, a sound of excitement.

Sam warned, "Stick with Angel. Do whatever he tells you and you'll be safe."

She whipped around and grabbed Sam's arms. "I will. Bring Hallene back, please."

"I won't come back without her." That was the most honest answer he could give, but since Phoebe now believed he and his team were invincible, she nodded.

Sam walked over to Angel. "I'll get the phone and clear the door. You get her out safely." Then he raced out of the room to find the guard laying on his side with blood running from his face, arms, chest ... hell, everywhere.

Where was his fucking phone?

Rifling through the guard's pockets turned up nail clippers, cash, and a small ring of keys, presumably one to the lock on their cell and maybe to a vehicle. He pocketed the keys and took his handgun to shove inside his waistband.

But no phone.

No, no, no. Sam rolled the guard over again.

Angel spoke softly to Phoebe as they emerged. "Don't look at the guard."

"Why not? I want that bloke dead."

Angel chuckled at the future Hallene.

Sam scrambled and peered through the clearing smoke to see the phone lying at the edge of the stairs. He dashed forward, lifting it on his way down the stairs while dodging debris. He thumbed through recent calls.

Thankfully, the guard had not called anyone in the last thirty minutes, but one phone number was marked W.

Sam made it down the four flights of stairs by taking two at a time. Just as he suspected, the door had been rigged for any attempted breach.

His fingers were shaking. Not from the adrenaline rush but from fear he would not find Hallene in time. He drew in a deep breath and calmed himself as he'd done many times in the past, then quickly dismantled the trigger system.

Unlocking the door, he opened it to face weapons drawn.

"Good to see you, too, Cuz," he said as Nitro and Blade lowered their weapons.

Sam explained the situation quickly, finishing with, "I've got to go."

"We'll all go, Partyman. Logan sent in three more members from ULFBR team." Nitro told Blade, "Need boots for Sam."

"I'm on it." Blade took off running toward a Humvee.

Shit. Sam trusted Logan and everyone on FALCA, but he would not risk Hallene's life with any unknown operators. "No. W will have eyes everywhere. I'll keep you posted so you can follow close enough for a takedown. I have to get to her first or he's going to kill her and get away with a massive hit on this soil."

"Damn, Sam. First you want the freedom to run with an unknown operative and now you think we're going to stand down?"

"Not asking you to stand down, Nitro, but I am telling you we have one chance of stopping a terrorist attack and getting to Hallene first is key because I think he's going to use her in the attack."

Nitro cursed up a storm.

Blade returned, handing Sam a pair of boots. His gaze slid to the side beyond Sam. "Is that girl okay?"

"Yeah, she's tough."

Angel walked up with Phoebe and explained, "I will take her to a safe location."

What Angel didn't say in front of Phoebe was that he'd lock her up somewhere safe and then rejoin the team. Sam could only ask for so much right now and Phoebe had proven herself to be resilient. She absolutely would be okay.

"Got a phone with W's number," Sam said, shoving his foot into the second boot. He lifted the device. "Get a trace on that number and don't crowd him. Let me insert and give you a sitrep."

One thing about Nitro was that he would not argue when they had a chance to take down a threat. "Give me the number."

While Nitro called the phone number into their tech support, Sam looked around for wheels. "If that Humvee is yours, what's the other one?"

Blade twisted around to stare at the only other vehicle. "Bad guy's, I'd think."

That one was a black SUV like the Feds used. Wouldn't it fit for W to use federal vehicles to commit crimes?

Sam dug the guard's keys out and clicked the button.

Lights blinked in response.

Nitro ended his call. "We'll have a location in the next couple minutes. I also called in the other team to bring another vehicle for Angel to drive."

"I'm leaving now," Sam announced and started for his ride.

"You don't have a destination yet," Nitro reminded him.

"I will by the time I get turned around." No one was stopping Sam at this point.

He jumped in and cranked the engine. As he swung around, Nitro and Blade climbed into their truck.

The guard's phone dinged with a message.

Sam grinned at the quick tracking. He opened the text and his stomach dropped. The text was not a tracking link, but a message from W that read:

Take the two captives to the next location and confirm delivery.

How soon would W expect that confirmation?

CHAPTER 41

———◆———

HALLENE RODE THE CONSTRUCTION ELEVATOR up twelve floors with nothing to force her to obey except W's finger hovering over his phone. If he tapped the button beneath it, Phoebe would be killed immediately.

Air swirled around her the higher they went in the unfinished high-rise intended to be homes for those wishing to live closer to their jobs in Washington, D.C.

W kept a content smile in place.

He held the world by unbreakable strings and intended to pull one to destroy a section of his playground. "I rarely look at unexpected fortune as a positive thing. I tend to be suspicious of gift horses, but I must say your selfless urge to protect your half-sister is going to benefit me quite well."

She leaned back, hoping the elevator would break and delay what was coming.

The worst part was not knowing what would come next.

Now that she thought about it, she'd like to find out what to expect. "I just don't see how you plan to succeed at your terrorist attack."

"Speculate all you wish."

Shrugging, she said, "I thought you'd entertain me with your delusions."

His smile remained, but his eyes warned she would pay for insulting him. "I would never have reached this point if I were delusional."

She kept poking at him. "I heard about the other attacks. If you were so brilliant, why wait a year between? That's why the teams hunting you think someone else is probably the top dog," she lied, hoping he'd be more incensed over elite teams discounting him. "Makes sense that they believe the big guy is letting you be the front man. An important man would not get his hands dirty, would he?" She gripped the metal bar she leaned against. The squeal of gears begging to be lubricated was lost in the louder whistling wind at each level.

That storm was building fast.

Maybe a tornado would come up and ruin his plans.

She looked around as if interested in half-constructed buildings. "We can talk about something else. I just thought if you were the true genius behind all this, you'd want to tell someone." She brought her attention back to him. "Or don't you know all the details?"

"You are digging for information."

"Why not? You don't plan to let me live."

"You are correct."

"I thought offering to take Phoebe's place would earn me at least a good story about what will happen once I'm dead."

"You want a story?" He crossed his arms while still holding his finger over the death threat.

She'd pricked his temper. Would he say more?

"Here's your story, little girl. My people in law enforcement uniforms will clear an area around the Liberty Bell in Philadelphia with a bomb scare. A boom truck will drive in and a body already hooked up will be lifted above the ground. The driver and my men will leave so citizens can sneak in to start taking pictures. I'll have a live feed going that will be released afterward. Ninety seconds later ... boom! This plan allows all those stupid creatures who go rushing around gawking to be killed as well. People are sheep. I am cleaning out bad genes of idiots. If you tell them someone is dying in the street, they all pull out their phones and rush forward to take a photo. None will have the survival instinct to realize their lives are threatened as well."

His eyes lit with excitement over being a master manipulator.

A true sociopath.

"That's nice of you," she commented in a complimentary tone.

He frowned. "What are you talking about?"

"Only killing a few people around the body."

"You are yet another simpleminded plebian," he muttered. "This event is so much greater."

Would he finish before this elevator made it to the top? She assumed that's where a megalomaniac would want to be.

Letting out a long sigh, she said, "All I'm hearing is a dead guy hung by a crane hook and an explosion. I've heard about more creative attacks in the Middle East."

"That's because your mind is incapable of thinking on a grand scale."

Opening her arms wide with her palms up, she said, "I'm ready to be impressed."

"That doesn't matter to me."

"At least finish the story."

He sounded bored. "The body hanging from the crane hook will have my face and stature. The abdomen will be carved with VV."

She startled at that. "What do you mean VV?"

"I was born Viraaz Vicha."

"Viraaz sounds Arabic," she said, thinking out loud.

He ignored her, too invested in laughing at everyone hunting him. "I find it amusing that those investigating the first attack thought the carving was a W. I should have thought of that in the beginning. They made it even easier to shield my identity once I adopted the moniker. I grew up here, earning my natural American speech honestly, but I was not born in this country."

That was the only thing this man had done honestly. She wished Sam could hear all of this.

Then she realized what this senator was doing. "You're faking your death."

"Ding, ding, ding. A winner. Finally, you came up with a clever thought." He grinned with true delight. "Everyone knows my persona as Senator Turner was hated by this elusive W villain. Notice I used the word villain for your enjoyment."

She'd enjoy a chance to use a move that would break his neck. Instead, she said, "It's a nice touch." She looked around and guessed they had eight more floors to go.

The air became cooler up here with a front moving in.

She could feel the building sway.

"Where was I?" he asked no one in particular. He wasn't even looking at her.

"You were going to tell me why this attack is far more brilliant and creative than the others." She realized he had not mentioned someone. "What about Kovac? How can he be involved in this? If so, you discovered a capability in him I never knew existed."

"Kovac is a tool. One step above a blunt weapon. He's greedy."

"Agreed."

"His greed and shipping empire aided me in facilitating this project. It's how I covertly moved a new secret Chinese submarine from the coast of Africa to sit three hundred miles off the coast of Pennsylvania. It rests on the bottom of the Atlantic Ocean hidden beneath one of Kovac's container ships. In fact, the submarine sailed beneath the container ship the entire way once they crossed paths. This has been one of my most amazing ideas. Sadly, that brilliance will never be discovered once China and the US go to war."

He possessed both sides of the knife blade known as insanity and intelligence.

She had no words. The senator had shocked her beyond speech. Kovac had voluntarily aided a terrorist. Worse than a terrorist, this man was single-handedly going to destroy the world when two superpowers clashed.

Forcing herself not to start screaming at his insanity, she said, "That's a hell of a plan."

He preened.

Being that he'd charmed so many, he might actually be a psychopath. He was so proud of himself.

"How'd you get a Chinese submarine out of China's hands?"

The elevator stopped six floors short of the top.

Her heart thumped in fear. She'd strode into dangerous situations to save children, but like any sane person, she did not want to die.

She wanted to be assured Phoebe had escaped.

She wanted another day with Sam, or a million days.

Coop had been right about one thing. She'd wasted too much of her life with her head down working and keeping any potential relationship at a distance.

Sam had blasted past her walls.

She knew what it felt like to have that one person, the only person, she'd want to spend a lifetime with.

On the other hand, she would die here. Why put someone like Sam in the position of losing her?

Always confident, he would dismiss that and tell her he would not lose her.

Even Sam couldn't save her now.

"Walk." The senator waved his phone toward the exit side.

She watched for sharp objects like nails or industrial staples to avoid even though her feet had plenty of cuts she couldn't think about.

Thankfully, someone had laid a plywood floor up here where it appeared meetings were held on-site. She entered a huge room with two large rectangular holes on each side for picture windows but no glass. A corner office with floor-to-ceiling windows for the person who had made it halfway up the prestigious ladder to the top of a business.

Wind howled around the building and swept through quickly, lifting dust particles.

Standing near a window opening, she could see shorter buildings, a crane, lots of trees, and cars moving at a normal pace. People living their lives with no idea of the malevolence surrounding them.

"Take a seat behind your desk," the senator instructed, breaking her from the moment.

Her mind did not want to accept this was happening on a Saturday when she should be anywhere but here. Hallene took in the pieced-together room with a chair placed behind a desk made of two sawhorses and an unfinished wood door.

A laptop sat in the center facing the chair.

When had he placed that? She walked over and realized the evil W had others to do his bidding.

He glanced at the phone where his finger remained ready, probably checking the time.

"You were at the point in the story about how you wrangled a submarine from China. Don't leave me hanging." Keep him talking. Anything to avoid what he wanted her to do.

"I shall wrap this up quickly as you have little time left."

Her throat squeezed tight against the urge to shout and tackle him. She gave him a polite smile and tilted her head to indicate she was waiting.

"Everyone has a weakness just as we've discovered yours is Phoebe. My contacts knew the captain assigned to the secret training mission for the new sub. He was to take it through secret maneuvers in foreign waters. The captain follows only my orders at this point while his wife, mother, and two children are being held. He has been promised by someone whose word is without question that if he performs as ordered, his family will be taken out of China to live a safe life somewhere else."

"But the captain and his crew are forfeit, correct?"

Now the senator shrugged. "I do not create stories with happy endings for everyone."

She doubted the ending would be happy for anyone except W. She could not keep thinking of him as a US senator. "How are you going to hang Kovac with this?"

"No one would believe he could have orchestrated this."

"True." She crossed her arms and leaned back in the chair to give off confidence her jittery insides didn't feel.

W cocked his head. "Why would you voluntarily finger Kovac?"

She leaned forward with her forearms stretched past the laptop yet to be opened. "He screwed my mother, literally, then mentally destroyed her. She's very sick with an unknown illness now. I think he poisoned her. I would gut him if he was right here, and I had a knife."

"Ah, the scorned stepdaughter."

She really hated being called any kind of daughter to Kovac. "What do you need me to do? If I'm going to die, I want to be sure to take him with me."

"My, I do love your enthusiasm." W stepped closer but stopped in the middle of the room. "You will open the laptop."

She did.

"Now tap the power key."

The screen came up fast with a control panel of some sort loaded.

"I will tell you when to click the green button at the bottom right."

She moved her finger toward it as she looked.

"*No!*" he shouted.

Yanking her finger back, she dropped her hand to her lap. "I wasn't going to tap it, just looking for the correct button."

"It is *obvious.*"

"It is *now* that I've looked but this control panel thing is like nothing I've ever seen. Is this the panel controlling the sub?"

"Just when I thought we were having an intelligent conversation, you ask a stupid question."

"Either that or someone else programmed this and you don't know how the button works." She fought the panic rising in her. How could she push a button and kill innocent people or not push it and kill Phoebe?

"It sends a message to the captain. End of story time as yours is almost over."

CHAPTER 42

—◆—

SAM PARKED HIS SUV A street away from where W's phone location had pinged in a building. The only one on that block was under construction. He took off on foot and sent a text to Nitro. *I'm at the site.*

Can you see either one of them? came back.

No. Sam spotted a crane. *Got an idea how to get high enough to see if they're in a building under construction.*

We're coming on foot. Be there in a couple minutes.

Sam shoved the phone in his pocket and secured the weapon inside the back of his jeans. He snuck from spot to spot, watching for any of W's people.

Lightning ran across the sky. Then the boom followed. Black clouds heavy with rain moved closer, swallowing the sun.

Not seeing his team worried him more than someone taking shots at him. Where were his people?

Sam ran for the crawler dragline crane. An older one from a construction job like the place he'd been brought in as labor to clean the site along with three other grunts. At sixteen, he'd never considered all those odd jobs of any value beyond the cash he pocketed, but he'd always been curious. During a lunch break, the crane operator had shown him how the machine ran.

This one appeared to be used for unloading transported materials since the building had a tower crane in place for building each floor.

The dragline's boom was not set in the right place for him to use it as a way to see inside the building.

He leaped up on the track pads and reached inside the cab where he found butter-colored and well-used construction gloves, then took a seat to start the diesel engine. It cranked up with a low rumble. Thunder boomed again and again. He worked the gears to turn the cab and lifted the boom straighter up.

Leaving it running, he swung out of the cab and climbed up the boom.

Halfway up, he saw her.

Hallene sat at a makeshift desk. Wind whistled through the windows and blew strands of hair around her face.

Where was W, that traitorous senator?

Sam was to her right. She kept her attention focused straight ahead. She had to be facing W. She said something then opened a laptop he hadn't noticed yet.

She had to be shaking over taking directions from a terrorist.

Sam's phone buzzed. A text from Nitro. *Look down.*

Nitro and Blade waited.

Not sure how much time Hallene had, Sam texted: *Both inside sixth floor. Blade covers me and watches building exit. You pull the ball up to me. I'll climb on and you swing me into the big window opening.*

Nitro read the text and looked at Sam as if he'd snapped.

Sam scowled at him and did a quick thumb jerk toward the window as *in hurry the fuck up.* They were out of time.

He was not Evil Knievel Angel, but he could do this.

He *would* do this.

Blade took up a position behind a large roll-off dumpster where he could cover Sam and watch the bottom floor of the building.

Nitro jumped into the crane operator's seat and the cable began winding the ball above the hook up to Sam's level. Being this far from the building with a storm blowing in would hide the cable noise.

He hoped.

Sam dropped down to climb through the widest gap in the boom so he could climb out and scurry back up the outside.

Nitro brought the cable closer to Sam. He held his fist out for Nitro to see as a signal to stop the ball.

Thankful he'd pulled on the gloves, he gripped the cable and climbed on the ball. Easier said than done. He did a dance to gain his balance and glanced at Hallene to see if she was staring his way.

Nope. All good.

Sending Nitro an all-clear sign, the crane boom began to lower until Sam was slightly higher from the ground than the bottom of the window. Sam eyed the cable. Looked to be long enough, but he wouldn't know until the last moment.

Nitro swung the boom away from the building.

Sam bent his knees and tried not to think of all the ways he could die doing this not even counting W shooting him.

As soon as the ball reached the pinnacle on the backswing, Sam shook off his right-hand glove to fish out his gun and leaned hard forward as Nitro swung him toward the building.

For a slow machine, this cable and ball were flying fast at the window opening.

He was thirty feet out when Hallene turned her head and her mouth opened in an O.

CHAPTER 43

———

HALLENE'S HEART LUNGED AGAINST HER chest. Sam was flying on a cable toward the opening.

The senator shouted, "Stop looking that way."

She tried to get a word out, anything to help Sam, but it all happened like a slow-motion nightmare. He leaped away from a cable as it barely reached the building and hit the floor, rolling forward three times.

He came up with his weapon pointed at W.

"Don't, Sam. *He'll kill Phoebe!*" Hallene shouted, panicked at losing Phoebe and watching Sam die. "Please stop."

The senator had a dumbfounded look on his face that would be hilarious in a different situation.

Sam sidestepped as if dizzy from that stunt. Sweat broke out on his forehead. His left arm hung loose. Had he broken his arm? He was breathing hard but said, "This ends now, Turner."

"You'll shoot me in cold-blooded murder?"

"Not when I can put you in prison for the rest of your miserable life and destroy your operation."

"Did you not hear her?" Turner acted totally in control of his world. That was the face of insanity. "I hold Phoebe's life in my hands as well as many other lives. Which will it be? Save Phoebe and the world or arrest me?"

"Sam?" Hallene pleaded.

He was heaving each breath. "Phoebe is safe. You know it's true for me to be here."

"Oh, thank God." Hallene caught her breath, but her hands were shaking like an addict in need of a hit.

Turner grinned. "Once again, I am dealing with people who

have no creative genius even if your minds were combined into one."

Hallene had been watching Sam but pivoted her gaze to the senator. "What are you talking about?"

"Do you really think I would leave only one guard to watch my captives? Clearly, this one escaped and one of his people took Phoebe somewhere safe. Sounds like she will get a happy ending, right?" He smiled broadly. "But no. A second guard has remained outside every location we have to oversee that any operational glitch is fixed. I had a tracking device inserted into Phoebe's clothes when she was first drugged. My second guard will find her and terminate that problem. She only had limited use for me once you stepped up. If I do not reply to a text when he has her, he'll kill her right then."

A tear ran down Hallene's face. They couldn't win, no matter what they did.

"Hallene?" Sam called out softly.

"Yes."

"Trust me?"

No question about that. "Yes."

Sam said, "It's over, Turner. Your men have been neutralized."

The senator didn't appear sold. "Liar. You can't get out of this. I would not put myself somewhere I could not get out."

"You did this time."

Hallene said, "He's got a body double being lifted to hang next to the Liberty Bell in Philadelphia. Once that goes up, he wants me to push this button and activate a submarine to shoot a missile at Philadelphia."

Turner said, "The body is being raised into the air now and media has been alerted. Nothing can stop this."

"I won't push the button," Hallene declared.

"Have you not finally realized that I believe in backups everywhere? Kovac has the same instructions as you. If you do not push the button first, he will do it thirty seconds later."

Sam called out, "Where you at, Cuz?"

A voice speaking from a phone on him replied, "On the way."

Turner paled. He pressed something on his phone with his thumb.

The phone voice called out, "*Sniper!*"

Hallene screamed, "*Sam! W pressed a button!*"

Sam roared, "*Get down!*"

She dropped to the floor as a shot ripped through wood on the wall to the side of her.

The senator was frantically typing.

Sam shot the phone out of Turner's hand. The senator howled, grabbing his hand.

Twisting to Hallene, Sam asked, "Are you—"

Lying beneath the plywood table, Hallene's eyes were fixed on W who was reaching inside his jacket. "Behind you!"

Sam spun his 9mm back to the threat as the senator pulled out a weapon.

They both shot.

CHAPTER 44

———

KOVAC TAPPED HIS FINGERS NERVOUSLY and watched the countdown on the laptop that had been delivered to him last night. He kept checking the time.

The clock was closing in on three in the afternoon here in London.

That would make it almost ten in the morning in Philadelphia. All correct.

He rubbed his hands together.

Seventy seconds. He could do this. He *could* do this. He ... felt powerful and ready to join W's operation. Sweat ran down his face. He yanked his tie loose and pulled the stinking collar open.

He'd never wear another bloody suit in his life.

Powerful men did as they pleased. He'd have a dozen women clamoring to please him.

Fifty-eight seconds.

Breathe. Keep calm. He was ready to rule his own empire. W could rule the world and Kovac would be more loyal than anyone else in his circle.

Why was this damn clock so slow?

Forty seconds.

He'd be wealthy beyond his imagination, which would finally have no limits.

With Phoebe and Hallene permanently out of the way, he'd send someone to finish off their mother as well. Get rid of two ball and chains at one time.

Had W dealt with Hallene? Kovac couldn't believe his man Crusher had failed, but W sounded confident he would terminate all headaches connected to this mission. The minute Kovac punched the button, he had to wait fifteen seconds then punch in a code that would completely wipe this laptop.

He could not wait to have the ability to pay the best hitman and find someone with the level of computer knowledge who created W's program.

Someone easy to corrupt.

Eighteen seconds.

Yes!

Sixteen!

Noises erupted outside his door. That bitch assistant had been instructed to not bother him under any circumstances.

Twelve seconds.

The door burst open.

He stood and shouted, "Get out!"

Something hit him in the chest and sent a charge of electricity through his body. He flopped on the ground like a caught fish, crying and shaking.

A large man walked over to stand above him. "My name is Logan and you're under arrest as an international terrorist."

Kovac peed himself.

CHAPTER 45

———

SAM DROPPED TO HIS KNEES, still holding the gun on Turner who stared at him as if shocked anyone would shoot him. He wouldn't die from the wrist wound, but neither would he be able to hold a gun again any time soon.

"*Sam!*" Hallene scrambled around the desk.

"Stay down, hon. There's a sniper trying to kill you."

She didn't stop, just kept coming on her hands and knees. When she reached him, tears poured down her face. "How bad is it?"

"He barely grazed my side." But Sam's shoulder would hurt like a bitch until someone popped it back into the socket.

She pulled up his bloody shirt. "That's not a graze, dammit."

"I'll live."

Footsteps pounded toward them. The building elevator had been groaning its way up.

She jerked her head around and moved in front of Sam.

Hell, he loved this woman even if she did crazy things like that. "It's okay, Hallene. That's my team."

Nitro strolled in with his weapon drawn, took in the situation, and started directing everyone. He had Blade and two men Sam didn't know.

Sam said, "What about the sniper?"

One of the men he didn't recognize who had to be from ULFBR team said, "Our guy took him out."

"Thanks." Sam didn't ask names. They would not share HAMR Brotherhood names in front of an enemy.

Putting his weapon down, Sam reached around Hallene's shoulders with his right arm and tugged her back.

Hallene asked, "What about Phoebe?"

Sam held his breath. He'd trusted his people to keep that girl safe no matter what came after her.

Nitro paused in issuing orders to calmly answer her question. "She's fine. Our man took her to a place where we had surveillance. When someone showed up who was not one of ours, he was neutralized."

Her shoulders slumped and she scooted next to Sam, then she surged forward again. "There's another way to activate the missile in the UK. A man named Kovac has it."

Nodding, Blade said, "We know. Once we located Turner's phone, our people heard what he planned. You did terrific getting that out of him. Our boss has been on standby in the UK. He took care of Kovac. Law enforcement in Pennsylvania also has Turner's double. He's bleeding badly, but he'll survive."

Relief must have swamped Hallene because she never let her control slip in front of others, but she buried her face against Sam's good shoulder and cried. He felt the same overwhelming relief at holding her close.

The only thing in his world that mattered now was holding onto her. He wanted to sit here for as long as she needed. His heart would never get over seeing her dodging a sniper's shot.

He kissed her head and rubbed his hand over her arm.

He had no idea what his future would bring, but he'd made his choices knowing he would face the music when this was over. He had never thought to have to choose between duty and a woman, but Hallene was not just any woman, and this had not been just any duty.

He'd tried to do his best by both.

Adrenaline did crazy things to a man's body. Now that it was draining from Sam's, he wanted nothing more than to get out of here and find a place to take his time with Hallene's body. To relax her until the horrors from today slowly faded.

He needed to feel her close.

Having skated so close to death had his mind wanting to be anywhere with her except here. Now he'd have to figure out how to stand without the bulge in his pants giving his completely inappropriate thoughts away.

He'd get another one of those you've-lost-your-mind looks from Nitro.

Sam didn't care. Men in love were crazy.

He was damn sure in love.

Once the senator was contained and on his way to a hospital where the federal authorities would take possession of him, Blade came over to Sam. "Your left arm isn't hanging right, Cuz."

"You noticed, huh?"

"Yep. Time to fix it."

That was going to take the starch from Sam's dick.

CHAPTER 46

HALLENE HUGGED PHOEBE, UNWILLING TO let go.
Phoebe's voice came out smothered. "You're suffocatin'
me, Sis."

Rolling her eyes at the exaggeration, Hallene eased up. "I may
suffocate you with attention for a while."

Phoebe had showered and changed into jeans and a lightweight
red pullover. "Does that mean you're gonna 'over?"

"I might hover."

"This is so not you, Sis. Neither is that crazy curly 'air. Never
seen you without perfect 'air before."

Hallene touched her hair, smiling because Sam loved her curls.
"You saw it in the tower when we were locked up together."

"Yeh. I thought it was part of a disguise. Speakin' of bein'
captured, wot do we tell Mum?" Phoebe sounded worried. "I
don't think she can take learnin' about this just yet."

Any other time, Hallene would have thought Phoebe was
trying to pull a fast one on their mother, but she heard sincere
worry in the girl's voice.

Softening her tone, Hallene said, "Mother is going to be okay.
You remember that guy on Sam's team named Blade?" Hallene
glanced around the safe house where his team had brought all of
them. Phoebe had a room with clothes and personal items. They
understood the need for her to feel normal and have her own
space after the traumatic situation.

"Yeh, that big guy over there. That one's a 'ottie." Phoebe
pointed.

Hallene gave Blade a quick glance, catching his bright grin
at her little sister calling him hot. Good grief. "Yes, him. We
talked. He said his boss had sent a team to pick up mother and

take her to a medical location to run blood tests and see if they can determine what is happening to her."

That had been over four hours ago. Would they know anything?

For the first time, Hallene saw yearning in Phoebe's face. The girl could barely talk. "You think ... they can figure out ... uhm ... you think she'll live?"

"I hope so, Phoebe. I suspected Kovac of poisoning her because he paid for her medical services which gave him control over who did what. I tried to take her away by saying I wanted to take her to lunch, but the medical center said Kovac wouldn't allow it. I wanted to get her fully tested somewhere out of his reach."

"That bastard."

Hallene couldn't hold back a chuckle.

"Wot?" Phoebe could be an adorable teen when her guard was down, and she smiled.

"Bastard was the code name I gave Kovac for intel gathering." She sobered and added, "I may hover some. I don't want to leave you alone. As for our mother, I think we will eventually tell her everything when both of us agree to do it, but not anytime soon."

"I'll be okay with you 'angin' around more, but you took out the only real threat to me if I don't make a stupid decision."

"You are right, and I believe in you, Phoebe. You'll do just fine with decision-making."

Phoebe stood up straighter. "When we get 'ome, I want you to teach me to be a super spy. I'll 'ave to learn to talk American like you, yeh?"

Hallene flinched at the word home.

She did not want to return to London right now, but she'd just said she wanted to keep an eye on Phoebe. Plus, her mother would need her soon.

"I'm not a super spy, Phoebe. I rescue children." Then a thought hit Hallene. "You can help with that and get some experience."

Phoebe grinned. "I'll do it. Wot about Sam and 'is team? Can I train to be like them, too?"

Sam walked up still favoring his left arm. "Okay, the first thing you have gotta do is never talk about this team. Don't share our names. Things like that. If you keep our secrets, then when you're out of college and after you've got plenty of experience with Hallene's operation, come talk to us."

"Deal." Phoebe's eyes lit up. She put her hand out to shake.

Sam took it and held on. "You did amazing with all this, Phoebe. I told Hallene we couldn't have broken out of that place without you. Really proud of you."

Was that pink in Phoebe's cheeks? She mumbled, "Thank you. I listened to wot you told me."

"See? You're already training to be an operative."

Blade called over, "Phoebe, would you come here?"

"Oh, yeh, the 'ottie is talkin' to me." Phoebe took off without another word.

Hallene laughed.

Sam brushed his hand over her hair. "I like that sound."

She loved his touch and hearing his voice. She had no idea where they went from here though. "What is next for you?"

"Not sure until I meet with Logan, but I have no regrets so don't you dare worry."

She would have a huge one if he lost his place with men he clearly respected and cared about.

Nitro walked over to them. "How's the shoulder, Partyman?"

"Sore, but usable by tomorrow."

Shaking his head, Nitro said, "You have to let your body heal."

"I may have lots of time for that," Sam admitted with a sad smile. "Thanks for all you did when I put you in a spot I never meant to do."

"No thanks needed. It's what we do, Cuz."

Hallene asked, "What about the Collector? Did anyone find him?"

"No, and I would have been surprised if we had," Nitro said. "The Collector hasn't been known for kidnappings of this level before and never kept a captive near him for more than three days. In the past, he took contracts for powerful cartels and some in the Middle East."

Sam said, "We won't stop looking for him."

Nodding, Nitro said, "He just moved higher on the international most wanted list and your intel is going to help, Hallene."

"Thanks." Hallene appreciated the way Sam's team gave honest answers on what they could share. She asked, "What about the submarine? Will the US and China be in conflict over this?"

"Hopefully not," Nitro replied. "Our boss interacts with governments in different countries and has been talking to the State Department here. If things go as expected, China and the US will remain in neutral positions."

So much fallout from all of this. Hallene wondered about the captain of the Chinese sub who had to sail it home to face his superiors even if he had been blackmailed. Then there was the senator's family. After suffering the media blast that trashed her family after her father's scandal, she felt for the senator's family who would have it far worse.

Then Nitro went over to check on someone else.

Thinking back on Nitro's words, Hallene turned raised eyebrows at Sam. "Partyman?"

Curling his lips, Sam said, "The team has always made fun of how I'll sit around reading during downtime instead of partying. They stuck me with that nickname."

She put her arms around his shoulders. "I like that you're a bookworm."

"If you're up for a little trip to Clercville, I might put my books aside." He hooked his right arm around her, pulling her close. "I'd like to read your body right now, starting with those lovely titties and kissing my way to—"

A trip with him that didn't include people shooting at them sounded wonderful. She kissed him, cutting off his words before he said more. She whispered, "Do not speak like that in front of your team. They hear everything."

Grinning big time, he said, "They aren't paying any attention to us."

She cut her eyes to the side. "Every one of them except Blade is watching us." Blade stood with Phoebe who held a phone to her ear. "Oh. Blade is waving me over."

Sam released her but walked with her.

Nitro caught him on the way and held Sam back to quietly say, "Logan wants to see you in the morning. He's flying in."

Heaving a deep breath, Sam said, "I know what this means. Thanks. I can never repay you."

Tears pooled in Phoebe's eyes. She handed the phone to Hallene. "I talked to Mum. She sounded weak but glad to 'ear from me. A doctor wants to talk to you."

Hallene took the phone. "This is Hallene Clarke."

"Hello, Miss Clarke. I've completed most of my tests on your mother and ... told her what I found. I explained the treatment to clear her body of toxins. It's not an easy treatment and there is risk since she's so weak from how long her body has been under attack. She's asked that you and Phoebe come home. Now."

CHAPTER 47

———————

SAM STOOD ON HIS BOAT after two hours of cleaning everything he could. He even polished all the cleats on the dock for this side of the marina. That frowny woman from the office had stepped out to watch him.

He'd smiled and waved.

She turned around and went back inside.

He looked around the deck that still had maintenance work to do, but his heart wasn't up to a major task yet. He couldn't use the excuse he wasn't healed. His arm and side were fine after a week of Angie's fussing and cooking.

He'd hated the fear he'd seen in her eyes when he walked in wounded.

She'd hugged him and shook with emotion. Once he told her what he could, iron-willed woman that she was, she told him she would never divulge anything he said so long as he let her know when he would be gone each time.

She wanted his agreement that Clercville was his home.

He'd taken a second thinking then nodded, saying, "I like that this is home for me."

Since then, she griped at him when he tried to fix the rest of the trim on the inn this week. That would change next week.

That's why he'd been cleaning on the boat today.

She'd kicked him out to get fresh air.

He could stand only so much fresh air when he had to breathe it alone. Stepping up on the dock, he walked down to the end and sat with his legs dropped over the side. The eastern horizon had little left to do except grow darker with bands of red and purple.

A different story behind him where the sun was exhausted

after shining all day and hurried to set.

His chest ached. Not from an injury, well maybe. Just not a bullet or knife wound. He'd had a slice of happiness for almost a week, even in the middle of danger, and he missed it.

Missed her smile.

Missed her curly hair.

Missed the way she made him feel.

Something cold touched his neck. Not a gun this time. A cold beer.

His heart went into overdrive, and he begged for it to be her. He reached up and grabbed the arm holding the beer and swung her around into his lap.

Hallene laughed out loud.

That was the picture he needed to see every day. He felt like a schoolboy who just found out the girl he'd been crushing on all year had shown up at summer camp.

His throat wouldn't work right. "Hi."

Her eyes were bright and happy. Her laugh slowed to a sweet smile. "Hi."

He took the beers she held in each hand and sat them next to him. His hands refused to wait anymore. He cupped her face, holding her there to prove she was here.

Then he kissed her.

Their lips were so damn happy to find each other again. She came willingly, a soft woman when she wasn't kicking someone's butt.

She moved closer to him, putting a hand on the back of his head and hugging an arm around his neck. Her lips were in conquer mode and he was a willing captive. Her tongue teased between his lips, and he laughed, then sent his to play with hers.

He'd dreamed of holding her like this, just being together and smooching.

He'd dreamed of her every night.

Dreams could never match what having his hands on her felt like.

When they came up for air, she leaned her head down on his shoulder. "I missed you."

"I can't think of words to tell you how much I missed you."

His gaze dropped to her hand smoothing over his chest. He could see her smile. "How's your mother?"

Sighing softly, she sat up to face him. "We were warned the treatment would be difficult. Kovac was some kind of monster. Logan's people are amazing. By the way, he is quite intimidating even when he's being nice."

"That's one way to describe him. Did you meet Margaux by any chance?"

Hallene made a face of shock. "That woman is scary and crazy about Logan."

"You nailed both of them."

"But I owe them for my mother's life. She is doing well."

He played with a curly strand. Just couldn't keep his hands off her. "What about Phoebe?"

"She is really pretty special once you get to know her."

"You two are getting along good?" He was happy at that news.

"We argue, which is more like sisters than sharing silent contempt. But she's the one who cornered me and said, 'You insult me ability to care for Mum by stayin' 'ere and not goin' to Sam. Aren't you serious about 'im or is 'e just a whim?'" Hallene said, mimicking Phoebe.

He held his smile, but inside he wondered just how Hallene had answered her.

"Don't look at me that way, Sam. I don't need two of you making me feel like I'm letting you down."

"Hey, you could never let me down." He leaned and kissed her. She was here. In his world, that meant she wanted to be kissed.

When she said nothing else, Sam couldn't take it. With his heart crawling up his throat, he squeezed out, "Are you serious or am I a whim?"

She rubbed the palms of her hands over her face then dropped her hands. "I am here sitting on your lap."

True, but he couldn't think past this minute, couldn't consider his future without knowing if she'd be in it some way.

He had to take a risk and find out her flinch factor for staying together. "I'm okay with however you want to move forward ...

if you're saying you *do* want to move forward." He gave her a hopeful glance.

She crossed her arms and stared at him.

He cursed.

"What do *you* want, Sam?"

His heart might explode at how fast it was beating. He put his hand on her cheek. She closed her eyes and leaned into his palm. "I want you to be happy."

She didn't open her eyes when she said, "Sitting here is pure joy for me." She blinked and leaned in for a smoldering kiss.

Man, if she kept that up, she'd find out just how happy he wanted her to be right here on the dock.

She started laughing. "I can read your mind."

"What? Really?"

"Maybe not, but you are hard as stone. Reading the mind of a man in that condition is pretty easy."

He reached up and cupped her breast.

She made a sweet noise. Her voice went up an octave. "I think you read my mind."

"I want to take you to my boat and spend all night in the cabin with you, but it's not shipshape yet for you."

"We should get a room."

"I have one at the local inn I believe you've seen."

"We should drink to that."

Was she dancing around telling him this long-distance thing would be sporadic at best? He popped the top on a beer and handed it to her then opened his.

She took a drink and gave him a sassy look. "How long will Angela allow me to stay?"

"Forever." That came out of Sam's mouth before he realized he had just made his greatest gamble and left himself raw. What would she say?

"That's a long time, Partyman." Hallene toyed with the paper around the lip of the beer. "Are you sure you won't become tired of me?"

"Not a chance. I'm hoping you could get used to me."

She hooked the hand with her beer over his shoulder. "I don't need to get used to you. I know you and love all the parts."

Her words climbed inside of him and clutched his heart. "You would really stay?" he asked. "Wait. You love me?" He had never allowed anyone to see him be vulnerable, but he did now.

There came an arched eyebrow. "I told you that when I was leaving the tower. Did you forget what you said to me?"

Worried he'd get this wrong, he fumbled his answer. "No, I mean, yes. I thought you were just saying that to make me feel better."

"Oh? Why did you say it to me?"

He'd never been a gambler, but he was going all in. "Because I can't imagine life without you in it. Because I want to wake up to see your face every day. Because I want to hear you laugh. Because ... I truly love you."

"I said it for the same reasons," she murmured, her eyes brimming with tenderness.

Relief smacked him in the chest, but he wanted to tell her everything.

He smiled and quickly clarified just what he was willing to do. "It's not fair of me to ask you to move here, so I'm going to ask Logan to let me go from the team. Then we can be together in London."

Her face fell at that news.

What had he said wrong?

"You will *not* quit your team!" She grabbed his shoulder then her eyebrows shot up. "Wait. Is Logan letting you stay?"

Sam smiled the relief he'd felt after talking to Logan. "He told me I still had a place with my team because they all spoke up for me. Said they still trusted me and didn't want to see me leave." Swallowing hard to push the thick emotion back down his throat, he had replayed the part about his team going to bat for him over and over in his head. He'd never been so humbled.

"Thank goodness," she breathed out, easing her grip on his shoulder. She shook her head. "I can't allow you to throw that aside for me. You would never be happy."

"Happy comes in a lot of colors, babe. The brightest one in my box has your name on it."

When she spoke, her voice was music to his soul. "I want everything you want because you are my world."

You are my world.

Four words sent his heart soaring.

"I also want you to stay with HAMR Brotherhood. I do not like the idea of you being hurt, but I believe your team is the safest net to wrap around you. I would never take what you love doing from you. I have to spend time in London during the year to help with the organization I've built to search for and protect children, but I would like to start a new branch here. I think Phoebe will be ready to step into my shoes in London in a few years at the rate she's maturing."

He couldn't believe his ears. "You'll live *here* some of the time?"

"No."

His heart broke.

"I will live here almost *all* of the time. When I do travel to London, I want it to be when you have time off. I want you to meet my mother and see my organization. In fact, Logan said he hoped you would take time off because of me."

"Hell, yes. I'll get this break extended."

She laughed. "That might be a problem. Margaux said I could *not* take you from HAMR Brotherhood for long and that woman scares me."

"Margaux is possessive, but no one in HAMR Brotherhood will ever harm you and all of them will put their lives at risk to keep you safe once they know you are mine. I just want to give you what you need."

Her gaze leveled his with her unyielding one. She whispered, "I'm possessive too. You are mine. You are what makes my heart sing." She brushed hair off his face. "I don't need any more than you have to offer."

He let out a harsh breath and believed her. She used her money for children, not yachts and jewels. "Man, this is ..." He held her gaze, hoping she heard what his heart was saying and not his clumsy words. "Love was not a word tossed around at home. I never thought I'd experience it other than from how Angie loves me like her own child. Never expected to care this much for a woman, not until I met you. Now I'm going to say something I sure as hell never intended to say. Will you marry me?"

Another woman wouldn't understand him like Hallene because she'd seen him, had really seen him. She might say no or not yet, but she deserved to know the depth of his commitment to her.

Smiling through her tears, she said, "The answer is yes. I want to be your wife and those are words *I* have never intended to utter either."

He looked forward to walking into the inn to tell Angie about the two of them. Angie had a huge heart. She would love Hallene the way she had loved Sam all these years.

Then Sam and Hallene would sit out on the inn veranda in Adirondack chairs with fresh beers and watch as the last bit of daylight vanished.

FROM DIANNA

I hope you enjoyed the HAMR Brotherhood FALCA Black Ops team. There will be more books in this series. If you have not read the Slye Team Black Ops Romantic Thriller series, you'll see this HAMR team for the first time in KISS THE ENEMY.

MORE BOOKS

Thank you for reading my books. If you enjoyed this story, please help other readers find this book by posting a review. To stay informed on all my books, sign up for my monthly (only) newsletter at ...

https://authordiannalove.com/connect

You can also follow me on Amazon and BookBub.

For SIGNED & PERSONALIZED print copies visit *www. DiannaLoveSignedBooks.com* where you can also preorder upcoming new releases.

AUTHOR BIO

New York Times **Bestseller Dianna Love** once dangled over a hundred feet in the air to create unusual marketing projects for Fortune 500 companies. She now writes high-octane romantic thrillers, young adult, and urban fantasy. Fans of the bestselling Belador urban fantasy series will be thrilled to know more books are coming after soon with the new Treoir Dragon Chronicles. Dianna's Slye Team Black Ops and HAMR Brotherhood Black ops are both romantic action-adventure series. She also writes League of Gallize Shifters paranormal shifter romance series. Look for her books in print, e-book, and (most) audio. On the rare occasions Dianna is out of her writing cave, she tours the country on her BMW motorcycle searching for new story locations. Dianna lives in the Atlanta, GA area with her husband, who is a motorcycle instructor, and with a tank full of unruly saltwater critters.

———

Visit her website at
AuthorDiannaLove.com and
DiannaLoveSignedBooks.com

ACKNOWLEDGEMENTS

Thank you for reading *WRECKED* and thanks also to all the readers who sent me messages wanting this series.

As always, thank you to my husband, Karl, who makes it possible for me to write my stories.

A special thank you to Judy Carney who gets better with every book she goes through, Stacey Krug who jumps in super early to read pages before they're totally clean. Tina Rucci sees the very early copy and her feedback is so helpful. Also, I appreciate Jennifer Cazares and Sherry Arnold for being terrific beta readers who catch a number of small things missed by all of us even after multiple editing passes.

I want to send a huge thank you to my Super Read-and-Review Team peeps, who read early versions then share their opinions – you rock!!

Sending a shout out to Candi Fox and Leiha Mann, who work hard to support me in so many ways. Thanks to Joyce Ann McLaughlin, Kimber Mirabella, and Sharon Livingston, too.

As always, the amazing Kim Killion creates all of my covers and Jennifer Litteken saves my butt time and again with great formatting just when I need it. Much appreciation to both of you.

Thank you to my peeps on the Dianna Love Reader Group on Facebook. I love coming out to visit with you.

Dianna

Printed in the USA
CPSIA information can be obtained
at www.ICGtesting.com
LVHW020812280924
792391LV00027B/719

9 781940 651057